MW00625544

DIAMONDS *and* DANGER

DIAMONDS *and* DANGER

a novel

Lynn Gardner

Covenant Communications, Inc.

Published by Covenant Communications, Inc.
American Fork, Utah

Copyright © 1997 by Lynn Gardner
All rights reserved

Printed in Canada
First Printing: May 1997

Cover Photographs
    San Francisco: ©1997 Digital Vision
    Diamonds: Grant Heaton Productions

03 02 01 00 99 98 97   10 9 8 7 6 5 4 3 2

ISBN 1-57734-108-2

Prologue

In the wake of a near-fatal Hawaiian honeymoon, Allison and Bart are just beginning to unwind and enjoy married life in their cozy California honeymoon cottage. The haunting memories of Scarlotti Scaddano, the madman who had kidnapped Allison and plotted the murder of her family as a diabolical act of revenge, are finally fading. Besides, all the evidence points to Scaddano's violent death on the treacherous rocks of his island estate. Allison believes she has nothing more to fear from this evil man, and she can now concentrate on being happily married and taking a closer look at Mormonism. Bart had learned about this fascinating religion while in a Tibetan prison camp, and is anxious to share his new-found faith with Allison. Now that their life is finally under control, they'll be able to enjoy a wonderful future together.

On the other hand, Bart's line of work could make short shrift of their future. When murder, mayhem, and mystery rear their ugly heads in San Francisco, what's a secret agent to do? Dodge bullets and put the criminals behind bars, of course. And take his bride into the jaws of death.

Chapter 1

"News from San Francisco today is grim. A third body, in as many days, has been discovered but police have wrapped the killing in a shroud of silence, refusing to release further information. A rash of robberies and plague of fires, the number escalating each day, has officials working overtime to . . ."

"What's going on?" I asked, plopping on the sofa beside my handsome husband of less than two weeks. The snug caretaker's cottage just above Santa Barbara that Mom and I had called home for the last twenty years was now a honeymoon cottage. Mom and Dad had moved into the mansion on the estate just up the hill.

Bart's intense blue eyes never left the TV screen as he pulled me close and idly kissed my forehead.

"San Francisco's just been hit by a murderer, a serial arsonist, a stickup man bent on hitting every Mom-and-Pop grocery store in the city, and increased gang activity. Strange it should all happen at once. Police can't tie any of it together, but, I wonder . . . ," Bart broke off.

I could almost hear Interpol's wheels turning inside Bart's head. He ran a sun-tanned hand slowly through his short, white-blond hair, a gesture I'd already learned to identify with a state of deep concentration.

"That can't possibly concern your job, or mine," I said. "We've already had enough bad guys for a lifetime, and your job targets terrorists, not arsonists and stickup men. Speaking of jobs, I'd better call Saroya in New York about mine. Will it disturb you if I call now?"

Guess not. Bart was totally absorbed in the broadcast.

"Saroya, it's Allison. How's my crippled roommate?"

"Alli! It's good to hear from you. Leg's healing properly. I can get around on crutches now. What happened to your 'peaceful' vacation on that beautiful estate? Are you really married? What about your fiancé, Milton? I couldn't believe it when I saw you on national news. Of course, all I've been doing is watching TV since I've been laid up. Tell me what happened."

I pictured Saroya, exotic dark eyes illuminating a lovely oval face, waist-length dark hair cascading down her back, and a broken leg propped up on pillows in the New York apartment we shared, her hands waving excitedly as she spoke.

"It would take hours to relate everything that's happened since I left New York," I said. "I've been to Greece and Hawaii, gotten married, been kidnapped, fallen into a volcano, and survived a hurricane and a ditching at sea, all in the space of three weeks."

"You're kidding! No, you're not kidding," Saroya squealed, her voice high with excitement. "You always have all the fun. Tell me every single detail."

"Later. I need a favor. Are you up to going back to work already?" I asked.

"I owe you for doing my job on top of yours at the United Nations when I broke my leg. What do you need?"

"Can you cover for me? Our honeymoon was cut short and, frankly, I need time to recuperate from all the excitement. Mom's had a pretty serious injury, and I'd like to keep an eye on her for a few days. Could you handle that? My boss gave me a week without pay if I could find someone competent to fill in for me. I immediately thought of you."

"I'll do it on two conditions. First, there are no kinky ambassadors coming to town I'd have to baby-sit, and second, that you tell me the whole story from start to finish the minute you get back in town."

I laughed. "I promise. Look at my calendar and see when Ambassador Hana is arriving. I think it's Wednesday. Check my files for his wife's favorite flowers. Order them, on my account, delivered to the embassy Wednesday afternoon with a note: 'Welcome to New York. See you next week. Allison.' Then call the embassy that evening before dinner and explain I'm on my honeymoon. Do I have any interesting mail?"

"An oversized postcard from the school thanking you for speaking on why everyone should learn a foreign language, with 'thank you' in twenty different languages! Your phone bill, reminder card from your dentist, and a florist bill that feels like you'll have to come into an inheritance to pay. There are envelopes from the French, Japanese, and Thai embassies. No wonder you're everybody's favorite interpreter. You spoil them all."

"Just want them to have a pleasant experience when they come to America," I laughed.

"Say, do I need to be looking for a new roommate?" Saroya asked.

"I'll let you know in a couple of days when Bart and I have had a chance to talk about it. Thanks a bunch, Saroya. Talk to you later."

"*. . . the sudden flurry of activity has police baffled. City officials are worried about tourist reaction to the rash of crimes hitting the city,*" the news reporter announced.

Wanting attention from my husband, I snuggled closer and unbuttoned the top button of Bart's shirt, ran my hand suggestively over his chest, and reached up to kiss his freshly shaven face. The only sign he was even aware of me was a tightening of his arm around my waist.

I unbuttoned the second button, then the third, and the fourth, and pulled the shirt open. His other arm went around me, but his attention to the news broadcast was so intense that he hardly seemed aware of me.

What would it take to bring this man back from his special-agent mode? I kissed his cheek again, and nibbled on his ear. No response.

I tickled his ear with my finger, something that usually drove him crazy. Bart's only reaction was to trail his fingers up and down my arm, his concentration uninterrupted. I was about to try something extreme when Dad knocked at the door and called, "Can I come in?"

"Might was well. The honeymoon seems to be over," I said.

Bart finally looked at me and raised an eyebrow.

"Must be if I can't even seduce you away from the news," I laughed.

"That's what I came to talk about." Dad frowned as he strode into the center of the small living room, his dusky gray eyes reflecting his serious mood.

As head of Anastasia, an elite anti-terrorist branch of Interpol, my father, Jack Alexander, stayed alert to unusual signs that signaled new problems anywhere in the world.

"Is that the news from San Francisco?" Dad asked, perching on the edge of a chair. Of medium build, medium height, and slightly graying hair, he could be any man anywhere with a minimum of change in appearance.

"Yes. They're showing the location where the last body was discovered. Jack! Look!" Bart's exclamation punctuated his astonishment.

The television camera panned the crowd. A dark-haired man standing behind the group turned away quickly as the camera zoomed in on the spectators, but for an instant his profile was silhouetted against the bright background.

Dad muttered an expletive under his breath. "The Roach!"

"I thought we'd seen the last of him in Syria," Bart said with disbelief.

"The Roach?" I questioned as Dad and Bart sat in stunned silence.

"He's a nasty little assassin who could dart in, do his dirty work, then disappear faster than anything you've ever seen. We thought he was blown to bits in the Lebanon bombing last month," explained Dad.

"That's a batch of trouble Anastasia doesn't need, especially now that our ranks have been decimated," Bart said.

Dad was silent, thoughtfully rubbing his chin. "I don't like this." They turned their attention back to the newscast's final segment.

When it was over, Bart leaned forward, his hands clasped with elbows on his knees, and asked, "What do you think?"

"It's too much at once on too many fronts. Looks like a smoke screen. But for what? Nothing's going on in San Francisco. And what's Roach doing there? He's a specialist. Expensive. It's got to be big if he's involved."

"Look's like somebody's got an agenda we're not going to like," Bart said.

"But terrorists don't usually announce, don't call attention to themselves beforehand. And I have a hard time believing this is coincidence. The murders, maybe, but the harmless little fires to keep the fire department busy, and the neighborhood stickups and gang activity to keep the police tied up?" Dad shook his head. "Penny ante stuff. Roach's presence ups the ante considerably. What's going on up there?"

"An exclusive diamond exhibit at the new Museum of Modern Art," I interjected.

Dad and Bart turned and stared at me.

"What kind of exhibit?" Dad asked.

"To celebrate the anniversary of the new museum's opening, the world's famous diamonds will be exhibited. The Smithsonian's lending their collection, monarchies are sending crown jewels, and private collectors everywhere are loaning their diamonds for the show."

Dad looked at Bart.

"Financing," Bart said.

"Hold the diamonds hostage for ransom?" Dad asked.

"Why not? They'd get more money that way than trying to sell to private collectors or to break up the stones."

"Who?" Dad shot back.

"Who needs it the most right now?"

Silence. Deliberations in progress. Dad paced the length of the fireplace.

"IRA is low profile right now," Bart said. "PLO? Abu Nidal?"

"No." Dad thought for a minute. "Qaddafi is still nursing his hatred of America since his daughter was killed in the bombing, but it's not his style."

"Peru's Shining Path has been pretty well annihilated," Bart said. "That leaves the obvious."

Dad nodded. "Early this year a presidential order froze all funds of Hamas, Hezbollah, and Islamic Jihad units in U.S. banks. They'd be feeling the financial squeeze right now."

"Jihad," Bart said with finality in his tone. "It's gotta be Jihad. Not only the most active but the most ruthless. Also Roach's last known employer."

Dad quietly resumed his pacing. Bart turned down the volume on a sports report, then with a wave of the remote control, clicked off the TV. He leaned back on the sofa, fingers locked behind his head, and stretched his six-foot-four length toward the fireplace. Dad stopped and leaned against the mantel, frowning.

"I think you'd better go up and take a look. I had a bad feeling about this when I first heard the report, but with Roach in town . . ."

"And you?" Bart asked. He hadn't changed position, but his body tensed, his face became alert and alive with anticipation and his blue eyes gleamed. Body language revealed what he nonchalantly attempted to hide. He couldn't wait for a new case, a new challenge.

"I'll feed you information as I find it. I'm not budging from here until Margaret's fully recovered."

"How's Mom feeling this morning?" I asked. "Must be better or you'd never have left her side."

"A little stronger." Dad's face softened a bit. "I made her promise to stay in bed until noon today. I can't believe how fast that wound is healing. Must be the old Hawaiian Kahuna's special medicine. She'll be back on her feet in no time." The scowl returned. "It's a good thing Scarlotti Scaddono is dead, or I'd track him down and slowly kill him myself, a piece at a time."

Fear and anger shuddered through me at the mere mention of the name. I wasn't surprised at Dad's hatred of Scaddono. He'd almost killed my mother. Remembering how close she'd come to bleeding to death from the arrow that pierced her breast and arm left me shivering. If Scarlotti had put anything on the tip, like he had on the dart that killed the policeman . . . it was too horrible to think about.

I didn't like being reminded of Scarlotti, never wanted to think about him again or the time I'd spent captive on his island.

"Catch the first flight to San Francisco and nose around," Dad said. "Find out what's happening. See if you can find out what Roach is up to, who else is in town and from where. Check out the diamond exhibit and the museum's security system. That could be a magnet for all sorts of low life, all with the same idea."

"Will do." Bart jumped to his feet.

"Ahem. Have you two forgotten something?"

They looked at me, then at each other. It was classic.

"Did you forget so soon that Bart now has a wife? And the little item of an unfinished honeymoon?"

"Bunny . . . ," Dad began, his hand rubbing the back of his neck in a 'what do I do with this daughter I'm not used to having to deal with?' gesture. After twenty years of being an absentee father, I'm sure it was a little hard getting used to having me around.

"I don't have a problem continuing our honeymoon in San Francisco. It's one of my favorite cities," I said.

"Princess," Bart started, a pained look on his face.

"Don't even think of leaving me behind. It's not a consideration. Dad let Mom work with him. I can help you," I stated flatly.

Bart recovered nicely. "Of course. You didn't think for a minute I'd go without you, did you? I'll need all the help I can get." Grabbing my hand, he pulled me to my feet, gave me a quick kiss, and pushed me gently toward the stairs.

"Call and book us onto the next flight into the Bay Area, then get your bag packed. Travel light. Oh, and call Bishop O'Hare with our apologies and cancel our dinner invitation and discussion for tonight. Tell him we'll have to reschedule when we get back in town."

He and Dad conferred while I called the airport. We couldn't make the next one, but I got reservations on the noon flight.

I threw some essentials into a suitcase, then ran up to the big house to see Mom. She was propped up in bed with pillows everywhere. Shoulder-length black hair was loose from its usual bun and spread on the white pillowcase, which made her face seem paler than it should have been. Mom's big dark eyes lit up with pleasure when I bounded into the room.

"I see Dad's been trying to make you comfortable. How do you feel this morning?"

"Suffocated. Return a few of these pillows to the linen closet, will you, please? What's going on? Something on the news set your Dad off. He made me promise to stay in bed, then flew out of here without a word of explanation."

"I can identify," I called over my shoulder as I stuffed pillows back on the shelf. "Dad just told Bart to get on the first flight to San Francisco, forgetting about me completely. It's a good thing I have a healthy ego. I think even Bart forgot he was married."

I picked up Mom's brush and she gingerly moved so I could brush her hair. "If the purpose of a honeymoon is to solidify the marital relationship and set the tone for the marriage, we're in trouble already. We can't settle down long enough for anything to gel. Bart was so busy on our honeymoon either protecting me or pulling me out of trouble, I don't think he had time to discover we now have a different relationship than the one we had growing up, when his role was my 'big brother' and protector."

"It will come," Mom laughed. "I just won't make any promises when. What with your propensity for adventure, the nature of Anastasia's work, and based on our own experience in this business, I think I can accurately predict the next few years will be as tumultuous as the last few weeks have been."

I groaned and flopped on the bed beside her. Mom took my hand and squeezed it affectionately. "Give Bart time. The 'protector' phase will pass and the 'partner' phase will kick in soon enough. Enjoy discovering each other and savor each new stage of your relationship."

"Thanks, Mom. I guess that's the down side of growing up together. I'd hate to think of him still seeing me as the pesky little tag-along he used to put up with all the time." I sat up cross-legged on the bed. "There is a bright side to this new development for you. Now Dad will have something on his mind besides smothering you with TLC."

"Maybe I can direct his energy to helping the work crews repair the fire damage to the other wings of the house. It's a good thing we installed the fire walls and doors. We could have lost the whole house in the fire when Antonio Scaddano tried to destroy everything."

"By the way, how does it feel to live in your own house and sleep in your own bed after twenty years of pretending you were simply the caretaker? And living openly with your husband instead of pretending he was dead?"

"Strange and wonderful at the same time. The arrangement is perfect, though, with you and Bart in our cottage. Have you two decided where to live? Are you going to keep your job and apartment in New York?"

"We'd planned to settle all that in Hawaii, but since that didn't happen, we were going to make some decisions in the next couple of days. Saroya's covering for me this week. I couldn't face plunging back into work after the frantic pace and exertion of the last three weeks."

"More on those killings in San Francisco . . ." a television news reporter intoned in the background.

"Turn it up, quick," I said, anxious to hear any new information from San Francisco.

"Police have no comment on the report that all three bodies found in the city this week had been pierced with a diamond earring after the time of death. No identification has been made on the corpses, but a reliable source reported the killings had occurred elsewhere and the bodies dumped where they were discovered."

"Diamonds everywhere. First an exhibit full of them, and now they're showing up on dead bodies. Gotta run. Hurry up and get better." I kissed Mom's cheek and ran to the door. "Oh! Do you know anything about a man called Roach? Dad and Bart just saw him on TV in San Francisco and it upset them. Why?"

The hand Mom raised to wave good-bye froze in midair. Her wan face paled even more.

"Roach is dead," she whispered. "I saw the explosion. He couldn't have survived."

The tone in her voice drew me back to her bed. "Who is he?"

Mom stared absently at the TV, shaking her head in disbelief.

"Who is he?" I persisted.

Margaret Alexander, the third surviving member of Anastasia, laid her head back on her pillow and answered quietly. "An assassin with an outstanding contract on Anastasia."

Chapter 2

Midafternoon we descended into San Francisco International Airport through a hazy blue sky. I had mixed feelings about this trip. I was delighted at the unexpected opportunity to continue our honeymoon in one of my favorite cities. The special ambiance of San Francisco, elegant, enticing, sophisticated, intrigued me. But something told me it wouldn't be a honeymoon at all.

"Whither first, Sir Galahad?" I asked as Bart maneuvered our rented convertible toward the airport exit.

"Check the map and get me to the Museum of Modern Art. We'll give it the once over, then find a hotel close by."

"I feel foolish asking this question to my husband, but when was the last time you were in San Francisco? Five years of your life are a mystery . . . where you were, what you were doing, who you were doing it with. Oh, just stay on Highway 101 until we're into the city."

"I haven't been here since college." Bart gave me a teasing glance. "During your carefree college career, I slaved away testing and training for Interpol, then plunged into the business. Most of that time I was in Asia, including the year in Tibet, half of which I spent in prison, then six months in Nepal healing from my near fatal beating. I worked with your Dad first. I figured they put me with a pro to learn how to stay alive."

"Glad it worked. The museum's in the SOMA District on Third Street between Mission and Howard. Does that help or do you need specific directions?"

"I know the general direction, but keep your finger on the map in case I get turned around."

"What are we looking for when we get there? Do you have a game plan? How on earth do you know where to start?"

"My inquisitive princess," Bart laughed, pressing my hand to his lips. "You never cease to amaze me with your endless questions."

"Never ask, never learn."

"You should be beyond brilliant, approaching genius by now. Find some news on the radio, and let's see what's happening in the City of Love this afternoon."

"*. . . Police refuse to comment on the mysterious murders of the last three days. The first body was found Monday in Diamond Heights at a still undisclosed location, the second in the Financial District, and the third was discovered yesterday on the steps of the Mission Delores. Police have not identified the bodies, nor will they reveal the cause of death. An unidentified source claims each had a diamond earring pierced into the body after the time of death. More on the news on the hour.*"

A chill shivered through me. "Do you still think the deaths aren't connected to the diamond exhibit?" I asked. "A body dumped in the Diamond District with a diamond pierced into it? That's pretty blatant. What are they trying to say?"

"Mmm, I don't know. It may be too blatant, too obvious. It would take a lot of audacity and ego to call attention to a jewelry heist like that."

"What kind of people are you dealing with? Aren't they filled with ego? Don't they hold everyone in contempt . . . the authorities, other cultures, just about everybody and everything not associated with their own beliefs?"

"That part's true enough. I'll reserve judgment until I have a little more to go on." Bart reached for my hand again and squeezed it. "But I will keep it in mind. You seem to have an uncanny ability to find the hot spots and plunge into the middle of them, so it wouldn't surprise me if you were right on this one." He laughed. "No pun intended. When I said that, I wasn't thinking of your plunge into the volcano."

"To save you from Pele's bubbling cauldron, I might add."

"I still can't believe you'd jump out of a helicopter hovering over a volcano to save me." Bart shook his head.

"Wouldn't you have done the same for me?"

"Of course, but . . ."

"Why would you throw yourself out of a helicopter to save me?" I persisted.

"Because I love you."

"Enough said."

Bart opened his mouth, then shut it.

"Yes?" I asked, expectantly. "You don't think for a minute I'd let you fall into another woman's arms, especially a goddess with supernatural powers. I didn't wait all those years for you to turn up again just to lose you to some fiery female throwing flaming lava around. Whoa! We leave 101 right up here. Veer right."

Bart executed the turn and headed for the SOMA District, the new South of Market Area being rejuvenated by the arts complexes and software companies that had moved there in recent years.

"What you just said indicated jealousy made you take the plunge." Bart tried to keep a straight face, but his teasing blue eyes gave him away.

"Here's Third Street. Turn left. There's the museum . . . and a parking lot right next to it." I ignored him, not wanting to acknowledge jealousy as a major motivator.

Looming over the Yerba Buena Center like a watchtower, the art deco Marriott Hotel had a sweeping view of the San Francisco Museum of Modern Art, Moscone Convention Center, and the Center for the Performing Arts. Bart immediately pegged the hotel as our base of operations.

The museum was a modernistic, five-story building with a white and gray-striped cylindrical skylight rising periscope-like from its center. Natural light from the skylight rendered a rich golden glow to the wood in the entry, and cast shadows from a catwalk suspended overhead.

Inside, I watched Bart wander, looking, probing, envisioning problems. He was as interesting as the exhibits.

I also observed a tall, striking redhead on the second floor who was intent on the paintings, making notations in a black leather portfolio. The ultra short skirt of her chic, oatmeal-colored suit revealed long, shapely legs. I experienced an immediate dislike of her, then laughed to myself. That was my initial reaction to all willowy females who towered over my measly five feet four inches.

Thick, straight, shining cinnamon hair brushed her shoulders as she moved, or fell across her face as she bent to write. The second area of envy. My naturally curly black "gypsy hair," as Bart calls it, is totally unmanageable. Generally wild and unruly, it has a mind of its own. It will not be styled, can not be made straight, and usually looks like I've just stepped out of a windstorm. Why did I always feel so inferior to these gorgeous creatures?

I was glad Bart hadn't noticed her . . . yet. Bart was right. I was jealous.

In the middle of my mental muttering, I was interrupted by the uncomfortable feeling someone was watching me just as I'd been watching the girl. I looked around, but the few people in the museum were occupied with other things. None seemed interested in me.

When Bart called me, I forgot the sensation. He'd finished his cursory examination of the museum and security system.

"What now, Sherlock?" I asked as we left the museum.

"Let's walk through the park and get a room at the Marriott. Then I'll be ready for dinner. How about you?"

"Thought you'd never ask. My rumbling stomach was about to set off earthquake alarms."

"Then we'll save the walk through the park for another time and drive to the hotel. We can unload our luggage right there and not have to come back for the car. I'd never want to be accused of starving my petite princess." He grinned lasciviously. "We must keep your energy level up."

But Bart's plan was foiled at the start. The Marriott was hosting a convention of gemologists coinciding, of course, with the historic exhibit of diamonds. A group of historians filled the remaining rooms.

The historians were scheduled to leave at the end of the week, three nights hence, so Bart reserved a room, beginning Friday, that overlooked the arts complex.

"I can't believe I didn't call ahead for reservations. You've addled my brain, Princess. Any druthers for the next three days?" Bart said, a trace of disappointment in his voice.

"There's a quaint little hotel I used to frequent on getaways. Want to try it? It's unlike the Marriott in every way. Not new, not big, European instead of American. Like I said. Quaint."

"Why not? Lead on, Watson."

We found ourselves in the middle of the five-to-seven o'clock traffic crunch. Bart parked in front of the little Abigail Hotel on McAllister Street with a sigh of relief. He stopped short when we entered Abigail's intimate lobby.

"Not quite like the Marriott's spacious lobby," I said.

"Like comparing grapes to watermelon."

Two people plus suitcases filled it completely, and they had to move to make room for anyone getting off the elevator.

We ended up in a delightful room on the fifth floor with big windows overlooking the street below. Bart called it tiny. I called it intimate.

"Old-fashioned," he said.

"European," I responded.

"Umm. Comfortable," he murmured, pulling me down onto the bed beside him.

"Premature," I purred in his ear as he kissed my neck.

He leaned on his elbow and looked down at me. "Your response was supposed to be 'perfect.' What's with the 'premature' bit?"

"Our car's parked in a twenty-minute loading zone, in danger of being towed away, and if you don't feed your starving wife, she won't have the energy to respond to your amorous overtures."

"No one can ever accuse you of being overly romantic," he laughed, rolling off the bed and pulling me to my feet.

"Unfortunately, my reputation as a pragmatic, practical person follows me everywhere. I guess you'll just have to teach me a whole new way of life. Is this how I start?" I pulled his head down and kissed him, teasing at first, then warming to the occasion. His arms wrapped around me, pulling me close against his lean, hard body.

"Maybe I'm not so hungry after all," I whispered breathlessly.

"Have I told you lately how very much I love you?" Bart murmured.

"No. Tell me."

"Maybe I'd better do it while we move the car and find dinner."

"Now who's being pragmatic?" I laughed, grabbing my purse and jacket.

The charming, antiquated elevator, christened "Elliot," was not the most time-efficient conveyance, but beat sharing five flights of stairs with other arriving hotel guests. I wanted to remember to ask the desk clerk where the name "Elliot" came from. Probably a public relations device to keep hotel guests from being irritated at its idiosyncrasies.

Bart opened the convertible door for me and bowed low in mock obeisance. "Your car, m'lady."

"Thank you, James." As Bart walked around the car, I settled back contentedly, wondering if anyone had a right to be so perfectly happy.

A glimpse of a tall, slender figure dressed in black with long, straight dark hair blowing in the breeze shattered my contentment. The man disappeared before I could get a second look. I shuddered. No. It couldn't be. Scarlotti Scaddono was dead. There must be dozens, hundreds of men in the world who resembled him, I told myself.

As we drove by, I watched the area where he'd vanished. No one was there.

"Looking for something in particular?" Bart asked, studying my face curiously.

I shook my head, trying to shake away the memory of that dreaded figure and the terror it invoked.

"Kahuna said I'd suffer paranoia from the drugs Scarlotti gave me. I think I'm also hallucinating. For a second, I was sure Scarlotti was standing across the street, then he disappeared."

"Allison, Scarlotti is dead." Bart clasped my hand tightly in his, his tone strong and certain. "It's probably normal to see ghosts everywhere after what you went through on his island. I saw my captor everywhere I looked for months after he tortured me. Even some of the lamas nursing me back to health looked like him at first. Don't worry about it." He laughed. "Your knight in shining armor has pledged to save you from all dragons, real or imagined, from now on."

"Thanks, Lancelot."

Bart was right. Scarlotti couldn't have survived the fall onto the rocks in the hurricane or the wild peccary that had torn him to pieces.

"He has an ugly habit of spoiling my honeymoon," I pouted, "even from the grave." I shuddered again. "By the way, have you talked to Kahuna lately? Did he find any remains, and is there a grave? I know it's foolish, but if I just knew for sure . . ."

"Sorry, Princess. I forgot to call when we got back to California. I promise I'll do that first thing in the morning. Now, what can I do to restore that honeymoon glow I was enjoying just minutes ago?"

"Take me to Boudin's at Fisherman's Wharf. A cup of their clam chowder and chunk of sourdough bread heals all ills. Turn right at Van Ness."

We drove silently through evening traffic, watching the lights of San Francisco come on one by one as people returned home after a day at work, shopping, or whatever they spent their time doing.

Bart slowed the car to stare out of my side window.

"What is it?" I asked, seeing only an empty building.

"Check out that beautiful old building. What a shame somebody isn't doing something with it. Look at the stonework, the pillars, the carvings up there."

A horn behind us put a quick end to our twilight perusal of the ornate work high above the huge door. I had time for only a glimpse of the old building that looked hauntingly empty.

Chapter 3

The clam chowder and sourdough bread at Boudin's was all I remembered. Bart and I were laughing about some silly memory when I suddenly experienced again the feeling someone was watching me. Goose bumps spread down my arms.

Everyone in the noisy little room seemed intent on their own intimate conversations. Large front windows mirrored the room, preventing me from seeing into the darkness beyond.

I shifted my chair closer to Bart's till I was touching him. I needed his strength, his warmth, his closeness, the reality of him. It was as if I could see Scarlotti's face leering at me from the dark, hear his sensuous voice saying, "I'm glad you feel my presence, Allison. I want you to know I'm here, right outside the circle of light. I'll be here, wherever you go, until I'm ready for you."

"Princess! What's wrong? You look like you've just seen a ghost!"

"I just heard one."

"One what?"

"Ghost. Bart, it was eerie. My antennae started quivering. I knew someone was watching me, but it wasn't anyone in here. Then it was as if Scarlotti was laughing at me, telling me he was out there, watching, waiting, until he was ready for me." I shuddered at the memory, at how real it seemed.

Bart started to stand up, to run outside and look, but I grabbed his sleeve.

"He's gone."

"How do you know?"

"I can feel it. It's almost like my telepathy with Dad. I get impressions, images. On the island he told me he'd never met anyone with my sensitivity. Could I actually share telepathy with him, like I do with Dad?"

"I don't know, Princess. Not my area of expertise. I do know protecting you against flesh and blood is hard enough. How do I protect you against a ghost?"

He sat back down and pulled me close against his chest. His heart pounded as fast as my own.

"Are you okay?" he asked, tipping my chin up so he could look into my eyes. He didn't really have to ask. He was becoming adept at reading what he saw there.

I nodded numbly.

Bart paid our bill and we went warily into the night. But the specter was gone. I no longer felt anything except the fear he'd left behind.

"First thing tomorrow, I promise I'll call Kahuna and see if he found Scarlotti's body. I think I'd better call your Dad and have him check with the Hawaiian police to see what they turned up. I can't believe Scarlotti could have survived. Did Kahuna say how long before the effects of the hallucinogens wore off completely?"

Mutely, I shook my head. I hoped it was simply hallucinations. I could live with that. I couldn't live with the idea that Scarlotti was still alive, and after me again.

Bart's arm went around me protectively as we walked the dark street to our parked car. He tried to lighten the conversation on our way back to the Abigail to take my mind off the terror that had dampened our first evening in San Francisco,

"After I'm through nosing around the police station tomorrow, what do you want to do? Play tourist and take a ferry around the bay, go hike Angel Island, or drive up to Sausalito and have dinner?" Bart asked.

"Mmm, I'll have to think about that. How long has it been since you've been to Muir Woods?"

Bart reached for the radio dial to pick up the news. "Actually, I've never been to Muir Woods. Want to educate me?"

The radio announcer blared his bad news into the semidarkness of the car's interior, injecting an even greater feeling of melancholy and gloom into the already dismal evening.

"Police are being tight-lipped about a body discovered this evening on the Golden Gate Bridge. The presence of a small diamond imbedded after the time of death links this killing to three others in the city in the last three days. The first body was found in the Diamond District on Monday, the second in the Financial District Tuesday, and the third yesterday at the Mission Delores."

Bart was pensive, so lost in thought he almost ran a red light. A fire engine howled across the street in front of us, lights flashing, sirens screaming through the night. Bart immediately whipped the car around the corner and followed the speeding vehicle.

"Do you chase fire engines often?" I asked, surprised.

"I'm just curious to see if this is a legitimate fire or one of those 'brush fires' that's plagued the city lately."

At the end of the next block, the big red and white engine screeched to a halt beside the fire chief's car. Bart pulled in behind the fire truck and jumped out of the car without a word. It was as if he'd forgotten I was along. I followed him.

A huge plate glass window in an old abandoned building had been broken and a fire built in the middle of the concrete floor. It looked like it might have burned itself out and not even damaged the building. Firemen quickly extinguished the small blaze.

Bart found the captain. "How many of these little fires have you had?"

"Too many," snapped the big man. "Move along. There's nothing to see here."

Bart produced his Interpol identification. "I'd like a couple of answers, if you have a minute, sir."

The captain snorted. "Bartholomew Allan, you don't have enough to keep you busy in your jurisdiction? You got to investigate our little annoyances?" His deep, rich voice resonated with disgust.

"I think your 'little annoyances' are a smoke screen for something big that's going to happen in this city . . . soon."

Dark eyes narrowed in the flashing lights. "Blaise Bronson." The captain thrust his hand toward Bart as he eyed him carefully. "What?"

Bart shook his head as he took the extended hand. "I don't know yet. Still working on that. But you've got fires, gang activity, murder, stickups, all disturbances designed to keep police and firemen busy while the biggest diamond concentration the modern world has ever seen is being organized. Tell me about the fires. When did they start? How frequent are they? Is there a pattern?"

"They started probably ten days ago. We get a dozen calls a day all over the city, scattered, no particular pattern we can see. All contained like this one. Never anything big or dangerous. Just a pain to answer the call, and expensive in the long run."

"Who calls them in?"

"Somebody calls 911. We've listened to the tapes. All different. Sometimes men, sometimes women, young, old. Usually somebody from the neighborhood just happened to catch it."

It was fascinating watching Bart in action. I'd had little opportunity to observe him at work, to see his professional side. He was focused, efficient, probing.

"Who do you think's behind the fires, and why?"

"At first we thought it was just some neighborhood kids getting a kick out of hearing the sirens and watching the fire truck roll in. Now I'm sure it's not, but it doesn't have the markings of an arsonist, either. Not big enough. They like the really big ones."

They were interrupted when a portable phone was thrust in Captain Bronson's hand.

"We'll talk more tomorrow. I'll find you," Bart promised, and strode purposefully back to the car. I hesitated only a second before following quickly on his heels, realizing if I wasn't in that car when Bart started it, I'd be left behind. Bart had forgotten me completely!

I jumped in and slammed the door, jarring Bart from whatever far plane he'd been on. The look on his face was priceless, as long as I retained my sense of humor.

"You forgot me, didn't you?" I laughed. "You would have left your bride standing right there on the sidewalk without another thought."

"Allison . . . ," he started lamely.

"Better I find out now that I play second fiddle to a case while I'm still basking in the glow of our honeymoon instead of later when I've convinced myself I'm your only love."

"Alli . . ."

"It's all right," I promised, leaning across the gear shift to kiss the chagrined look from his face. "I knew what I was getting into when I married an agent intent on saving the world instead of a millionaire with nothing to do but spoil me. I'll let you make it up to me when we get back to the Abigail. We are going there sometime tonight, I assume."

"Anywhere your forgiving little heart desires," he laughed, shifting into reverse and backing away from the fire truck.

"Home, James. I'm ready for bed, or whatever else you can conjure up to ease a tired body. All this excitement can be exhausting." No reply. He was gone again, off somewhere pondering this mystery.

I reached for the radio, hoping to find some soft, romantic music to regain the mood we'd lost as we left our room. Only a news report.

"*. . . the latest of the exquisite gems to join those already pledged for display at the museum. It was one of the highlights of Geneva's sales last year when Sotheby's sold the 64.42-carat, D-category, heart-shaped diamond for 5.2 million dollars. The new owner will remain anonymous until the exhibit opens. The magnificent diamond is the biggest and most flawless to ever be put up at auction.*"

"D-category is supposed to be the best there is," I said.

"How would you like to help me with this puzzle?" Bart asked.

"Love to!"

"While I do a little digging at the police station and fire department, will you hit the library and do some digging on diamonds? Find out all you can about these beauties that are coming in here? Didn't I see a library in the vicinity of our hotel?"

"Actually, I think the Abigail is immediately behind it. Sounds fun."

We parked the car and walked arm in arm around the dark block to the hotel. One of the inconveniences of a small hotel—no parking garage attached. I caught myself staring into every alley, every dark doorway, examining every shadow for a tall, slender phantom. Maybe if I hadn't been looking so hard, I wouldn't have seen the movement in the shadows across the street.

Suddenly Bart whirled me into the entryway of a darkened store and crushed me against the door frame. In that same instant something zinged against the wall where we'd been seconds before. Tiny fragments of brick exploded around us like flak.

Bart's body pressed solidly against mine. I felt him reach for the gun he wore in a holster near the small of his back.

For a brief moment everything was quiet. The city seemed to hold its breath right along with me. Then the headlights of a car slashed through the darkness, followed by another, lighting the street, illuminating the shadows. The pulsating bass of a too-loud radio shattered the quiet. Teenagers spilled from both cars, laughing, calling to each other, filling the street with life, light and noise.

"Was that what I thought it was?" I asked breathlessly as Bart tried to slip his gun back into place unnoticed.

"What did you think it was?"

"I think someone just shot at us."

"Now why would anyone want to do that?"

"I don't know. You tell me. Maybe you could start with Roach and the contract he has on Anastasia, and how he knows you're in San Francisco."

Bart's only answer was to grab my hand and hurry me down the street through the dancing, noisy teenagers. I wanted to stop and thank them. I figured we owed them something. Probably our lives.

"You're not talking," I said as we whipped around the corner toward the Abigail.

"Just had a sudden surge of passion. Can't wait to get you upstairs. You're irresistible, Princess."

He could play that game if he wanted, but I knew he'd seen something in the shadows, just as I had. I knew with equal assurance that we had been shot at.

As we stepped inside the lobby of the Abigail, I whirled and faced my husband with quiet determination.

"Bartholomew James Allan, we're in this together, for better or for worse, like those marriage vows we made two weeks ago. Now you can tell me what we're really up against here and I'll help in any way you need me to, or I'll find some way to help on my own. Either way, you've just acquired yourself a partner, whether you want one or not."

Bart stood without speaking for a minute, just staring at me with those intense blue eyes as if searching into my very depths to see of what stuff I was made.

"I think I'll like this arrangement, Princess. I've never taken a partner to bed before."

Chapter 4

San Francisco's many faces enchanted me. I wasn't sure which I loved more—warm, sunny days when the city sparkled above the bay or gray, foggy ones like today when the mist hung low and heavy.

A mystical magic cast a spell on the city as long slender fingers of fog crept down the streets, filling alleys, transforming street lights into flickering candles and trees into goblins with outstretched arms, and smothering the world with a cushion of expectant silence.

I crawled back into bed and snuggled next to my sleepy husband. One arm pulled me closer as Bart buried his nose in my hair, his breath warm on my neck.

"Time to get up?" he mumbled.

"Not for hours yet."

Bart leaned up and peered over my shoulder at the travel alarm on the dresser.

"I can't see the clock."

"That's because it's still dark outside. You can't see the sun so we don't have to get up yet."

"Something tells me not to believe you," Bart murmured.

"Would I lie to you?"

"Not outright. But your phrasing was very suspicious. What do you mean, 'you can't see the sun'?"

"It's foggy. I was just offering you an opportunity to begin a sybaritic lifestyle."

"Translation?"

"Sybaritic—devoted to luxury and pleasure. We could start by staying in bed another couple of hours, having breakfast sent up, and then . . ."

"A long, leisurely shower," Bart finished.

"You know me so well already," I laughed.

"That's the only predictable thing about you. What did you do before I became your personal back scrubber?"

"Suffered immeasurably. What time do you have to leave this morning? And what are you going to do while I'm at the library?"

"I want a printout of the location and times of the fires from Captain Bronson. From the police, I want the location and times of the holdups, and description, if they have any, of the stickup man. I also want to know what kind of gang activity has been going on, where, how often, and why. I'll need to alert the police to Roach's presence in town, too."

"Will you get all that done this morning?" I asked.

"No. Especially not the whys. But I hope to get the rest. Then I'll pick you up and we'll go back to the museum and check their security. This time we'll be official."

"We? That means I'm now an acknowledged partner?"

"No. Nothing more than keep me company when I check out the museum. Jack's bad feeling about this is contagious. I've caught it. I don't want you involved, especially with Roach in town."

I sighed heavily. "So much for the honeymoon."

"I think we can squeeze a little of that in here and there," Bart teased. "I'll pencil you in my schedule for the next hour."

I hit him with a pillow. The ensuing pillow fight ended on a honeymoon note, and after a quick but satisfying back scrub in the shower, we had a hurried bite of breakfast in the tiny little dining room downstairs.

"I'll walk you over to the library."

"Of course not," I laughed. "It's only around the corner."

Bart cupped one hand under my chin and tilted my face so I was looking directly into his concerned blue eyes.

"I know you're an independent spirit, Princess, but I don't want you on the street alone."

"Let's hurry up and get this investigation done, 007, so we can play today. I'm determined to get a honeymoon out of this trip one way or the other."

Bart insisted on walking me to the library. As we stepped into the street, a car roared out of the mist, heading straight for us.

Instead of slowing when the driver saw us, he accelerated.

We threw ourselves back against the building. The car bumped over the sidewalk, barely missing us and taking out the twenty-minute parking zone sign in front of the Abigail. We looked at each other as the car disappeared in the fog.

"You okay?" Bart asked, reaching for my hand.

"Yes. Are you?"

"Great way to get your heart going in the morning," he said with a wry smile.

"Accident or attempted hit and run?" I asked, my knees suddenly weak.

"What do you think?"

"I think I'll call it an accident. I don't like to think someone is trying to kill me."

"Good idea," Bart said, looking at me carefully. "Ready to get on with it?"

"Why not? I don't hear it coming back so I assume he's not going for a second try."

"You're catching on." Bart put his arm around my shoulder and we hurried across the foggy street to the library. He kissed me good-bye at the bottom of the stairs and watched as I walked into the library, then turned and left.

It's okay. You're perfectly safe with all these people around. It's not like you were alone here, I told myself. *Scarlotti is dead. No one's even looking at you, and Bart would never leave you alone if there was any danger.* That made me feel better.

I was surprised to see guards on duty. Was that to keep the street people that gathered in the area from bothering library patrons, or to keep patrons from 'lifting' the books?

The climb up two flights of marble steps was a good warm-up. My body was overdue for a strenuous workout. My daily jog hadn't found its way into my new schedule yet.

It took several frustrating minutes to decipher the library's system and find the books I wanted. Tables and study cubicles filled quickly, so I found a quiet, sheltered corner and sat on the floor, piling my books around me like a barricade to ward off heavy-footed, inattentive wanderers.

I'd just lost myself in fascinating diamond lore when little prickles started on the back of my neck and shivered their way down my arms. I glanced up quickly, expecting to find every eye in the room glaring at me for nontraditional library behavior, but no one was paying the least bit of attention.

In fact, I was quite hidden from most areas of the room by bookshelves, copy machines, or tables. Only half a dozen people could have seen me from where they sat, and each was absorbed with his own studies.

I looked around again, puzzled by the sensation I'd just experienced. I had a keen sense for peril or threat of any kind and was rarely wrong when my danger antennae tingled. Why now? Why here? After watching for a minute, and seeing nothing amiss, I shrugged and went back to my research. The drugs Scarlotti slipped me in Hawaii must have messed up my system much more than I'd thought.

Finally settling back into my subject, I became lost in the world of incredible diamonds. The Orlov diamond, associated with unrequited passion and unachieved power was connected with Prince Orlov and Catherine the Great, and was now in the Russian imperial scepter in the Kremlin.

Greeks saw diamonds as fragments of stars fallen to earth. Romans thought diamonds so hard they could break iron. Chinese treasured them for their engraving ability. Today they're used to pledge eternal love in engagement rings. Fascinating.

The 3,106-carat Cullinan diamond was so enormous that even cutting it into 105 stones, plus 9 more carats of polished bits still yielded the first and second largest diamonds in the world, namely, the 530-carat Great Star of Africa and its little sister, the 317-carat Lesser Star of Africa.

The rough, uncut stone was presented to Edward VII on his sixty-sixth birthday in 1907 and given to Joseph Asscher to prepare and cut the stone. After a year of extensive study, Joseph placed the cleaving blade on the jewel and tapped with a weighty rod. The blade broke; the stone didn't. But the second tap was perfect. The jewel split exactly as planned—and Asscher fell down in a dead faint.

I wasn't sure the British crown jewels were ever let out of the

Tower of London except to be worn by the royal family. Would they be exhibited?

Cramping knees and a sore tailbone demanded a change of position and some stretching. I unwound my legs from the piles of books, glad I'd worn jeans and a sweat shirt for this excursion instead of a skirt. As I straightened and stretched, the tingling at the back of my neck started again. I glanced around the room and caught a glimpse of long, silky, straight black hair disappearing down a staircase in the hall. Was it Scarlotti? I had to know.

Rushing across the room, I knocked the books from the arms of a ponytailed, bespectacled young man who rounded a corner at the wrong time.

"Sorry!" I apologized quietly over my shoulder and raced for the stairs. I flew down the narrow wooden staircase without a thought of what could await me at the bottom—until I was there. A long, dark corridor, lit only by a dim recessed light, stretched toward the red exit sign at the far end where a door was just closing as I reached the bottom step. Was I hallucinating, or had I actually seen Scarlotti Scaddono disappear through that door?

A frisson of fear quivered through my body from head to toe. *What are you doing down here, you idiot? Don't you know better than to fling yourself headlong into something without looking where you're going first? What if that had been Scarlotti? What if he had lured you down here to take you back to his island?*

I wheeled and raced back up the stairs, back to my hidden corner, trembling from head to toe. I hugged myself tight, trying to calm the tremors that racked my body. That was incredibly stupid! *Why did you do that?* Because I needed to know for sure whether Scarlotti Scaddono was really dead. *I had to know.* But how could I find out for sure?

I tried to focus back on diamond research, but it was difficult. My mind jumped back and forth between Scarlotti and the bodies, each imbedded with a small diamond stud. Why were they being left where they were? I grabbed a couple of books on San Francisco history and plunged into that research. A spot cleared on a table nearby and I moved my books there, wanting Bart to be able to find me immediately when he came. I was ready for him to come—now.

A scuffling and shifting of chairs nearby broke my concentration. Someone tall and slim, dressed in black with long, dark, silky hair covering slender shoulders sat down at the table directly in front of mine.

I dropped the book. I couldn't breathe. My heart pounded in my chest. My veins suddenly felt transfused with ice water. Would Scarlotti brazenly show himself like this? Yes!

Placing sweating palms on the table, I pushed myself up on unsteady legs, leaning against the table until I stopped shaking, then took one faltering step around the table, and another, until I was in front of the black-clad figure at the next table.

Was it Scarlotti?

Exquisite, almond-shaped brown eyes stared at me from an exotic, oval face. This elegant creature was certainly not Scarlotti—unless he had a new mask.

"Pardon me for staring, but you're incredibly beautiful. I know this sounds strange, but may I touch your hair?"

The young woman stared, unblinking.

What reason could I possibly give that would sound sane? What would my reaction be if a stranger had made that request of me? I'd think they were slightly off their rocker and run for the door. I was ready to beg her forgiveness and turn away when she smiled shyly.

"Yes, of course."

"It looks like spun silk," I offered lamely, reaching to stroke it while touching her cheek as if by accident. Definitely no mask. Her skin was soft and pliant, the real thing. Her voice was also authentic. Not The Voice I'd come to fear and loathe.

"Thank you. Forgive me for bothering you." I grabbed my purse and notes, leaving the books on the table, and fled the room, eager to be away from there and the memories that flooded back. I flew out the front door and down the steps, right into Bart's arms.

"Princess! What's the matter? You look like you've seen a ghost."

I clung tightly to him, savoring the safety I felt in his warm, strong arms, waiting for my trembling legs to steady, my heart to return to a normal beat, and to compose myself somewhat before I looked up at him. I didn't want him to know just how truly frightened I was.

"I thought I had for a minute. I saw Scarlotti—thought I saw Scarlotti. It turned out to be a woman, an extraordinarily beautiful woman. I had to touch her to be sure it wasn't Scarlotti under a mask. Bart, I think I'm losing my mind!"

Fog swirled around us as he held me close, stroking my hair, murmuring assurances that I wasn't.

"Let's get back to the hotel. You can tell me what you found and I'll tell you what I didn't find." He put his arm around my shoulder, guiding me down the steps.

I took a deep breath. "No luck on getting your information?"

"Not much. How about you?"

"Lots of it, but I had a hard time concentrating. First I had this awful feeling I was being watched, then I saw, or thought I saw, Scarlotti leave the room and go downstairs. I followed . . ."

"You what!" Bart grabbed my shoulders and whirled me to face him.

"I know it was stupid. As soon as I realized what I was doing, I ran back upstairs. Bart, I have to know. It's driving me crazy. Is he dead or not?"

"Oh, Princess." He wrapped me in his arms and held me so tight my ribs hurt. "Please don't do anything like that again. I can't stand the thought of . . ."

I pushed him away and looked up into his face.

"Then you aren't really sure he's dead, either."

"No. Yes. Look at me. You've got me so shook, I don't know what I'm saying. Yes, I believe he's dead. No, I don't think it was humanly possible to survive that fall, the storm, and the peccary."

I shuddered involuntarily.

"I'm not sure he *was* completely human. There was something almost . . . supernatural about him."

"Come on. We'll go call Kahuna right now and see what they've found. He'll have buried the remains already and you can put the nightmare behind you."

We walked arm in arm through the mist that seemed to have no intention of dissipating, though it was nearly noon. It was the perfect atmosphere for my mood. Haunted.

Bart headed for the lift, but I couldn't stand the thought of being confined in a small space just then, even with my handsome husband. I needed room, air, distance between me and my surroundings. I was feeling decidedly claustrophobic and tiny "Elliot" would have me climbing walls.

Bart picked up the phone as soon as we reached our room and called Kahuna in Hawaii. No answer. He dug out Lt. Nakamura's number on Oahu and tried that.

"Lt. Nakamura, this is Bart Allan in California. I'm trying to reach Kahuna, the gardener on Scarlotti Scaddano's island. Do you know where I can find him?" A long, pregnant pause. "Maybe you can help me. Do you know if they ever found Scarlotti's body? I know the Hilo police were handling this, but since all the investigating officers were killed, and you were the first one involved, I thought maybe . . ."

Bart was quiet, listening intently to whatever Lt. Nakamura had to tell him. I sat on the edge of the bed and hugged a pillow, trying to be still, trying to be patient until he could report the conversation, but I was screaming inside.

Tell me he's dead. Tell me they found the body and buried it and I'll never have to worry about him again.

"I see. Sure. Those were his exact words? Read it to me from the report."

I held my breath, heart throbbing till I thought it would leap from my breast. I leaned forward and put my ear against the phone, trying to hear the report.

"Thanks, Lieutenant. That's what my wife's been waiting to hear. Have Kahuna call us at our Santa Barbara number when he gets back. We'd like to talk to him. I'll be in touch." Bart hung up the phone and opened his arms to me.

"Tell me! What did the report say? What did Kahuna say?"

Chapter 5

"He read it directly from the report. Kahuna's exact words were 'I buried the remains I found in the garden he loved.' You're free, Princess. The nightmare's over. Scarlotti is dead. Now you can put it all behind you and stop seeing him in every shadow. Let's celebrate. I'll take you anywhere you want to go for lunch before we head for the museum!"

Bart grabbed me and swung me joyously around and around, squeezing the breath right out of me. Then he plopped on the bed, pulling me on top of him and kissed my nose.

"Where would you like to celebrate, Princess?" He brushed a stray lock of hair from my cheek, then was still. "What's the matter? You don't look like someone who's just heard the good news she's been waiting for."

Bart rolled me onto the bed and leaned up on one elbow so he could look down into my eyes. "Out with it. What's the matter?"

"I guess it just takes a minute to sink in. Scarlotti's been such a fearful presence in my life, I can't believe it's finally over. Tell me again what Kahuna said."

"I buried the remains I found in the garden he loved."

"It wasn't 'I found Scarlotti and buried him in the garden' or 'I found what was left of Scarlotti'? It's almost too vague to . . ."

"Allison. Listen to me. Scarlotti's dead. Put him out of your mind. Okay? Repeat after me, Scarlotti is dead."

I couldn't answer. The words just wouldn't come. Bart feathered a fingertip across my bottom lip, then up the side of my face and around an errant curl.

"What can I say to convince you?" he whispered, cradling me securely in his arms.

I sighed, forcing myself to say the words my concerned husband wanted to hear. "Okay. Scarlotti is dead. I don't have to worry about him anymore."

Bart brushed a kiss across my nose, then my lips. He searched my eyes, studied my expression, trying to decipher my feelings.

"No more shadows hanging over us," he said softly. "We can get on with our honeymoon and our life, and go catch some bad guys before they commit the biggest diamond heist in the history of the world. And have lunch. Does that appeal to you? I'm starving."

He rolled off the bed and, taking both of my hands in his, pulled me up, but he didn't let go. His hands gripped my shoulders so I couldn't turn away and his blue eyes narrowed as he scrutinized my face. Then he pulled me close and held me against him, so tight I could hardly breathe.

What was he thinking? That he had a paranoid wife who was letting her imagination run away with her? Or did he understand how truly terrified I was of Scarlotti? Lighten up, lady. Don't let your phobias spoil your honeymoon!

"I like your plan," I laughed, reaching up to plant a quick kiss on the corner of his mouth. "I'm famished, too. But let me change first. I'd feel grossly underdressed at the museum in jeans and a sweat shirt."

I turned quickly to the closet to get my emotions under control. If I could convince Bart I believed him, maybe I could start believing it, too.

I searched for something chic and sophisticated through the limited wardrobe I'd hurriedly packed. Not much choice. I settled on a hunter green suit with Chanel's classic lines and a white silk blouse. I wouldn't feel like Cinderella, pre-fairy godmother, when we met some gorgeous doll all decked out like a fashion plate. Bart watched with amusement.

"What are you laughing at?"

"Just wondering if that long-legged beauty taking notes in the museum yesterday had anything to do with your dressing to the nines today."

"You saw her?" I cried with dismay.

"Of course, I saw her. And everyone else who was there. That's my job. But she wasn't half as pretty as you, Princess, so she didn't rate a second glance."

"By the way, you didn't tell me what you found, or didn't find, this morning. Any luck with the police and firemen?"

Bart frowned and pulled off his shoes. "Unfortunately, they don't want to let go of what they have. The chief wasn't in, so I couldn't go to the top, and no one else wanted to cooperate with an outsider. I need to deliver something that'll help them before they'll be glad to see me coming, I'm afraid. Captain Bronson was helpful, though. I got a printout on the fires. We'll do a little analysis on that later. What did you come up with?"

"If only a fraction of the famous diamonds end up in this exhibit, it will be worth millions of dollars—but that's just the monetary value. Their historical and sentimental value is off the charts. I'll bring my notes and answer your questions over lunch."

Lunch was delightful, a welcome change of pace from fast food and grabbing a bite on the run. Linen tablecloths, crystal water goblets, and fresh flowers on each table, a romantic background of live piano music—all you could possibly ask for and more.

I was finally able to relax and refrain from examining everyone at other tables, to stop scrutinizing those walking by on the sidewalk, and to concentrate on Bart and his work—finally able to stop looking for Scarlotti behind every pillar and post.

"Are you sure you can afford this place on an agent's salary?"

"If I can't, I guess you'll just have to dip into a few of your millions to keep us from washing dishes to pay for it."

"Do I detect a note of irritation?"

"Not at all. I've come to grips with the fact that my lovely wife is an heiress with more money at her disposal than I'll ever make in a dozen lifetimes." Bart leaned across the table and took my hand. "I've also come to the conclusion that since you're sensible, level-headed, and generous to a fault, you won't let it change you from the Allison I've always known and loved. So why let my macho genes refuse to allow you to enjoy doing whatever you want with it?"

"Thanks, Vanderbilt. We'll make a great team! Your good looks and good sense and my money." I sighed. "I'll miss this when I go back to work. Lying in bed in the morning, leisurely lunches with my husband . . ."

"What do you mean, when you go back to work?" Bart interrupted, picking up the check. "You'll have a full-time job taking care of me."

He laughed when he said it, but it disturbed me that he would tease about it nevertheless. I loved my job at the United Nations. It was important to me. Like the issues of where we were going to live and religion, this was another subject that needed time for discussion, time for delving into it. There never seemed to be enough time.

At the museum, Bart asked to meet with the curator as well as the head of security. While he waited, I wandered, enjoying the current exhibit.

Suddenly, there she was again, even more of her long, gorgeous legs bared today in a microskirted suit of celery green that set off her shining cinnamon hair.

I turned to see if Bart had spotted her yet. His back was to us as he talked with the security guard on duty. I walked to the other side of the room so I could watch unobserved. She was taking notes again in the black leather portfolio, oblivious to my perusal of her.

Her casual elegance fascinated me, along with the way she tossed her hair when it fell across her face, then tucked it behind her ear. She stood as if she were posing—long, shapely legs wide apart, then close together, one rubbing against the other, a celery-colored shoe pointing, heel tapping. She moved down the room like a dancer in slow motion, dipping and swaying, pausing, wheeling. I followed at a distance, watching as she studied each room, making extensive notes and sketches.

I was intrigued. Who was she? A reporter doing a story on the museum? An art critic? My musings were cut short when Bart appeared.

"Enjoying yourself?"

"Just watching Legs do her thing, whatever that is. She's fascinating. Did you get to talk to your people?" I asked.

"The curator isn't in today and the head of security is at lunch. I made an appointment with both of them for tomorrow. Let's do a little prowling and get intimately acquainted with this place. I want a feel for the soft spots."

"Soft spots?"

"Vulnerable areas. Places it might be hard to protect. Easy access or escape routes. That sort of thing."

We wandered the museum, examining the huge round skylight and the catwalk below it on the fifth floor, paying special attention to the exit doors that led out back. He prowled the fourth-floor balcony, scowling at what appeared easy access for an expert second-story man.

While Bart checked for soft spots, I checked people. Always an avid people-watcher, I'd become acutely aware of those around me since I'd been stalked so often lately.

I watched a tattered old man, bent with age, tap his way around the gallery leaning on a beautifully carved cane that seemed totally out of character with his raggedy appearance.

Two small children hurried their reluctant mother through the exhibit much faster than she wanted to go, her blonde ponytail flipping back and forth as she tried to catch all the paintings before they dragged her to the next room.

A trio of studious-looking young people, college art students on assignment, I guessed, were sketching a Matisse, probably copying it for an art class.

I was intrigued by two fellows who strolled casually by, stopping, examining, discussing the paintings. They seemed an odd pair—poles apart in appearance. One was tall, muscular, bearded, with dun brown hair slicked back close to his head and a ponytail hanging down the back of his somber mud-brown shirt. Hostile dark eyes scrutinized his surroundings more closely than the paintings.

The other was totally opposite. Short, stout, close-cropped, maize-colored hair and laughing, friendly, pale eyes so fair I couldn't tell whether they were blue, gray, or hazel. He seemed oblivious to everything around him but the exhibit, visibly savoring the beauty of each painting before him, seemingly hungry for each new work of art.

Bart interrupted my people-watching.

"In the mood for some more library research?"

"What do you need?"

"A place to sit quietly and examine the fire stats Blaise gave me."

"We could go back to the Abigail."

Bart flashed a foolish grin. "We could, but there's too much distraction there to concentrate. An emerald-eyed Lorelei keeps luring me away from my investigation. I think at the library, I can keep my mind on business and not get sidetracked so easily. While I'm trying to find a pattern to the fires, you can finish your diamond research."

"Lead on, Lochinvar. Whither thou goest, I will go," I laughed, looping my arm through his. "I promise to not lure you away too soon."

As we rounded the stairs overlooking the atrium, I was suddenly glad we appeared so intimate. We ran smack dab into the gorgeous Legs.

"Oh, I'm so sorry," she cooed in an accent I couldn't place. Not quite French, not quite . . .

Bart immediately instigated introductions. My green eyes blazed greener at Bart's bright, animated smile and attention to the beauty who towered over me, making me feel like a dumpy, frowsy little girl playing dress-up.

I pushed the hated feelings of inferiority away and offered my hand, hoping my smile masked the emotions struggling just under the surface.

"I am Elekta Apotheosis. I'm so sorry. I was not watching where I walked."

"It was as much our fault. I'm afraid we were concentrating on each other and not enough on where we were going," Bart apologized.

I could have hugged him for that comment. My cheeks pinked with pleasure and I grew about one foot in that instant. The bitter taste of inferiority sweetened as my sense of worth increased.

"I'm Allison Alexander . . . Allan," I hastened to add, glancing at Bart with a smile.

"You're recently married?" Elekta ventured with a smile that lit luminous brown eyes. Her flawless, creamy complexion glowed with a minimum of makeup. How could any one person be so totally stunning? It wasn't fair!

"Is it that apparent?" Bart laughed, his arm tightly around my waist.

"There is an aura, a radiance, that surrounds you. It gives you away." Her low, husky voice was smooth and cultured, her manner of speaking careful and studied.

"I'm trying to place your accent. Your name is Greek, but your accent is not. Forgive my curiosity, but where are you from?"

For the briefest instant her big brown eyes flickered and flashed darker. Then she laughed.

"You are a student of the Greek?"

Before I could reply, Bart answered for me.

"My wife is a linguist. She speaks a dozen languages, and has had a lifelong love affair with words. It's second nature to her." He kissed my forehead in a gesture of pride that endeared him to me forever.

She hadn't answered my question, implying that I had guessed correctly. But I'd spent half my life in Greece, had grandparents who had lived there all their lives. Hers was not a Greek accent, despite her Greek name.

"I was hurrying to meet an associate. I will be late." She extended a well-manicured hand with long, tapered, unpolished fingernails buffed to a high gloss. "I'm so pleased to meet you. I wish you a happy life."

She shook Bart's hand, dipping her head slightly as if in salutation, then took mine and repeated the slight bow, tilting her head so the auburn hair fell across her face. She flashed an enigmatic smile, spun on one celery-colored high heel and glided toward the entrance with the grace of a skater.

"Bartholomew James Allan," I said, standing on tiptoe to brush a quick kiss on his cheek. "Have I told you lately how wonderful you are and how very much I love you?"

"As a matter of fact, Mrs. Allan, you haven't. But I have time right now if you'd like to take care of that little matter."

He pulled me around the corner away from the atrium and drew me into his arms.

As I opened my mouth to tell him, slippery little fingers of fear slid up my arms and down my spine, leaving me quivering in their wake.

"Allison! What is it?" Bart demanded as I whirled to see what had caused my danger antennae to set alarms tingling through my system. There was nothing, nobody in sight that should have triggered such a tremor through my body. My flesh was still crawling with goose bumps when I heard—felt—his voice. The Voice. Soft and sensuous.

"Allison, I'm here."

Chapter

6

I flew into Bart's arms and clung tightly to him.

"Hold me and don't let go," I whispered, trembling all over.

"Princess, what's the matter? What happened?" Bart's arms folded instantly and securely around me.

I shuddered.

"He's here. He's not dead. He called my name. He said, 'Allison, I'm here.' It was his voice!"

Bart's body went rigid; his heart thudded faster in his chest as he pressed me close to him. He rotated us slowly so he could see in every direction, one hand stroking up and down my back, the other firmly holding my head against the taut muscles in his chest.

"Let's get out of here." Bart hurried me from the museum, straight through the dense, gray fog to the car. He guided me gently down into the seat, then slammed and locked the door.

As he strode swiftly to the driver's side, I watched him instinctively reach for his gun, touching it as if to reassure himself he'd remembered to bring it. He jammed the key into the ignition and the little blue convertible's engine roared to life. I jumped, startled by the sound, then realized I'd expected Scarlotti to have disabled the car, stalling us, trapping us.

Bart tossed a ten-dollar bill out the window at the parking lot attendant as we peeled out of the lot into busy Third Street, forcing a Mercedes to a screeching halt when we pulled in front of it. I buckled my seat belt as he raced around the corner, flew through a yellow light and fishtailed another quick turn on the fog-dampened street.

I stared at Bart, trying to read the expression on his face, to know what he was feeling, his reason for the urgency of the flight. Was he disgusted with me—or afraid for me?

Aware I was watching him, he turned, flashed a sympathetic smile, and reached for my hand, squeezing it reassuringly.

"Just wanted to make sure we had a head start on your ghost. If he finds us, I'll know you're being haunted for sure. If he doesn't, then I'll suspect he's human after all, or . . ." He let the sentence fall away unfinished.

I picked up the thread. "Or your wife is certifiably crazy and should be committed." My quivering voice betrayed the fear flushing through me that the thought might be true.

"I don't believe there's anything wrong with your mind, Princess, unless you're experiencing a little leftover paranoia from the hallucinogens Scarlotti fed you. I'm certainly no expert, but I know you can experience flashbacks for some time. You're too much together, too strong to be imagining something this real. So either Scarlotti isn't dead and he's trying to torment you or his drugs are haunting you."

Bart concentrated on the road again as he swung onto I-80 toward the Oakland Bay Bridge.

"Where are we going?" I asked, peering through the fog that enveloped us in a smothering blanket of mist. It seeped and oozed into and around everything, obscuring traffic signs until we were nearly past them, shrouding the bridge above, cloaking the city and bay beneath, even penetrating the convertible top. I imagined tendrils of fog creeping in around the windows, searching for me, reaching for me.

Get control, Allison! Don't let your imagination send you over the edge. Scarlotti would love that. Calm down. Breathe deep. That's better.

Bart squeezed my hand. "Are you okay?" he asked, his voice filled with concern.

"Am I that easy to read?"

"I was holding your hand, remember. Your grip nearly broke my fingers. What's going on in that perceptive mind of yours?"

"My vivid imagination just got out of control for a minute. The fog must have set off my claustrophobia. Where are we going? Did I already ask that, or just think I did?"

"Actually, I think you did," Bart laughed sheepishly. "I was lost in thought, too." He pulled my hand to his lips and kissed the back of it lightly, then turned it over and kissed my palm, sending little shivers of pleasure through me. A nice change from the fear that had chilled me.

Bart's voice became serious. "The thought that Scarlotti could still be alive shook me. I'd buried him and filed him away. Case complete. But if he did survive, you're in very real danger and so are the rest of us. He'd planned to kill us all. Instead, his magnificent pet lion is dead and we don't know the extent of his injuries. If he's further disfigured, he'll certainly blame us, and be all the more determined to do us in."

"What can we do?"

"If Scarlotti *is* a ghost, he's definitely not a benign, friendly one. Right now I'm taking you where evil spirits don't go. On the other hand, if he's alive, I don't think even he could have followed us, so either way you're safe for now."

My fear of Scarlotti Scaddano was consummate. He had connections everywhere and the money to hire as much help as he needed. He was evil, cunning, Machiavellian, with a not-quite-human way of slipping silently in and out of rooms and a voice so hypnotic, it compelled you to obey. Images of a modern-day phantom filled my senses when I thought of Scarlotti.

Bart exited the freeway and we wound through hilly, fog-shrouded residential areas above Oakland. He pulled into a parking lot where palm trees lined some kind of promenade. Mist obscured all but a glimpse of the gleaming white building beyond. He parked, facing the gated entrance, watching to see if we'd been followed, and began his explanation.

"The first time I met Bishop O'Hare, we were seated together on a flight from Washington D.C. into LAX. When a delay kept us on the ground at Dulles, we got acquainted. In the course of the conversation I discovered he was a bishop in the Church of Jesus Christ of Latter-day Saints. I told you Emile converted me in Tibet before he died, but I'd never had a chance to be baptized."

I nodded. He'd said that had changed his life, had kept him alive through six months of torture before he escaped.

"We spent the whole flight talking about the Church, how it was restored exactly as it had been when Christ was on earth. We explored doctrine, the commitment required to be a good Church member, forever families. I told him about Emile, how he died knowing he'd be with his family after death, how I wanted that for you and me. It came out we were in the same line of work—FBI and Interpol. I rented a car to drive back to Santa Barbara and offered him a lift since he was headed there, too."

Bart stopped his story. "Looks like we're okay. No one followed us. Let's go."

Bart got out of the car and came around to open my door, continuing his narration as we walked.

"He asked if we could stop at the Los Angeles Temple just off the 405 on Santa Monica Boulevard, a detour of only a few minutes. I'd seen the spire from the interstate dozens of times, but never been there. I parked and settled back to wait while he took some computer discs filled with genealogy inside, but the sunshine and a huge ancient tree enticed me out of the car. While sitting on a bench under the tree, I watched an old Asian couple get out of a car, cross the street, and as they reached the temple grounds, kneel down and take their shoes off."

"Why?" I asked, stopping at a great circular fountain with water splashing gaily in the gray vapor that swirled around us.

"I think they felt they were on sacred ground. The feeling I had as I watched them . . . I can't even think of a word to describe it. Awesome, incredible, peaceful, sacred. None of them do it justice. I just sat there, absorbing the spirit I felt all around me. I closed my eyes and . . ."

He stopped, struggling to control his voice. I squeezed his arm but didn't speak.

"Alli, I couldn't stop the tears. It was as if a spring inside me had burst open. A cleansing took place. I even felt . . . ," my big, strong husband looked at me through misted eyes, ". . . something I can only describe as a heavenly hug. Does that make sense to you?"

I remembered the feeling in the tunnel in Hawaii, paralyzed by claustrophobia, desperate to get to the police, yet not being able to move. I'd had that same sensation in answer to a fervent plea to God for help.

"Yes. I know exactly what you're talking about."

"I don't know how long I sat there. I was vaguely aware of people passing, but I clung to that feeling, yearning to keep it as long as possible. I prayed again for a confirmation that this church was true, that I was doing the right thing in seeking baptism. I got it."

Bart turned to me again, but this time it wasn't tears shining in his clear, cobalt eyes. It was the fire of faith. He'd asked. He'd received. He knew.

"You brought me here so I could have that same experience?"

Bart stood thoughtfully for a minute before he answered, then slowly shook his head.

"No. You'll find your answer in your own way, when you're ready to ask. I brought you here because I panicked. I didn't have control anymore. I couldn't stand the thought of not being able to protect you from Scarlotti—to keep you safe from real or imagined threats. I needed a haven, a refuge, a safe house," he laughed lamely, lapsing into familiar jargon. "This was the first place I thought of. And the safest." He took a deep breath. "Want to see the place?"

"Sure. I love romantic meanders through the mist." Stopping at the elaborate white wrought iron gates that served as the temple's entry, Bart turned me to face him, tilting my chin up.

"Do you know how very much I love you? My greatest fear is that something or someone will keep us from having our marriage sealed in the temple and I'll lose you. The thought makes me wild."

He pulled me close, pressing me against his warm, hard body. I slipped my arms under his jacket and clung to him. What would I do if anything happened to Bart? I'd loved him since I was five years old. If this religion could actually offer all Bart said it could, that seemed almost reason enough to embrace it. But I needed to know for myself, just as Bart had discovered for himself.

Wandering silently toward the towering white temple with its spires peeking in and out of the mist, we found a staircase and climbed it. Peace as tangible as the fog swirling around us encompassed me, warming my heart, calming my mind, touching my spirit.

"Can you feel it?" Bart asked softly.

"Yes. Thank you for bringing me here, for loving me, for not doubting my sanity. So many doubts have plagued me. Am I sane or crazy? Am I hearing things that aren't there or are they real? Will you love me if I'm crazy or will you go away and leave me? The questions alone are enough to drive me insane!"

Bart stopped walking and turned to me. Pain flashed across his face.

"I feel so helpless. I know the priesthood has the power to heal, to preserve, to safeguard. But *I* don't have it. I can't give you what you need. I keep letting other things get in the way of my baptism. I wish I could just walk in the front door and say, 'I'm ready. Baptize me. And my wife. And marry us forever.' Do you realize when we're baptized," he paused, "if you are, it would be an entire year before we could come to the temple? A whole year! We're wasting so much precious time."

He turned, pacing in a tight circle in front of me. I stood mute, helpless at his frustration.

"I got so excited about the hunt, the chase for the bad guys. Stop the evil. Safeguard the world. And my own world could fall apart under my very nose," he lamented. "Where are my priorities?"

I waited while he did another turn, mentally whipping himself.

"You were right in bringing us here," I offered. "I'd forgotten in my own state of fright and panic how many times in Hawaii God answered my prayers and came to my rescue. If you feel that strongly about it, your baptism shouldn't wait."

Bart stopped pacing and looked at me, blue eyes filled with agitation. Then his expression softened.

I opened my arms and he walked into them, sweeping me off my feet, twirling me through the mist, sending it swirling around the benches and over the ledge into the invisible valley below.

"Princess, you have such a nice way of putting things in their proper perspective. Whatever would I do without you?" His kiss, warm and sustained, was balm to my jagged nerves.

"I'll do my best to make sure you never have to," I promised.

I was glad he hadn't pressed me about *my* decision to be baptized. I wasn't ready to commit one way or the other just yet.

"Ready to face our demons now?" Bart held me at arms' length and looked at me.

"Ready when you are, Saint George. I just hope our dragons are of the flesh and blood variety."

Chapter 7

Nearly soaked to the skin from the dense, wet fog that had turned to a drizzle, we clambered back into the car in a mood much different from that of an hour before.

Bart pulled over at the first public phone he saw and motioned me out of the car with him.

"I'm going to assume, until we get a definite decision from the police, that Scarlotti is alive."

"I'm sure Scarlotti knows about the secret passages in the house," I said. "If he slipped in when Dad was gone, Mom would be helpless."

"Your folks need to get out of the house. Now."

Bart punched the numbers into the phone with confident precision.

"Jack, Bart here. We've reason to believe Scarlotti isn't dead and is here, ready to finish what he started in Hawaii. Allison thinks he knows about the secret passageways in the house. You'd better get Margaret to a safe house pronto. I'll assume there's no secure line to or from the estate and that there may be a bug on our car and in our room. Possibly yours, too. Will you see what you can find out from the police in Hilo? We need a body. An identifiable one."

Bart listened to Dad on the other end.

"Not good. How about that specialist in Athens? Leave a message at the Abigail Hotel or with Chief Saddler of the San Francisco police so I'll know where to find you."

Another pause. I didn't like Bart's end of the conversation. Something was wrong with Mom.

"Yes, Allison's fine." His arm came around me and pulled me close. "Let me know how to contact you."

"What?" I demanded as Bart hung up the phone.

"Your mom's not responding as well as she did at first. Jack's worried and was about ready to get her to a specialist."

"In Athens?"

"The 'specialist in Athens' is our code for total security. That was simply telling him to get her under cover so he's the only one who knows where she is. Not even we'll know. It's coincidence he's planning to take her to a specialist."

"What's the matter with Mom?"

"Jack said she's been plagued with headaches and so exhausted she couldn't get out of bed, after he'd been fighting to keep her down the first few days."

"But Scarlotti could get the message when he leaves one," I said.

"Jack's message will be coded when it comes. We'll only talk on secure phones."

Bart gave me a quick hug and brushed the strands of wet hair from my face.

"Don't worry, Princess. She'll be fine. You know your dad will get her the best help possible."

I bit my lip. Was this a temporary relapse or had Scarlotti put something on the arrow tip that just now commenced its dirty work? I wanted to be with Mom. But how much help could I really be? And I needed and wanted to be here with Bart.

"So what's the plan, Mr. Bond, while we wait to hear from them?"

"First, some dry clothes, then how does dinner sound?"

"A man after my heart! Sounds wonderful."

"Actually, I'm after more than just your heart. I want your body, too."

"You know all the right answers." I wrapped my arms around his neck and pulling his wet face down, kissed him.

"Mmm. I could use a whole lot more of that. Let's get back and dry you off before you catch pneumonia. One sick member of the family is enough."

In the car, the soft music on the radio was interrupted by the report of the discovery of yet another body. I turned the radio off before I heard the location. We could find out later. Right now I needed a break from all the violence.

We had three messages waiting for us when we got back to the Abigail. Fire Captain Blaise Bronson and Police Chief Jim Saddler each informed Bart they'd scheduled a joint meeting for seven o'clock the next morning. They wanted his ideas on the trouble in San Francisco and planned to explore the necessity of a task force to deal with it.

The third was for me from Saroya. "How do you do all this? Come as soon as you can. It's more than I can handle!"

"So much for the honeymoon!" I moaned ruefully. "They're putting us back to work."

"Only if you let them. You're not going back, are you?" Bart said incredulously.

"I won't if you won't," I teased as we climbed the stairs to the fifth floor.

"Princess, it's not quite the same thing. What I'm doing has international implications."

I didn't like the condescending tone in his voice.

"And my work at the U.N. doesn't have international implications? I work with diplomats and ambassadors from a dozen different nations every day. That's not international?"

"I guess I should have said my work concerns international security."

"You could certainly say the same thing for mine. If I misinterpret or mistranslate some of those high-level meetings, I could be the cause of World War III."

I couldn't believe we were having this conversation! It seemed petty, each insisting that our job was the most important. Actually, I didn't think my work was more important than Bart's, but I felt he was simply discounting my work, brushing it aside as frivolous, superfluous.

Bart turned the key in the lock and stepped to the side before pushing the door to our room open. He blocked my way so I couldn't enter.

"Yes?" I asked, letting a little petulance creep into my voice.

Bart turned at the tone.

"Just making sure no one was waiting for us with some kind of nasty surprise. I didn't want you walking into any kind of harm."

"Sorry, 007. I forgot you're on duty all the time. Not that I'm not grateful! I certainly wouldn't want to walk into Scarlotti's hands again, or be caught by any of his little snares."

Efficiently and carefully, Bart searched the room from top to bottom.

"Looking for anything in particular?"

"Anything that's not supposed to be here," he replied. "Bugs, explosives, snakes, spiders . . ."

"You're kidding, aren't you?" I grabbed his arm and turned him around so I could see his face.

"Do they worry you more than a bomb?"

"I don't want to worry about any of that in a hotel room. I want to come back to a nice, safe, quiet refuge, change into dry clothes, and pretend I'm going to get to finish my honeymoon, all of which looks like a foolish dream at this point."

Finishing his inspection of the bathroom, Bart turned on the water to run a hot bath, then peeled off my soggy jacket.

"Now what are you doing?"

"Getting you out of these wet clothes, since you obviously aren't interested in doing it. After waiting all these years for you to grow up and marry me, I'm not about to take a chance on losing you to pneumonia, or anything else, if I can help it."

"You continually surprise me, Bartholomew James Allan. First you insult and demean me, then you undress me. Is there a message there?"

"Probably that I'm a typical thoughtless, unobservant male," he said as he gently shoved me back on the bed to remove my shoes. "When did I insult and demean you, and how?"

"When you implied my job wasn't important."

"Did I imply that?" he asked absently, his mind and his fingers concentrating on the tiny fabric buttons on my blouse.

"You did. You dismissed my work, brushed it aside as you would brush a fly away. I can do this myself, you know. I learned how to undress years ago."

"I know, but I'm rather enjoying it. How do I get you out of your dripping skirt? You're getting the bed all wet."

"You're changing the subject. Do you or do you not think what I do is important?"

Bart pulled me off the bed and stood me in front of him where he could reach the button and zipper on the soggy skirt.

"To be honest, Princess, I've really never given it any thought. When I pictured what you do at the U.N., I guess it was giving tours to interested tourists or translating mail from a grandmother back home in Greece for someone who didn't read the language."

I stepped out of the skirt and he draped it over the end of the bed.

"You're wet clear to the skin. Aren't you cold?"

"With a handsome hunk undressing me? Not exactly. Do you want to know what I really do?" I asked, retrieving the skirt from the wooden bedstead and hanging it on a hanger, as well as the discarded jacket and blouse.

"Sure," Bart said distractedly as he pulled my slip off and grabbed a towel to dry me.

"I personally greet each diplomat or ambassador to whom I'm assigned and welcome their family to America. I connect them with others from their country, familiarize them with the city and some of our more important laws and rules they might have missed in the briefing they should have received before they came. Mmm. That feels good."

Bart briskly rubbed my arms and shoulders with the towel, then pushed me back on the bed to peel off my panty hose and dry my legs and feet, warming them in the process.

"All that's really unofficial," I continued. "My official duties, what I get paid to do, is translate meetings between diplomats and help them communicate. To understand what the other is saying, not just the words, but the gist of the whole conversation. Sometimes that's the hard part. Making one understand what the other one is really trying to convey, and not what he or she is actually saying."

I took Bart's damp jacket off and hung it on the valet next to the dresser, then unbuttoned his wet shirt while he towel-dried my hair.

"I guess there's no way you'll know unless I tell you that I'm very good at what I do. I have ambassadors who schedule their visits to America to coincide with my availability."

I pulled off Bart's shoes.

"Guides take people through the United Nations building. I have translated letters from relatives in a foreign language, but that's not really part of my job." I peeled off his wet socks. "I've had diplomats refuse to come to a meeting if I was translating somewhere else, and," I struggled to unbuckle Bart's belt, "I even brought two feuding ambassadors together who hadn't spoken for twenty years to sign a treaty for their countries."

"How did you accomplish that feat?" Bart asked, sitting up so I could tug off his damp trousers.

"I told them I'd never work with them again if they didn't swallow their pride and meet with me and each other." I knelt on the bed behind Bart, drying his hair and shoulders with the towel. I dabbed gently at the scars that crisscrossed his back. Though he said they were no longer sensitive, they looked like they should be.

"Sounds to me like you're indispensable," Bart laughed, turning to take the towel from my hands.

"I'm not sure I like the patronizing tone in your voice," I pouted as I pulled it away and covered his head with it.

"Enough!" Bart cried, grabbing the towel from me. He whipped it around my waist and pulled me around in front of him. "I believe you are very, very good at what you do. How could you be anything else? I'm sure you're in great demand. Everybody who knows you should love you. How could they not be captivated by you? I believe you're going to be missed immensely when you quit your job. You'll leave a void ten people won't be able to fill."

He pulled me close, dropped the towel, and wrapped his arms around me, rolling back on the bed.

"What do you mean, when I quit . . . ?" But his mouth closed over mine before I got the rest of the question out, and in a minute, I completely forgot the discussion.

We barely caught the tub before it overflowed, but only because it was one of those huge, old-fashioned things with brass claw feet that held twice the water of today's tubs. Bart sprinkled in the last of the herbs Kahuna had given me in Hawaii to heal my blistered hands and cut feet and said he had to make a phone call before he joined me.

I settled into the steaming, scented bath, leaned back, and closed my eyes. What beat a hot bath on a dismal, foggy day?

Did I doze momentarily and dream, or did the herbs' aroma invoke unwanted memories? Goose bumps suddenly surfaced, tingling my fingertips and toes in spite of the hot water. I felt Scarlotti's eyes watching. His malevolent presence was overwhelming.

I quickly lost all interest in my bath and fled to the safety of the bedroom. I couldn't tell Bart what happened; I simply gave the lame excuse that he'd taken too long joining me.

What was happening to me? Was my mind playing tricks on me? Was I still suffering from the after-effects of the hallucinogens? Or was my sanity in question here? How could I possibly explain what I'd just experienced? I didn't try.

Chapter

8

I perched, fascinated, on the edge of the bathroom counter watching Bart shave. It was a ritual I'd missed because of my own father's absence while I was growing up. I understood now why Queen Victoria was so mesmerized each morning watching Prince Albert shave. Bart made one final swipe with the razor above his upper lip, poking it out with his tongue to get a better angle, then rinsed his razor under running water.

"If I end up in meetings all day, what are you going to do with yourself?" He sounded apologetic as he wiped off the rest of the creamy white foam.

"First on my agenda is a nice long run to get the kinks out. I've sorely missed my daily workout of a good swim or run."

Bart's eyes narrowed as he studied me in the mirror.

"And just where did you plan on doing this run?"

"I'm sure the *concierge* can suggest a good place."

Bart turned and gripped my shoulders.

"Sorry, Princess. I hate to curtail your fun, but if Scarlotti or Roach . . ."

"Speaking of Roach, how could he know we're in San Francisco?"

"The same way we keep tabs on him and guys like him. Spotters, surveillance, checking known addresses, travel plans, and so on. Are you worried about him?"

"No, just curious. Both incidents, the gunshot the other night and the car in front of the hotel, could have been random acts, totally unrelated and coincidence. But if it was Roach, I just wondered how he could know we were in San Francisco."

"If it was Roach, and we need to assume it was, he could have had someone watching the estate. Everyone in the world who watches TV knew where we were for the wedding. It would be an easy matter to have someone waiting for our return and report to him. That's why I don't want you on the street alone."

"You know I'll be careful," I laughed lightly, pulling the towel from around his neck to wipe a dab of shaving cream from his ear. "I'll run with my pepper spray in my hand."

"Allison, I'd rather you didn't leave the hotel." He waited for an assurance that I wouldn't leave.

Should I be flippant and say, "Sorry, Charlie. You're my husband, not my keeper?" Or should I acquiesce to his wishes? I was at a loss to know how to handle this newly-acquired husband-creature.

"I do have something you could occupy your time with," Bart said.

"Yes?"

Out of the pocket of his suitcase, he pulled a navy blue book with an angel embossed in gold on the front.

"This answered many of my questions, as well as raised a lot of questions for me to ask. I'll leave it for you if you'd like to read it."

"What is it?"

"It's the book Emile read to me over and over in the prison in Tibet. Not this copy, of course, but the book."

"*The Book of Mormon?*"

"Yes. I'd be happy if you'd read it . . . prayerfully."

"Thank you. I will read it," I assured him.

We walked down the stairs, Bart's arm across my shoulder. He paused, tilted my chin up, and looked down into my eyes.

"Promise me you'll stay in the hotel and be very careful, Princess. I couldn't live with myself if anything happened to you."

"I promise you I'll be very, very careful." I did not promise to stay in the hotel.

The desk clerk looked up and smiled. "Good morning."

We echoed his greeting as I walked Bart to the door of the Abigail and kissed him good-bye. I took the corner table in the tiny breakfast room where I could look directly onto the street from the tall, curved art deco window. Already, at six forty-five, there was a little bouquet of fresh daisies at each copper-covered table.

Opening the book to the title page, I started reading while I waited for the seven o'clock continental breakfast. By the time I read the last two paragraphs in the introduction, I knew why Bart wanted me to read the book.

I sipped orange juice and nibbled a bran muffin as I started the first chapter. "I, Nephi, having been born of goodly parents . . ." What a strange beginning for a book. Sort of catchy, though.

Engrossed in my reading, I completely lost interest in eating as I became involved in the story. I read, "I will go and do the thing which the Lord hath commanded, for I know that the Lord giveth no commandment unto the children of man, save he shall prepare a way for them that they may accomplish the thing which he commandeth them."

I stopped reading. Makes sense. If he wants you to do it, he certainly ought to help you accomplish it.

I glanced out the window directly into the intense dark eyes of a strange old woman with a purple felt hat squashed on top of her frizzy gray hair. Her face was lined with age, weary with life. Pain and sorrow were reflected in those deep-set dark pools. Her dress was covered with big faded yellow sunflowers, over which she wore a navy blue sweater and a red shawl.

Out of the deep pockets of a checkered apron came hands covered in dingy white gloves with the fingers cut out. They pointed at my breakfast, then at the sidewalk. I looked down. Winding themselves around her legs were a dozen cats in an assortment of kinds, colors, and sizes.

I mouthed an invitation to come in, motioning to let her know that she could sit at my table, but she shook her head, pointing again to the cats. I nodded.

The desk clerk doubled as kitchen help during breakfast, replenishing juice, coffee, muffins, bagels, and Danish as needed. I deposited a ten-dollar bill in front of the clerk, and asked him to please provide some milk and kitchen scraps for the cats and breakfast for the old woman.

"But, Madam . . ." he stammered.

"If you prefer to feed them around at the back door, you may do that, but please feed them."

He gestured broadly for the woman to go around to the back

door. She pumped her head up and down, a wide smile revealing a set of gleaming, even white teeth. Acknowledging her gratitude with a nod and a smile, I went back to reading as the old woman and her entourage vanished around the corner behind me.

I scarcely noticed time passing as I got caught up in the excitement of reading about Lehi's dream.

"Your Highness? Your Majesty? Excuse me." Aware of someone at my elbow, I looked around to see where and who the royalty was. The desk clerk was talking to me.

"I'm sorry to bother you, Your Highness." The tall, slender young man bent nervously over me, a tousle of glossy black hair falling onto his forehead as he nodded.

I must have stared open-mouthed at him. A self-satisfied smile lit his gray eyes and curved up his mouth at the corners.

"I didn't mean to eavesdrop but I heard your husband call you 'Princess' and I remembered seeing your picture. You're Princess Alexandra."

Speechless, I shook my head.

"I understand, Your Highness, you don't want anyone to know who you are," he dropped his voice a notch lower, "and I promise not to tell a soul. But, Princess, should you be here all alone? Where are your bodyguards?"

"But I'm not . . ."

"It's all right. I'll keep your secret," he insisted with a whisper.

Caught up in the humor and ridiculousness of the situation, I played along since my feeble attempts at denial weren't doing any good.

"I didn't think I'd be recognized, so I don't have any bodyguards."

"Will you be safe alone?"

"I'm sure I will. I'm not planning to go where anyone would see me."

"I have a friend who's a bouncer at a nightclub . . ."

"No, thanks. I really don't need a bodyguard. You can tell me one thing, though. When people want to run here, where do they go? Is it safe to run a few miles around the blocks?"

Shock blanched his long, narrow face. "You mean run, like, on the street?"

"Yes."

"Umm, well, most people, but Your Highness, you're not most people."

"Where do 'most people' run?"

"Probably the best place, Your Highness, would be Golden Gate Park, although there are nice trails along the bay and through the Presidio, and some like to run the bridge."

"Can't I just run to the park?"

"No, Your Highness. I'll call a cab for you when you're ready to go. Is there anything else I can do for you?"

"Please don't call me that," I insisted. "Someone is bound to hear you." It suddenly dawned on me this might be very helpful. I glanced at his name tag. Rick Reinalles.

"Rick," I said confidentially. "You can help me. No one but my husband is to know where I am, just in case someone does recognize me and tries to follow me. If anyone calls asking, tell them nothing, even if the caller says he's my husband. It just possibly might be someone who's been stalking me lately."

That was a mistake.

"Please let me call my friend," Rick pleaded. "He'd feel privileged go with you. He just lives around the corner, he could be here in ten minutes."

"No, Rick," I fibbed. "I'm sure it's just the *paparazzi* looking for a story."

Just then the old woman and her cats reappeared at the window. She knocked on the glass and mouthed "thank you" with a grateful smile, then waddled down the street a little unsteadily, I thought, talking to her feline friends as she went. "Does she live around here?" I asked, curious at her early-morning foray into the streets.

"I don't actually think she has a real home. Probably one of the city's homeless. I see her all around the Civic Center and the SOMA. She begs for food for her cats, rarely asks for food for herself, though she probably eats the scraps along with them."

"Rick, can you find out about her? Inquire discreetly so she doesn't know we're asking. I'd like to know something about her, why she's on the streets instead of bouncing grandchildren on her knee in some cozy little cottage."

"Of course, Your Highness."

"No more of that, remember? Just call me . . ."

"Alexandra," he interrupted breathlessly. "I'm sorry. It's just that we never get royalty here and I've always wanted to meet a real princess. It's such a privilege and a surprise. You're not what I expected at all, more just like . . ."

"Common folks?" I laughed as he broke off, flushed with chagrin. The phone rang at the front desk and Rick backed away to answer it, grateful I'm sure, to be extricated from his embarrassment.

"Call a cab for me when you're through there, will you please?"

He nodded as he picked up the phone.

I ran back up to our room to leave the book and retrieve my pepper spray. As I reached the top of the stairs, a dark figure was momentarily silhouetted against the glass door at the far end of the long hall, then disappeared.

I dismissed it without a second thought, still smiling about my "royal" encounter with Rick as I unlocked the door to our room. The smile vanished as a fist of fear hit me in the stomach, knocking the breath right out of me.

A single red rose in a silver vase on a silver tray sat incongruously in the middle of the unmade bed.

Whirling back to the hall, knowing it was empty, I looked anyway, then stared at the key in my hand. I did just unlock the door, didn't I? Yes. *Someone else had a key to our room.*

Could it just be coincidence the vase and tray were like those on Scarlotti's island, and the rose was the same dark shade of red as the Don Juan roses Scarlotti grew? Surely the envelope on the tray would solve the mystery. But I couldn't make myself enter that room. *You're being rather dramatic.*

I peeked into the bathroom and closet. Empty. Relieved, I closed and locked the door behind me and picked up the gray linen envelope with black edging. Prickles trickled through my quivering fingers as I removed the card from the envelope.

"In remembrance of another time, another place, and in anticipation of memories to come."

It wasn't Bart's handwriting.

Chapter 9

I tried to picture the figure at the end of the hall. Was it Scarlotti? I'd caught only a quick glimpse.

What to do now? Lock myself in my room and wait for Bart to come back? That didn't sound like a good idea, since whoever delivered the rose hadn't been stopped by a locked door. Find a lot of people for a safety in numbers sort of thing? No. I really needed to run or swim; both body and mind cried out for it. That was how I got myself together and, heaven knows, I needed to get it together now. Since the hotel had no pool, run it was.

The appearance of the rose shattered and stripped me of what little confidence and composure I had left after my episodes of the last couple of days. If it was Scarlotti, he was succeeding in making me doubt my own sanity.

Go for it, girl. Clear out cobwebs from your mind. Get the kinks from your body. Think through this thing clearly.

I gathered myself together, leaving the rose untouched in the middle of the bed. Trading the book for my fanny pack containing wallet and pepper spray, I said a quick prayer for both guidance and safety and left the room.

As I carefully locked the door behind me, the thought flitted through my mind—*This won't do any good. Ghosts walk right through doors. Stop it!* I chastised myself. *There are no such things as ghosts.* I shivered at the thought, not entirely convinced.

Rick had a cab waiting at the front door when I got downstairs.

"Let me call my friend," Rick insisted one last time.

I shook my head and asked for a city map.

He retrieved one from under the desk and spread it out for me to examine. It only took a minute to decide.

"Thanks. That's just what I needed to know. See you later. Remember," I flung back over my shoulder, "even if you think you recognize my husband's voice, you are to tell no one over the phone where I've gone. You can only tell Bart in person."

"Yes, Your Highness," Rick said morosely, unhappy at my leaving alone.

"Mornin', ma'am. Where to?" the cabbie asked over the back of the seat.

"The University of San Francisco. Drop me at the corner of Fulton and Shrader, please." That was only a block from Golden Gate Park. I'd make sure no one was following me, and the driver would report I was going to the university if anyone asked.

Who're you kidding? Not just anyone would ask. Be honest here . . . if Scarlotti asks. Roach wouldn't be interested in me . . . would he? One threat was enough. I wouldn't worry about the others.

The driver turned out to be a friendly soul with a running commentary on the marine layer hanging over the city that wouldn't dissipate. But it should in the next day or two, he assured me, so we could enjoy San Francisco's sunny side while we were still in the city.

I didn't mind the fog. After all, I'd been raised in Santa Barbara and we certainly had our share of early morning ocean fog. In the city it seemed romantic, mysterious, exciting.

No one was following us. In the fog, they'd have to stay close. Nothing was behind the taxi. It seemed only a few blocks before the cab pulled to the corner. How silly to call a cab to go running when I could have just been warmed up by now. I paid the cabbie and headed toward Golden Gate Park, feeling the exuberance of a thoroughbred given his head as I loosened up and fell into a rhythmic trot.

I entered the park on Conservatory Drive. The closer I got to the ocean, the denser the fog became. Deep-throated foghorns blared background bass notes for the chorus of bird song above me.

No longer did I try to see where I was, to read the signs as one path or road merged into another. Doubts of my sanity, fear of Scarlotti fell behind as the freedom and rapture of the run returned my sense of well-being, of control.

I'm not sure how far I'd run, or even where I was, but I heard voices for the first time since I'd entered the park. Someone babbled hysterically in French, repeating the same frantic, urgent message about a dead body on a statue over and over.

Leaving the path, I veered toward the voices. A statue of a man sitting on a huge domed pedestal was barely visible through the fog. The closer I got, the more gruesome the scene.

Across the cold marble lap of the statue, another man was draped, face grotesquely twisted in the agony of death. Sightless eyes opened wide in a terror he'd never divulge. And a diamond studded his forehead.

A young man, camera in hand, pointed, horrified at what he was seeing, trying to make a couple in jogging suits understand what he was saying.

"*Monsieur, pauve-vous m'aider?*" I asked.

He whirled toward me, grasped my arm and pointed again to the body on the statue's lap.

I asked if anyone had called the police. The young couple said no, they'd barely come upon the scene. I sent them to call the police and told them to have the dispatcher relay the message onto Captain Saddler in his meeting with Chief Bronson and Bart.

Guiding the upset fellow to a bench a few feet from the statue where we couldn't see the grisly spectacle above us, I asked his name and how he'd found the body so early when it was nearly obscured by fog. He was Reynard du Pre, a French visitor to America, and he'd come to photograph the statue of Francis Scott Key, hoping for a superb shot in the mist.

"Did you get it?" I asked, curious to see how committed a photographer he really was.

He shook his head and stared at me. "*Non.*"

"Why not?" I asked gently. "A good photographer would get all the pictures he could before everyone gets here. Reynard, you could sell your pictures to the wire services with a personal story of how you discovered the body and probably make a tidy profit."

I'd had time to observe the slightly-built Frenchman. He was late-twenties, I'd guess, maybe a little older, with a day's growth of stubble on his chin and neatly-trimmed brown hair that framed his sensitive features. Well-worn, almost shabby clothes led me to believe he could use the money.

"Avoir torte?" he asked with a hopeful note in his voice.

"I don't think it would be wrong at all. In a few minutes, there will be more photographers here than you can imagine doing that very thing, so why don't you take your time and get some really good shots. Do you speak any English at all?"

"Leettle beet," he offered in English and smiled for the first time, then lapsed back into French. "Not enough to converse with anyone. Since my parents were killed in an accident, I've been working to support my siblings so we could stay together. I had to quit school, so my English is poor, but I plan to continue my studies. I want to be a photojournalist."

He stopped as though suddenly embarrassed by this revelation of personal history, his big dark eyes luminous in the early morning fog.

"Get your pictures," I prompted gently, hearing sirens approaching through the fog, "but be careful not to disturb the crime scene. Do you develop your own?"

"Oui."

He warmed to his task, clicking a shot from every angle.

"What are you doing in San Francisco?" If he worked to support a family, how could he afford to come to America?

"I work three jobs," he said in stilted English. "I am the baker by night, store clerk by day, and tutor students in the evening in French composition and history. The people of my village give me a ticket to America to study how Americans do things—marketing for my employers so they can increase business. Then I go back and teach them and the children what I learn."

"How long have you been here?"

"I was three days in New York City, but it is too big for me. Too many people. I meet a truck driver coming to California. He show me America if I take pictures for him."

His dark eyes lit up with pleasure. "He bought film, give me tour of this big, beautiful country, pay for my meals, then drop me here and tell me he will pick me up in one week when he returns to New York. I give him the pictures then."

"Where are you staying?"

Reynard looked away, busying himself with another shot.

"Do you have somewhere to stay while you're here?" I persisted.

"I arrive late last night. I spend the night taking pictures. No time to look for a place to stay."

"Reynard, do you have money for a hotel room? Do you have money for food?"

He avoided my eyes and my questions. The police car pulled into the circle, lights flashing a warm red glow in the fog, sirens whining down.

"The police will want to know where you're staying. I'm going to tell them you'll be at our hotel. It's just a little hotel, not very expensive. I'll pay you to do some photography for me so you can pay for your room. Okay?"

"Zank you," he said in English. "Zank you veree much."

That ended his English. He was so flustered by the police questions he lapsed into French and I had to interpret every answer he gave.

Then it was my turn. As I identified myself, Reynard gasped, then coughed. "Ze fog gets me," he mumbled in English.

Captain Saddler called on the police phone for the report from the investigating officer, then Bart got on and they passed the phone to me.

"Are you okay?" Bart asked, his voice filled with worry.

I assured him I was and gave him a quick update.

"Allison, you promised you'd stay at the hotel."

"No, I promised I'd be careful."

Silence on the other end of the phone. "Semantics. Have the police car drop you back at the hotel. I can't believe you always end up right in the middle of the excitement."

"Just lucky, I guess," I laughed. "I'll be okay. I need to finish my run this morning."

"Oh, no! I'm ordering the police to deliver you back to the hotel, and I'll meet you there in one hour. This won't take as long as I thought. Don't leave our room. Promise me you'll be there when I get there."

I remembered the rose. "I'll meet you in one hour at the Abigail. I promise." I didn't promise to go back in that room.

As it turned out, I didn't have to worry about it. The investigation took longer than we thought. The police weren't ready to leave until the body had been photographed, examined, and loaded up for the ride to the morgue. Reynard and I watched the whole process with interest from the back seat of the police car where we had been relegated on Captain Saddler's orders, safely out of the way until we could be delivered to our hotel.

"Practice your English with me, Reynard. I know it's faster and easier for you to speak French, but you'll need to be understood while you're in America."

"I'm curious. You are not upset by ze body. Why?"

"I've seen several in the last few weeks and this was one of the least messy." That had struck me when I first saw the body draped across the lap of Francis Scott Key.

Sgt. Slade slid under the wheel and started the car. "Sorry to keep you waiting, Mrs. Allan. It's the Abigail Hotel, right?"

"Yes, thank you. I'm sorry to be so much trouble. I really could just run back, but . . ."

"Chief says we're to deliver you safe and sound to your hotel." He glanced at Reynard in the rear view mirror as we eased into traffic out of Golden Gate Park. "You'll be staying there, too, so we can get hold of you if we need to talk to you again?"

Reynard nodded. *"Oui."*

"How was he killed?" I asked.

"Same as the other three."

"And that was . . . ?"

"Very tidy and quiet. A thin wire around the neck. No noise and no blood."

"Did this one have a diamond like the others?"

"Just like the rest—above the nose right between the eyes," Sgt. Slade said.

"This man looked like some of the panhandlers I've seen on the streets. Was he homeless? Were the others?" It seemed a safe assumption since none of the bodies had family listed in the paper.

"Yes. So far we haven't ID'd any of them."

"Isn't there usually some sort of community of street people— they know each other?"

"If they hang around the same areas for long enough. None of the regulars know anything about these guys. They seem to have been loners, kept to themselves, didn't talk to anyone else on the street."

"Any idea why they were killed?" I asked. "And what about the diamonds? What's the significance of that?"

"Here's your hotel, Mrs. Allan. End of interview."

"Sorry. That did sound like reporters' questions, didn't it? My husband and I have differing opinions on the motives of the killings. Just wondered what you thought."

Sgt. Slade turned, put his arm across the back of his seat, and opened his mouth to tell me, but the crackling of his radio claimed his attention.

"Sorry. Gotta go."

"Thanks for the lift, Sergeant."

Reynard and I piled out of the police car and it sped off into the fog, leaving the morning mist swirling around us.

"Guess the first thing we'd better do is get you a room so you can get some rest. If you've been up all night, you're probably ready to crash."

"Crash?" Reynard asked with a puzzled look.

"Sorry," I laughed. "Get some sleep. Go to bed."

"Oh, I'm much too excited for that. I am ready to see this beautiful city. You said you wanted pictures. I want to start right away."

"Reynard, there's no hurry on the pictures. My husband was fascinated by a beautiful old building and I thought it might be fun to surprise him with a photo or two of it. Come on. We'll get you checked in."

Rick was hopping from one foot to another, bobbing back and forth behind the desk, waiting to find out why I'd been delivered in a police car.

"What happened? I was afraid it wasn't safe out there for you," he blurted as we opened the door.

"It's all right, Rick. I'm fine. Here's another customer. Reynard is a French photographer who'll be here for a week doing some work for me. Bill his room to us, please."

"Yes, of course, Your . . ."

"Rick!" I knew what was coming and didn't need anyone else under the pleasurable, but erroneous impression I was royalty.

"Sorry," he stammered. "I almost forgot. Oh, here's a message that was delivered while you were out."

Rick handed me a gray linen envelope edged in black with my name handwritten in flowing, perfectly formed letters. "Allison Alexander Allan." I took it with trembling fingers. The handwriting was the same as the note with the rose.

Chapter 10

"Reynard, if you're sure you don't need to rest first, let's get your things up to your room, and I'll show you what I want you to photograph for my husband. We have less than thirty minutes before I'm supposed to meet him, but it's not far, so we could get there and back before he comes." I shoved the envelope and my hands into my pockets so Rick and Reynard couldn't see them trembling.

"Unless you want to see your room first, I could just send your bag up and you can go now with Prin—, with Mrs. Allan," Rick offered.

"*Oui* . . . yes. Okay. We will do pictures first." Reynard nodded, reverting to English. He checked his voluminous jacket pockets to make sure he had sufficient film.

"Shall I call a taxi?" Rick asked.

"Heavens, no. We're only going to Van Ness and O'Farrell. Besides, my run was interrupted . . ."

"Yes! Why did the police bring you back? What happened?" Rick broke in eagerly, leaning across the desk anticipating a story.

"Sorry. Have to tell you later. I promised my husband I'd be here when he got back. Give me one minute, Reynard."

I stepped around the corner by the telephones, out of sight of prying eyes, pulled the envelope from the pocket of my jogging suit with quivering fingers, and opened it.

Do you like to play games, Allison? I'm biding my time, just out of reach but always in sight. When I'm ready, I'll finish what I started in Hawaii.

I leaned against the wall, stunned. It was Scarlotti! He was alive. Dead men don't send roses, and ghosts don't send notes. At least now we knew what we were dealing with. And my sanity wasn't in question anymore. Only my life. That I felt more capable of handling. I took a deep breath and squared my shoulders.

"Okay, Reynard. I'm ready." I shoved the note deep into my pocket and felt my pepper spray. *And I'm ready for you, too, Scarlotti, now that you've finally come out in the open.*

Glancing frequently behind me while Reynard and I briskly covered the few foggy blocks to our destination, I avoided close proximity to alleys and gloomy doorways, staying acutely attentive to our surroundings. He wouldn't catch me unaware if I could help it.

As we approached the two-toned building at 1000 Van Ness, I couldn't believe my eyes. Long, slender legs emerged from a taxi, then the rest of Elekta Apotheosis slid sleekly from the car. Cinnamon-colored suit and shoes very nearly matched her shining cinnamon hair. Her wardrobe was unbelievably chic—and short.

We approached the bottom step as she stood poised at the top, five steps above us, keys in hand.

"Mrs. Allan! What a surprise! And where is your handsome husband today?" She peered pointedly at Reynard, standing just behind me.

"Elekta Apotheosis, this is Reynard du Pre. He's visiting from France. We keep running into Elekta at the museum," I explained to Reynard.

Elekta unlocked the door, swept ceremoniously through and pirouetted into the center of the huge, pillared room, her long, lovely legs the center of Reynard's attention.

"Welcome to my art gallery," she announced, arms outstretched dramatically. "I'm the new tenant. You probably wondered what I was doing at the Museum of Modern Art every day. I was taking notes on how the paintings were displayed, the lighting, and myriad other details." She handed me her card, stared at me, then at Reynard's camera. "What are you doing here? What is your interest in my gallery?"

"My husband appreciates unique architecture and he fell in love with this building. Probably attracted by the bears on the columns outside. I thought I'd surprise him with some pictures of it— Reynard's a photographer. This is marvelous! Look at that ceiling, all molded and engraved, and the woodwork! These carved balconies look like they came from a medieval castle."

"Isn't it perfect?" Elekta's enthusiasm bubbled through her normally cool facade.

"Did you see my incredible fountain?" She drew us to a blue mosaic tiled fountain at least nine feet tall and three feet wide framed in spiraling wooden pillars, and crowned four feet above that with an ornate wooden shield and ornamental molding. A lion's head with open mouth had at one time spewed water into the tiled basin six feet below.

"I'll have that working, of course. Look at the pillars! Don't they add an Old World elegance to the showroom?"

I walked around the huge room. The ceiling, two stories overhead, was covered with rosette-embellished eight-point stars and Greek crosses set off in carved paneled sections.

Two rows of pillars with three-foot molded wooden bases reached to the ceiling. I'm not sure the three of us could have joined hands around the girth of a column.

"When do you open?" I asked, wondering how much work there was to be done.

Elekta drew in her breath sharply. "They tell me nearly five months. I think I can do it in less than one. I don't have to have all the floors finished to open. I'll start with this one and the next two. The rest will open as I acquire more artists and the workmen have time."

"Time!" I glanced at my watch. "I promised to meet Bart at the hotel. Is it okay for Reynard to take some pictures for my husband?" Then I had a thought. "What are you doing for publicity? Maybe Reynard . . ." I left it at that, thinking if she were interested and it worked out, Reynard could make a little extra money doing some photography for Elekta. If she wasn't, I wouldn't put either of them on the spot.

"Reynard, can I leave you here? Can you find your way back to the hotel?"

"Yes, if I may take ze pictures?" He looked questioningly at Elekta.

"Of course, and I'll want to see them when they're developed."

"*Oui,*" he beamed at her, then turned to me. "*Adieu. Merci.*"

I glared at Reynald. He laughed. "Okay. Ze English. Good-bye. Zanks for everyzeeng."

As I jogged back to the hotel through the fog, I glanced at the card I still held in my hand. Elekta was a Greek word meaning brilliant, shining star. Fitting. Apotheosis was also Greek for the act of raising a mortal to the rank of God, or deification. It was a perfect description of Elekta: a brilliant, shining star who acted like she'd been deified from mortal to goddess. Was that the work of a doting parent at birth, or had she adopted the name with its innuendos for a reason?

Her accent still puzzled me. Even with her Greek name, I was certain that wasn't her nationality, or at least that Greek wasn't her first language. I'd heard that unique accent before. Exactly where flitted just out of reach somewhere in the back of my mind.

"Allison!" The voice booming through the fog jolted me back to reality.

"What are you doing wandering the streets? You promised to wait for me at the hotel."

I looked up into the troubled face of my husband. He jumped down the six-foot drop from the parking lot to the sidewalk and took me by the shoulders. I knew what he was going to say so I started before he could.

"I promised I'd meet you at the Abigail in one hour. I have exactly one minute to be there before I'm late. But if you're not there either, I guess it doesn't matter." I reached up and kissed him, then before he could say a word, bombarded him with questions. "How was your morning? Productive? Did the chiefs agree there was a conspiracy here? What are they going to do?"

Bart didn't reply. He just stood, hands on my shoulders, staring at me as if he couldn't decide whether to scold me or kiss me. He hugged me close instead.

"What am I going to do with you? The idea of you out there in the park, in the fog, with those killers drove me wild."

"But I wasn't," I protested. "They were already gone."

"How do you know?" he asked, emphasizing each word.

He might as well have thrown ice water all over me. I hadn't thought of that.

"How can I protect you when you're constantly putting yourself in danger? Where are you coming from just now?" He held me at arms' length, his blue eyes filled with concern.

"Elekta—remember Legs at the museum—is opening her own art gallery and you'll never guess where. The empty building you admired the other night! It's even more wonderful inside, with columns and tiles and lovely carved wood balconies."

"What were you doing there?"

I stopped. I didn't want to ruin the surprise; neither did I want to lie to my husband.

"Allison?"

"I was working on a surprise for you, but I guess you'll have to know." I slid my arms around his neck, looked up at him coyly and asked, "Or can I just get away with that much?"

"Not on your life. I want to know what you were doing that was so important you had to go out alone in the fog, when I asked you to stay at the hotel. The police car did take you there, I assume."

"Yes, they dropped us at the hotel, but I wasn't alone. I had Reynard with me. I just left him with Elekta taking pictures of your—her—building. I thought I'd surprise you with some photos of the edifice you admired."

"But you were on the street alone," he scolded. When I was not repentant, he shook his head in resignation. "Tell me about Reynard. He's the one who found the body?"

"He's fresh off the plane from France." I linked my arm through Bart's and we walked back to the hotel. "He has no money, so I got him a room here, told them to bill us, and figured he could pay for it by doing some photography for me."

"Still collecting strays." Bart rumpled my hair. "You're a soft-hearted soul. As long as you don't get softheaded on me, I guess I can live with it. But you've got to be more careful. You could have stumbled onto the killer in the act."

I was glad we'd arrived at the Abigail. Bart was warming to a lecture, which I didn't need to hear. And I'd just thought of something I did need to hear.

"Rick, are there any messages for us?"

He checked. There were none. I turned to Bart with a sick feeling in the pit of my stomach.

"We should have heard from Dad by now, shouldn't we? I'm worried about Mom. Is there any way you can get hold of them?"

Bart shook his head, took my hand, and headed up the stairs. I was desperate to know how Mom was doing. I concentrated on telepathing a message to Dad, but received no answer. That could mean he was too worried about Mom to tune me in or he was too far away to receive my message. There was still so much I didn't know about this special gift I shared with my father.

The door at the end of the hall reminded me of Scarlotti, the rose on the bed, and the envelope in my pocket.

I hung back while Bart produced his key and opened the door, following the same careful routine he had before. I hesitated, not sure I wanted to confront the rose again, or the knowledge that our room had been entered by persons unknown, our privacy violated. Bart caught the hesitation and preceded me into the room, did a quick check of bedroom, bathroom and closet, then waited for me to enter.

I locked the door behind me and turned to face the rose. The bed was made, the rose gone. I looked around the room, then in the bathroom. The rose in the silver vase on the silver tray had vanished.

Bart quietly watched from the window seat.

"Like to tell me about it?"

"About what?" I asked with wide-eyed innocence.

"Why you were reluctant to come into our room. What you were looking for that you didn't find. What you're afraid of telling me. I don't like secrets, Princess, especially when they concern your safety. I have a feeling this does."

I sat down on the other end of the window seat facing Bart and hugged my knees, mostly to stop them from trembling. "After breakfast, I came up to leave the book and get my fanny pack. As I reached the top of the stairs, I caught a glimpse of someone at the far end of the hall, a tall, thin silhouette, nothing more. My mind was on something else, so I didn't think anything about it until I opened the door and found a rose in a silver vase on a silver tray in the middle of the bed."

"You opened the door . . . ."

"I unlocked the door. It was locked. I thought you'd had the rose delivered, or maybe the desk clerk had sent it up while I had breakfast. But the wording on the handwritten card changed my mind."

"What did it say?"

"'In remembrance of another time, another place, and in anticipation of memories to come.' When Reynard and I got back to the hotel, Rick said this had been delivered. It's the same handwriting as the card with the missing rose." I pulled the note from my jacket pocket and handed it to Bart. He studied it with a frown.

"The note gives us some good news and some bad news," I said. "The good news is that your wife is not losing her mind after all. The bad news is too horrible to contemplate."

Chapter
11

I jumped a foot when the telephone rang, a noisy, irritating jangle that shattered the quiet room and my nerves.

Bart strode, tight-jawed, across the room to pick up the offending instrument.

"Yes? This is Bartholomew Allen." A surprised look crossed his face. "Of course, we'll be there." He tossed the note on the dresser as he hung up the phone, then picked it up again immediately and asked Rick to call a cab. "We'll discuss the note and its sender on the way. Chief Saddler has just invited us to lunch."

"The Chief of Police of the City of San Francisco?"

"One and the same."

"Did he mention lunch this morning when you met?"

"Not a word. This is a complete surprise."

"Did he say why?"

"That was his secretary. She just said he wanted to meet the two of us for lunch at the Empress of China at twelve o'clock. That gives us just over thirty minutes to dress and get there. You'd better hustle."

"But I've got to shower. . . ."

"Then hop to it." He gave me a gentle push toward one of the quickest showers I've ever taken. Why would Chief Saddler want to meet with both of us after meeting with Bart this morning?

"You've used up five of your fifteen minutes already," Bart called as I turned off the shower.

Towel-drying my hair as I searched my meager wardrobe for appropriate apparel, I finally settled on a long-sleeved, cream-colored silk blouse and matching slacks. Too bad I didn't have long legs like Elekta that I could show off.

"Ready?" Bart asked, looking out the window. "Our cab should be here, but it's still so foggy I can't see whether he's down there or not."

"Why aren't we driving our own car?" I asked, wondering if it was a silly question or if I'd missed something.

"We won't have time to find a parking spot. The cabbie can drop us right at the door."

"Grab my black blazer, will you please, while I find my pearls?" Natural curl did have its advantages at times. There was no time for hair styling this morning. I grabbed my purse and flew out the door, while Bart locked it behind us, then knelt for a minute before joining me on the stairs.

"What were you doing?" I asked as we raced down the five flights of stairs. "Elliot," the lift, would have been far too slow today.

"An old spy trick James Bond made famous. Hair across the door at the bottom so we'll know if anyone enters our room."

"Our last visitor has been only too obvious. How about triple locks instead?"

The taxi crept along busy, colorful Grant Street in Chinatown, jammed with traffic. Bart kept glancing nervously at his watch, and when we finally arrived, he tossed the driver some money and flung open the door before the car stopped. I hopped out and we raced to take the elevator to the five-star, sixth-floor Chinese landmark.

Chief Saddler was just being seated. He arose while Bart made introductions and took my hand, his piercing dark eyes doing a general appraisal all the while.

"Did I pass inspection?" I asked, then could have cut out my tongue the minute the words passed my lips.

"Was I that obvious?" Chief Saddler laughed, his stern face softening with amusement.

"I'm afraid so. Am I what you expected or are you disappointed?"

"Actually I'm delighted. I'd never met anyone who jumped out of a helicopter into a volcano and my curiosity got the best of me when I found out you were Bart's wife."

I looked at Bart in dismay, but he held up his hands in protest.

"Honest, Princess. I didn't say a word."

"Your reputation preceded you, Mrs. Allan. We, of course, got the report from Honolulu PD on the deaths of the four policemen and Scarlotti Scaddono, along with the story of your kidnaping and the volcano episode. I imagine it was quite an experience."

"From start to finish, Captain, our honeymoon was quite an experience, or maybe ordeal would be a more accurate term. This trip to San Francisco was supposed to have made up for it, but I'm afraid it's turning into another 'experience.'"

Captain Saddler turned to Bart, one eyebrow raised in question, but before Bart could reply, a gold-jacketed waiter appeared to take our order. When that was out of the way, Chief Saddler plunged right in.

"Bart mentioned that you were convinced the murders are tied to the possibility of a diamond heist at the museum. What makes you think so?"

"It just seemed like the thing a defiant, egotistical group of terrorists would do," I answered. "Flaunt their prowess at breaking the law and not getting caught, or even possibly being connected to it."

"Are you a student of psychology, Mrs. Allan?" the Chief asked, broad shoulders leaning forward. Intense interest animated a tanned face outlined by slightly graying, short-cropped hair.

I could feel color rising in my cheeks. "No, sir, I'm a linguist with absolutely no credentials to support my theory. I have spent a considerable amount of time studying people, though, especially those in Europe and the Middle East and I guess that's what I based my conviction on."

"Allison's intuition is invariably right on the money," Bart added, giving my hand an affectionate squeeze, "probably because she's such a keen observer of people and situations."

"I'd like you to share your thoughts on these murders, Mrs. Allan."

"Please call me Allison. Why me?"

The chief leaned back in his chair and folded his big hands across his lean, fit stomach, a hint of a smile playing across his face.

"Sometimes as 'professionals' we get tunnel vision. It frequently helps to stop and take a look through someone else's less jaded eyes. In your case, however, I couldn't call it less jaded, could I?" He laughed at his own joke, then drained his glass of water, wiped his mouth, carefully arranged his napkin in his lap, and looked across the table at me, all sign of humor gone.

"I want to know what you think about these murders," he said, his voice matching the serious expression on his face. "Why they're being committed, why the diamond in each body, why they're being placed where they are . . . in short, every thought you've had regarding this case. And I want your thought process—why you came to that conclusion."

I glanced at Bart, received an encouraging look in return, took a deep breath, and plunged in.

"Dad and Bart were concerned initially at the heavy outbreak of seemingly trivial criminal activity. When I mentioned the diamond exhibit, something gelled for them. I picked up on their feeling it was terrorist operations instead of local hoods harassing the authorities. When the first body was found in Diamond Heights with a diamond pierced into the body, my mind just made the connection to the diamond exhibit at the museum and wouldn't let go." Hesitating, I looked at Bart, then back at Captain Saddler.

"Go on," he urged.

"While I was researching diamonds, I found a book on terrorists, their weapons, targets, and activities. That led me to believe they were using bodies to leave messages. All were killed somewhere else and dumped at a very public location where they'd be discovered immediately. The first drop called attention to diamonds, of course, with the name. Diamond Heights is a residential area, isn't it?"

The chief nodded silently, elbows on the table, chin resting on laced fingers, intent eyes never leaving my face.

"The second was the Financial District. Where?"

"Front door of the Transamerica Tower."

"The third was on the steps of the Mission Delores. That's the oldest structure in the city, Latin section, and also a church. The fourth on the Golden Gate Bridge, the fifth at the glass pyramid at the Palace of the Legion of Honor, and the sixth this morning was in Golden Gate Park, but more precisely on a statue in the cultural area of the park. That gives us family, finance, religion, possibly history and ethnic identity, transportation, and finally art and freedom. The body was draped across Francis Scott Key's lap. The statue is a tribute to the national anthem and 'the land of the free and the home of the brave.' That in itself seemed significant."

I glanced at Bart. His face was a mask of serious contemplation, but he winked one blue eye in encouragement and nodded his head slightly.

Chief Saddler cleared his throat. "Do you think they've made their statement? And exactly what is it?"

"I think they're blatantly saying they can hit wherever they want—whenever they want—and I don't think they're finished. If you were to list every area or focus in this town, there's military, environment, tourism, history, government and society left," I cataloged, ticking off the list on my fingers. "You could have another half-dozen bodies before they're through."

"And where else do you think they're going to leave us 'messages'?"

"Personally, I'd target the most obvious place in each category. What's the most prominent military installation in the area?"

"Since 1776 it's been the Presidio but that's now in the hands of the National Park Service. Basically everything in the city's inactive—Treasure Island, Fort Mason."

"My choice would be the Presidio because of its size and reputation in the area. For tourism, I'd guess Fisherman's Wharf. Although Chinatown . . ." I thought for a minute, watching the fog press against the window like a child with its nose to the glass. "Chinatown's a perfect drop for an ethnic category since there are two prominent spots to leave a message—under the Dragon Gate on Bush and Grant, or Portsmouth Square."

"Dragon Gate," the chief said. "Not many outsiders know the square's the hub of Chinatown. Continue."

"Environment? My guess would be Muir Woods."

Chief Saddler nodded silently, his finger tracing the gold crest on his glass. Bart's attention seemed to be on the antique wood pillar in the middle of the room with peacock feathers arching out of fan-shaped wooden holders. I knew he was mentally staking out each place.

Our lunch arrived and while the polite Asian waiter arranged our plates in front of us, I scanned the crowd and was surprised to note it seemed to be made up only of American or European tourists. I heard smatterings of French, Italian, Portuguese and Danish, as well as accents from Boston, New York, and the Deep South. Conspicuously absent were Asians. Did they avoid the Empress because of the tourists or the food? One bite convinced me it wasn't the food.

"Three more—history, government, and society," the chief prompted, deftly scooping rice to his mouth with chopsticks.

"History has a lot of possibilities in this city. Coit Tower, postcard row on Alamo Square, or one of the prominent old houses, like the Spreckels Mansion or the Haas-Lilienthal House."

"Your choice?"

"The Haas-Lilienthal House is the only historic Victorian open to the public, and it survived the fire after the 1906 earthquake which makes it even more special. All the houses on Alamo Square are privately owned and none especially stands out. I'd have to guess Haas-Lilienthal."

"Why did you rule out the Spreckels Mansion?" Bart asked, a piece of Mongolian lamb poised halfway to his mouth.

"Unless these are locals, they'd have had to do a little homework. The Haas-Lilienthal appears in more tourist brochures than any other."

"You've done your homework, Allison. And the society bit?"

"Nob Hill, of course, with six possibilities. The builders of the Central Pacific Railroad—Crocker, Stanford, Hopkins and Huntington—were the 'Big Four.' The Mark Hopkins Hotel marks the site of Hopkins' home. Crocker's mansion was torn down where Grace Cathedral stands. Governor Stanford's mansion was on the current site of the Stanford Court Apartments and Huntington's is now Huntington Park."

"The other two?" Bart asked as I paused for a drink of water.

"James G. Fair and James C. Flood were the 'Silver Kings' of the Comstock Lode. The Fairmont Hotel's on the Fair property. Of the six, only Flood's home remains. It's the big brownstone housing the Pacific Union Club. The only original left. I think that's where they'll leave a 'message.' As for government, I'd guess City Hall or the United Nations building. They're both imposing, prominent buildings."

There was silence at the table for what seemed a very long time. Chief Saddler moved his food around with his chopsticks but didn't eat.

Bart thoughtfully chewed a bite and I took the opportunity for another taste of lunch before it got cold.

"You really believe this," the chief said, leaning forward across his plate to look me squarely in the eye.

I sat back, smoothing crumbs from the white linen tablecloth. "I feel strongly those bodies are a communique from a ruthless, arrogant group stating they can hit any time, any place and we're powerless to protect families, environment, society, and art or historical treasures. They want us to know they disdain the military, can take out transportation, control finances, and, in short, do whatever they want to further their agenda."

"And this all stemmed from watching a news broadcast about a couple of murders, a diamond exhibit at the museum, and a bunch of little fires and robberies?" The chief's voice sounded full of disbelief—even derision.

My face flushed and I forced myself to meet his dark eyes again.

"Yes, sir," I said firmly.

He turned to Bart. "You're right, Allan. She's attractive, articulate, and imaginative, with the emphasis on the latter." He laughed, or more accurately, snorted and turned back to me.

"Terrorist messages, huh! I think you've been inhaling something besides volcano fumes. Why is it women think they have to have an opinion on everything? Have to solve all our problems for us? If you had a brain among you, you'd all be satisfied to keep your mouths shut and just look pretty. You'd better keep your eye on her, Bart, or better yet, have her committed. She's not playing with a full deck."

I stared at him. He was serious. There was no amusement in his eyes, no smile playing around the stern mouth. No joking. No teasing.

I stood. "Thank you so much for lunch, Chief. It's been . . . a real 'experience.'" As I picked up my purse, somehow my freshly filled water glass fell against his water glass, spilling both into the lap of the man whose leer suddenly disappeared.

I walked stiffly to the elevator, fuming at his insults. Bart rose from the table. "I'll be expecting an apology to my wife before the day is out, Chief Saddler. Your behavior is unacceptable even by today's low standards."

Chapter 12

"I can't believe he said that! My cat has more couth than that! There was absolutely no excuse for such blatant bad manners. Actually—more than that! I think I just experienced sexual harassment!"

Bart folded his arms and leaned against the elevator wall, wisely keeping his distance and his silence while I fumed and paced the little elevator. I wanted neither sympathy nor consolation. What I did want was to punch Captain Saddler right in his smirking smart mouth.

I stormed out of the elevator and into the street, the sting of the police chief's words driving me before them like a whip. Bart kept pace as I stomped down the street, the bitter taste of humiliation replacing rage.

"Why couldn't he have simply said, 'Thank you very much, Mrs. Allan? I appreciate your input. If we have any more questions, we'll be in touch'? What's the point in being so crude? So cruel? I've never felt so . . . so . . . put down . . . so humiliated in my entire life."

Bart grabbed my shoulders and jerked me back up on the curb and out of the path of oncoming traffic. I wasn't watching traffic lights, probably couldn't have seen them through the blur of tears that stung my eyes as Captain Saddler's taunts stung my ego. I hated my reaction. Hated the tears that probably made me seem weak.

Bart pulled me back against his solid chest, wrapping his arms around me, his chin resting on my head. I was glad he didn't turn me around, didn't try to look at me or make me face him. I wasn't ready for that just yet.

"If it's any consolation, Princess, I think he's a supercilious, salacious sap."

"You've been reading the dictionary!"

"My only hope of comprehending your conversation, my petite sesquipedalian." He released me as the light turned and we crossed the street, my fury spent, disgrace displaced by discouragement. Through my gloom, it dawned on me Bart was becoming very adept at discerning my moods and needs, even able to change them almost without my being aware of it.

"We've got humiliation out of the way already, so now that you've scraped me up off the sidewalk where Chief Saddler stomped me into inconsequential dust, what's next on your agenda?" I asked with resignation.

Bart looped my arm through his as we made our way under Chinatown's famous Dragon Gate through tourists, business people, and students crowding the sidewalk and crisscrossing the busy street.

"I'm supposed to brief our operative . . . who should have landed about thirty minutes ago," he answered, glancing at his watch.

I stopped in the middle of the sidewalk and turned him to face me, impeding the flow of foot traffic behind us. People streamed around us, a human river parting for an island.

"But . . ." I didn't know how to phrase the question for which I wanted, needed, only one answer.

"I believe you, Princess. From the beginning I've believed your notion made absolute sense. You only filled in some gaps for me when you explained the whole thing to the captain. Anastasia's proceeding on its own, whether we have the cooperation of the San Francisco Police Department or not."

"Thank you." I couldn't say another word. Who cared now if the callous Captain Saddler didn't believe me? Anastasia's confidence meant a whole lot more to me than some supercilious stranger. I liked that word. Captain Saddler had certainly been scornful and contemptuous, feelings caused, I'm sure, by his superiority complex.

Well, I knew I wasn't crazy, even if he thought I was. I couldn't have said that at this time yesterday.

"I still need you to finish up that research on diamonds at the library, but since Scarlotti's made his presence known, I can't let you out of my sight," Bart said.

"There's no reason I can't go to the library and finish," I protested. "I do have my pepper spray, and now that we know . . ."

"Absolutely not. You're not going to run loose where Scarlotti can grab you at will."

"Bart, you can't spend the rest of your life holding my hand. You have things to do and so do I. Besides, you know how Scarlotti works, how he plays his games. It's not his style to pull me into a car in broad daylight. He preys on the psyche, then strikes in the dark. I can take care of myself now that I know it's not the supernatural I'm dealing with."

"Maybe I wouldn't worry so much if it was supernatural. Scratch that. I would worry. Sorry, Princess. I can't take a chance. You're too precious to me."

"Bart, I'll be okay. I promise I'll be very watchful, very careful, and if it will make you happy, even carry my pepper spray in my hand 'at the ready'."

Bart wasn't entirely convinced, but finally relented. "You watch what's going on around you. Scarlotti isn't the only thing I worry about. San Francisco may be the City of Love but all its inhabitants don't read PR notices. I've seen some pretty scroungy characters loitering about." He checked his watch. "It's just after one o'clock. How about if I meet you back at the hotel about four? Then we'll take a little time for us."

"I'll be there with bells on!"

"That should be interesting, though I'd prefer even less than that," he teased in a low, lecherous tone. "Want me to call you a cab?"

I laughed at his innuendo and gave him a quick kiss.

"No, thanks. I'd rather walk or catch a cable car. Looks like the fog's lifting and the sun may make an appearance soon. I could use a little sunshine—and exercise."

We parted company at Market and Grant. Bart headed for the museum to meet and brief some welcome help, and I took off in the opposite direction for the library, my mind replaying the horrible scene at lunch. The more I thought about it, the madder I got.

What right did he have, did anyone have, to make fun of someone else's ideas, particularly when he had been so adamant about hearing them? I'd been more than candid. I'd laid out my entire thought process, bared my soul, so to speak. And he had stripped me of every dignity, every face-saving option with his derision.

Scarlotti had actually done me a favor by revealing himself just when he did. Confirmation that he really was alive had restored my faith in myself and my sanity. To have Captain Saddler state outright that I should be committed would have been devastating—would have really shaken my faith in me.

As it was, I felt naked. Humiliated. And angry. I experienced a resurgence of all the emotions I'd already been through, reliving the entire mortifying incident.

I charged around a corner, hating the humiliation I felt, my face hot with anger at being ridiculed, dismissed as mentally imbalanced—and collided with another body. The force of the impact knocked me off my feet and I hit the pavement with a painful smack.

"Oh, I'm so sorry. Please forgive me. Here, let me help you up. Are you hurt?"

I stared up into the pleasant, concerned face of a very English-looking gentleman, dressed in impeccable tweeds and corduroys, proffering an apologetic hand. I took it.

"My goodness, I am sorry. Are you all right? My most sincere apologies. I should have watched where I was going." He doffed his tweed hat and bowed a small, polite bow from the waist.

I brushed myself off, touching a very tender spot on my tail-bone and one on my elbow. My favorite black blazer now sported a jagged tear where the fabric had already worn thin.

"Oh, my dear. I've ruined your charming outfit." The man was truly upset, punctuating each sentence with a tap of his mahogany walking stick.

"It's all right," I assured him with what I hoped was my most forgiving smile. "I'll just put some leather patches on the elbows and it'll be like new."

"Please, may I offer you a cup of tea by way of apology and succor. I'm really not in the habit of assaulting beautiful young women and I'd like to make up for it."

"No, it was my fault as much as yours. I barged carelessly around that corner without looking. I'm fine, thank you."

"I insist. I want to make sure you really are all right." The old gentleman took my arm, guiding me gently but firmly away from the Marriott in front of which our accident had occurred, to a little English tea room just down the street.

"Really, I'm quite all right," I protested, wondering if he was as innocent and harmless as he appeared. "You needn't bother . . ."

"Oh, my dear. It is no bother." He pointed his walking stick at a table overlooking the street, steered me toward it, and pulled out the looped-back cherry wood chair.

I sat gingerly, deciding that he was authentic and had nothing to do with Scarlotti or Roach. He settled opposite me, put his hat on the chair next to him, leaned his walking stick properly against it, then turned his full attention to me.

"I should have introduced myself. I'm Arthur Bainston." He extended his hand across the table.

"Allison Allan," I responded, wincing as I reached to shake the nicely manicured hand.

"I have hurt you." His forehead creased in concern above clear, gray, sympathetic eyes. He had a distinguished face, small salt and pepper mustache turned slightly up at the corners and a matching immaculate goatee that came to a point just below his chin, giving him a elfin, almost mischievous look.

"It's only slightly bruised and will be just fine. I heal quickly," I assured him.

My benefactor suggested a soothing herbal tea which he ordered for us before he relaxed a bit.

"Now then, where were you going in such a hurry and am I keeping you from an important appointment?"

I liked the timbre of his voice and the charming British accent that was both clipped and lyrical.

"Actually, I was on my way to the library."

"You work there?"

"No. Just doing some research."

"Then you're a student?"

"No," I laughed. "I'm a linguist, a translator for the United Nations."

"In San Francisco?"

"In New York City."

"Then you don't live here?" He shook his head. The confused expression flitting across his face was quickly replaced by a cheery smile. "I have a habit of classifying people, putting them into neat little cubbyholes according to occupation, type, that sort of thing, you know."

"And into what cubbyhole do I fit?" I asked, curious to know how this intriguing Englishman would categorize me.

"I filed you under native Californian, career-oriented, with a generous nature and sense of humor that endears you to your friends and acquaintances. Now tell me where I went awry."

"Actually, you're quite right. Technically, I'm a native Californian, though I was born in Vietnam. My parents were living there at the time, but I was raised here. I guess I am career-oriented. I love my job."

"Well, I know I'm quite correct about the other two qualities. You didn't get angry with me for knocking you down, making light of the situation instead of berating an old man for his ineptitude. What are you doing in San Francisco?"

"I'm here on my honeymoon," I said, then added almost under my breath, "but my husband's here on business."

Arthur Bainston's expressive eyebrows went up.

"Our honeymoon in Hawaii was interrupted, so we're trying to finish it up here while my husband takes care of some business. What brings you here from 'Jolly Old'?" I asked, steering the conversation away from a subject I didn't want to discuss with a stranger. "I assume from your charming accent you're British."

"Right on. History is my vocation, but my avocation is gemology. I've spent my life in a study of diamond lore. Therefore, I couldn't resist the opportunity to combine my two loves when the occasion presented itself for me to view so many of the outstanding gems of the world together at one time."

"The diamond exhibit at the Museum of Modern Art?" I asked incredulously.

"Yes. Do I detect a note of surprise?"

"It's just that I was on my way to the library to research those very diamonds."

"And what is your interest in them?" He leaned forward,

sipping his tea, gray eyes gleaming with curiosity.

"What woman isn't interested in diamonds?" I laughed. "And as you said, what an opportunity! Some of the privately owned ones I'd never get to see otherwise."

"If you're really interested, I'm speaking on the history of some of these diamonds this evening at the Convention Center. I'd be delighted to have you and your husband as my guests. We've saved a couple of spectacular surprises to coincide with the end of the convention and the opening of the exhibit," he hinted slyly.

"Thank you! I'll accept tentatively since I'm not sure whether Bart's made other plans. Any hints on the surprises?"

"One concerns the known, and one the unknown," he said with a twinkle in his eye. He withdrew his wallet from his jacket pocket, placed a five-dollar bill on the table for the waitress, and handed me two tickets.

"If you can use them, please do."

"If we can't come, I'll leave them at the box office so someone else can use them."

"I have no one else to give them to. Please don't trouble yourself. I'd be pleased to have you come and to meet your good husband. I shall have to chide him for letting business take precedence over a beautiful woman. If I were a few years younger, I'd try to win you away for myself." Stroking his goatee, he slid his chair back slightly and laughed a very jolly laugh for someone who was clearly not of Santa Claus proportions.

Glancing at my watch, I was horrified to see it was well after two o'clock. I had less than two hours to finish my research.

"Good grief! I've got to go." I extended my hand as I stood up. "Mr. Bainston, thank you for an absolutely delightful time. I'll look forward to hearing your dissertation on diamonds tonight. And about the mysterious surprises."

He took my hand in both of his as he rose. "It was so nice running into you, Allison Allan," he said, kissing my hand in a very continental manner, his gray eyes never leaving mine while twinkling merrily at the pun.

"I hope next time we meet, it's a little less physical," I laughed.

"Perhaps less painful, but no less physical," he countered, his face crinkled with glee. "I'm lodging at the Marriott with my colleagues, if you desire to contact me."

I withdrew the hand he was still holding firmly in his and thanked him again, afraid to say anything else that he could turn into a punful innuendo, and hurried from the tea room.

Was that sweet old man propositioning me, or just stroking my ego? Whatever his intention, he'd made me forget the ugly encounter over lunch and replenished my self-confidence.

I hoped we could hear his talk tonight. His was probably knowledge not available in the library, possibly nothing that would be helpful, but I was sure it would be entertaining. And the surprise announcement sounded intriguing.

As I swung lightheartedly down Market Street, I realized the fog had disappeared completely. The sun shone bright and warm on my face, matching my sunny mood. Too bad there weren't more Arthur Bainstons and fewer Jim Saddlers in the world. It would certainly be a much happier place.

At the library I did a little digging in past issues of the local newspapers on the dastardly Captain Saddler and came up with some surprising, and some not-so-surprising items of interest.

Then I plunged back into the heady world of famous diamonds and the legends surrounding them. The Smithsonian was lending some incredible pieces for the exhibit—the Hope diamond being the most well-known because of its supposed curse.

Pure, deep sapphire blue, the Hope is huge and, according to legend, served as an eye in a statue of the Hindu goddess Sita. When a Brahman priest stole the stone, the angry goddess decreed that bad luck would befall anyone who wore her eye as jewelry.

In 1642, Jean Baptiste Tavernier acquired the 112-carat diamond, but apparently never wore it as jewelry. Tavernier sold it to King Louis XIV of France about 1669. Around 1673 it was cut into a sixty-nine-carat heart shape to bring out its brilliance, and named the Blue Diamond of the Crown. Louis XIV, it is said, wore the accursed crystal only once, then contracted a fatal case of smallpox.

His successor, great-grandson Louis XV never adorned himself with the French Blue, and had a long, successful reign. The curse must have been in full effect when Louis XVI and his queen, Marie Antoinette, wore it—they lost their heads in the French Revolution.

In 1792 the French crown jewels were stolen, disappearing for thirty-eight years, possibly ending up in the Spanish court. In 1799 Goya painted Queen Maria Luisa wearing a large blue stone.

At the beginning of the nineteenth century, a beautiful dark-blue diamond came from Amsterdam to London, having been cut down to its present cushion shape of 45.52 carats. Legend of the curse continued to grow with the story of the cutter's son stealing the diamond, then committing suicide and the diamond cutter dying of a broken heart.

Henry Philip Hope acquired the extraordinary gem about 1830 to add the rare blue stone to his collection of fancy-colored diamonds. The curse continued during the Hope family ownership, with tales of misfortune, suicide, bankruptcy, murder, and fatal accidents of subsequent owners continually surfacing.

In 1910, Pierre Cartier of the famous Paris house told Evalyn Walsh McLean about the diamond and its famous curse. Objects which brought misfortune to others had the opposite effect on her, she felt, but she wasn't interested in the stone. Cartier reset the diamond in a magnificent necklace which he delivered to the famous Washington hostess, requesting that she keep it over the weekend. She fell in love with the remarkable blue diamond, bought it, and as insurance against the curse, had it blessed by a priest. From that time, she rarely took it off, and when she did, it was either stored in the back of a tabletop radio or hung around the neck of her Great Dane, Mike. Rumor had it her son Jock teethed on it.

The curse seemed at its most potent during Mrs. McLean's ownership. Her marriage ended in divorce; her alcoholic husband died in a mental institution; her brother died an untimely death; her nine-year-old son was run over and killed; her only daughter overdosed on pills at age twenty-five and she herself died of pneumonia when only sixty years old.

The exquisite Hope diamond was bequeathed, along with her other jewelry, to Mrs. McLean's grandchildren who sold it to jeweler Harry Winston to pay estate debts. Winston gave the famous blue diamond, now notorious for its "Legacy of Doom" to the

Smithsonian Institution. The curse apparently was broken as it immediately increased attendance for the venerable old institution.

My danger antennae started tingling again. Chills ran down my arms and the hair on the back of my neck stood up. Was it activated by the murder and mayhem I'd just immersed myself in? No. I slipped my hand into my pocket and felt my pepper spray. Surely Scarlotti wouldn't try anything here in the library. Slowly I swiveled in my seat and stared straight into the mocking face of the man who'd vowed to kill my family.

Chapter

13

Scarlotti, face partially hidden in the shadowy hall, leaned against the railing of the staircase that led to the basement not ten feet from where I sat.

His long, slender fingers slipped slowly, deliberately, into the black jacket pocket, grasped something, then paused before bringing it out.

I sat rigid in my chair, frozen with fear.

Dark, cold eyes glinted with the hint of a mocking smile. I suppressed a shudder. I couldn't take my eyes from his, mesmerized by the malevolence I saw there. Scarlotti straightened, took a measured step toward me and stopped. So did my heart.

He moved another step closer, like a panther stalking its prey. His hand emerged from the pocket. Slowly, deliberately, he brought his hand forward, producing a gray linen envelope edged in black. He paused, statuelike, then with a quick flick of his wrist, sailed the envelope onto the table in front of me. I turned to follow its flight, looked back at Scarlotti, but the hall was empty. Only the shadows remained.

Grabbing the envelope, I ran into the hall in time to hear the door at the foot of the stairs click shut. I peered over the balcony at the same empty stairway I'd chased him down earlier. I had no intention of repeating that foolish act.

Weak-kneed, I leaned against the bannister and stared at the envelope, identical to those he'd left before. Only the delivery was dramatically different.

Taking several deep breaths to calm the frenzied pounding of my heart and steady myself, I opened the dreaded envelope on the way back to the table, and sank into the chair before looking at its contents, not sure my legs would hold me up any longer.

"My preparations are almost complete. Soon we'll finish what we started in Hawaii."

Not if I have anything to say about it, we won't. I thought defiantly, gathering up my notebook and fleeing the library and proximity to Scarlotti.

I needed Bart, the assurance of his calm strength, the security I felt with him, his knowledge of what to do. What if he wasn't back yet?

I glanced at my watch as I raced down the marble steps. No. Five o'clock. Where had the time gone? I was supposed to meet him at four o'clock. He'd either be furious or worried sick. I hoped he wouldn't call the police.

That was the last thing I needed—to give the misogynistic Captain Saddler reason to believe I was as addle-pated as he thought! Rounding the library corner, I met Bart storming across the street from the Abigail, fists clenched at his side and a scowl on his handsome face.

"Where were you?" he demanded, grabbing my arms. "I've been frantic!"

Wincing with pain, I pulled the envelope from my pocket as Bart's fingers touched the rip in my sleeve. When he saw my torn jacket and the envelope, he crushed me in his arms, squeezing the breath out of me.

"Princess, what happened?"

"First I ran into a very attractive man who literally swept me off my feet. Then Scarlotti delivered this—in person."

"When? Where?" he demanded, holding me at arm's length, examining me for wounds or injury.

"The attractive man or the delivery?"

"Allison, don't play games with me. Not now."

"Would you rather I collapsed with fear and trembling right here in the street after my confrontation with evil personified? I'm scared to death. I either have to laugh or cry."

Bart's blue eyes darkened with rage. "What did he do to you?" He indicated the torn jacket.

"That wasn't Scarlotti. That was Professor Bainston."

"I want to hear this tale, in detail, now." He rushed me back across the street but not to the hotel. Instead, with a quick check over his shoulder, he hurried me the half block to the hotel parking lot.

"Where are we going?"

"Where Scarlotti can't get his filthy hands on you."

"Good idea, Galahad. The farther the better." My heart still pounded wildly from the fright of Scarlotti's appearance and threat.

Bart's face was grim as he opened my door and waited for me to get in, then slammed it a little too hard. He wasn't just upset; he was livid. He started the car and pulled onto the street before he spoke.

"From start to finish, I want the whole story. Scarlotti first. Then you can tell me about a man who sweeps you off your feet, leaving you bruised and torn."

I took a deep breath, assessing the man at the wheel. Was this a loving, concerned husband asking for explanations or an Interpol interrogation? I was gratified to see the husband had taken precedence over the agent. Just barely.

"It was at the library. He came out of the shadows behind me like a cat ready to pounce, tossed the note, and disappeared down the stairwell."

"He didn't touch you, didn't come near you? Didn't speak?"

"No. I'm sure he knows his presence is terrifying enough. He doesn't need to do anything else."

Bart stared at me. I met his gaze without blinking. If he thought he was going to send me away . . .

"How do you do it?"

"Do what?" I asked, puzzled by the question.

"Stay so calm when the devil who plans to kill you has just handed you your death sentence?"

"Do I look calm? My insides are churning like a bread machine and if my heart doesn't slow down, it'll explode. If I wasn't sitting already, I'd have collapsed by now, my legs are shaking so badly. Frankly, I'm scared spitless."

Bart reached for my hand.

"Now tell me about your other encounter."

After telling my story, stressing the personal interest Mr.

Bainston had shown in a honeymooner on her own in the city, I produced the tickets he'd given me to the lecture.

"What do you suppose the surprise announcement is?" I asked. "The Russian crown jewels are coming? That might be the known. What could the unknown be?"

"It doesn't matter. You're not going to the lecture. I'm going to have you placed in protective custody. . . ."

"Bart! No!"

"Give me one good reason why not." It was not spoken in a friendly tone.

I'd have to soften his heart fast or this honeymoon was history.

"Let me stay with you," I pleaded. "You can protect me from Scarlotti."

"I've got a terrorist plot to unravel, then prevent. You're a magnet for trouble. I couldn't leave you alone for a minute without you conjuring up some kind of danger."

"Then don't leave me alone. That would solve the case of the missing honeymoon," I teased, "and we could expend our energies on the case of the about-to-be-missing diamonds."

"I don't want to talk about diamonds right now. I want to talk about . . ."

"But wait till you hear what I discovered about the Koh-i-noor! And about your self-righteous Captain Saddler."

"You're changing the subject." Bart maneuvered through traffic streaming across the Golden Gate into Marin County.

"I think you'll find it very interesting." If this didn't work, I'd find myself locked up who knows where, and Captain Saddler would laugh his pompous head off.

"Give it to me in a nutshell."

"It's thought to be the oldest of all known diamonds. . . ."

"No, the part about Captain Saddler."

"In checking back issues of the local newspapers, I found the callous captain is involved in a very messy, very expensive divorce that's still before the courts, questionable ethical practices regarding some high-profile cases, and surprise! Sexual harassment suits up to his eyeballs. This is the original woman hater."

I waited for his reaction. There was no change in his expression.

"I'll bet you're a good poker player," I said, running my fingers down the muscles on the side of his face. "These didn't move the least little bit."

Bart took my hand from his face, faked kissing my fingertips and put it back in my lap. He was warming to something I knew I wouldn't like.

"While you're feeding that bit of info into that computer brain of yours, let me update you on the Koh-i-noor," I said. "It's thought to be the oldest of all known diamonds, discovered more than five thousand years ago. Baber, first of the Great Moguls, acquired it when he invaded Northern India in 1526 and named it 'The Great Mogul' after himself."

"You're changing the subject."

I ignored him and continued. "Baber's heirs passed the huge gem down the line, but about 1665 the huge diamond vanishes."

"The Great Mogul disappeared?"

Ah, he was listening. "Yes, and the history of the Koh-i-noor picks up where the Great Mogul leaves off, even in the same collection. Muhammad Shah hid the stone in his turban to keep it from falling into the hands of the Persian invader, Nadir Shah."

Bart kept checking his rearview mirror. He was not easily sidetracked or distracted. Maybe I wasn't doing as well as I thought.

"Here's the good part. Nadir Shah wanted his low-born son to marry the high-born daughter of Muhammad Shah, so naturally, he didn't want to kill his son's future father-in-law to get the diamond. A woman servant snitched on its hiding place and at a grand state banquet, Nadir Shah suggested, as a good-will gesture, they trade turbans. By custom, Muhammad couldn't refuse. When Nadir Shah returned to his quarters and unwound the yards of cloth, out tumbled the coveted diamond. 'Koh-i-noor!' he cried."

"Which means?"

"Mountain of light. And thus began the long history of mayhem and murder associated with the 108.93-carat Koh-i-noor diamond."

If I could get him talking, distract him from the scare we'd just had from Scarlotti . . .

"What did you find out at the museum? Did you decide where they'll try to enter and how they'll get the diamonds? Did you meet your operative? Do I know him?" I hesitated before I asked the next question, almost afraid of the answer. "Did you tell him about my theory?"

Bart studied me for a minute before he answered, then concentrated again on the bumper-to-bumper traffic.

"Yes, I met him. No, you don't know him. Yes, I told him your theory."

"And?"

"Oz thought it sounded entirely plausible."

"Oz?"

"Oswald Barlow. We've borrowed him from the FBI. His area of expertise is foreign terrorist activity in the U.S., particularly Jihad and Hezbollah. He investigated the bombing of the World Trade Center in New York and initially, the bombing in Oklahoma City until they discovered it was domestic, not internationally instigated."

"Where is he now?"

"Setting up surveillance of the museum. We discussed the Marriott, but decided instead to take the empty top floor of a building across the street from the park in front of the museum. We'll have more room and privacy. Now back to the problem at hand: what to do with you."

He was within a breath of sending me out of here or locking me away somewhere. It would be the professional thing to do. I understood that. But it was the last thing I wanted right now. I needed to see this through, needed to redeem myself in the eyes of Captain Saddler. It had become a point of honor. *Or just foolish pride?* a small voice asked.

"Aren't you just a little bit interested in the diamond lecture tonight? It might give you some helpful insight."

"Did your Arthur Bainston reveal any clue as to this mysterious announcement?" Bart asked, exiting Highway 101 at the Muir Woods off-ramp.

"Only that one concerns the known, and one the unknown. I didn't think to question him further."

"No questions? That's a first. Either you were more injured than you let on, or . . . how old did you say this Bainston was?"

"Older than my father," I laughed, "but I will admit, he had a kind of sensuality that transcends age. He declared if he were a little younger, he'd try to win me away from my negligent husband, and hoped our next meeting was no less physical than our first."

An eyebrow went up. "Sounds like I have a rival. And speaking of other men, Rick Reinalles gave me this to give to 'Her Highness.'" He pulled a folded piece of paper from his shirt pocket and handed it to me. "What's the Highness bit?"

"Rick's convinced I'm Princess Alexandra. I finally gave up trying to persuade him otherwise. He probably heard you call me Princess. I asked him to find out about an intriguing little old lady who appeared on the sidewalk this morning, asking for food for her cats. I was curious about her."

I glanced over the neatly typed, one-page report Rick had prepared.

"What does it say?" Bart asked.

"Mmm. Not much."

"Read it to me."

"Name unknown. Commonly called 'The Cat Woman.' Been around the area for ten or twelve years. Feeds stray animals, mostly cats. Lived in an old hotel until it was torn down a couple of years ago to make room for a parking garage; now she's living on the street. No known family. Apparently has small income from somewhere as she's able to get a room somewhere when the weather's bad.

"Disappears occasionally at holiday time for a couple of weeks, but won't say where she's been. Friendly soul, talks to everyone but never reveals anything of a personal nature about family or past.

"Lost a great deal of weight recently and hasn't seemed well."

"What about her intrigued you?" Bart asked.

"I'm not sure. Maybe her eyes. Maybe the fact that she looked like someone who should be home baking cookies or doting on grandchildren. I guess I felt sorry for her with no snug home to go to and just her cats to love her."

"Another stray? You'd take care of the world if you could." Bart reached for my hand and squeezed it. "That's what makes you so special, Princess. You're unique, unlike anyone else I've ever met in my life. But you sure don't make it easy taking care of you."

"I'd ask you to define unique, but I'm a coward," I laughed, ignoring his last comment. "I'm not sure I want to hear your definition. I do want to hear your plan of attack. Did you figure out how you're going to approach this case?"

"Oz and I met with the curator, Helen Hunicutt, and Matt McMillan, security. Sheila Rogers, the rep from Lloyds of London, joined us at the end. They're grateful we're getting involved and they're fully cooperative, which makes our job much easier."

"Too bad Captain Saddler isn't of the same mind. Go on. What do we do next?"

"Tonight after the museum closes, we're going back in to check out the special security being installed for the exhibit and see how good it is—see if anything further is necessary or if they've covered all the bases."

"Or exits?"

"Exactly. Tomorrow Blaise will have his report ready on the fires, and we'll also have whatever he can get from Captain Saddler on the stickups, under the table, of course, and hopefully, something on the murders. That part'll be unofficial but Blaise thought he could get the info since he and the captain are good friends. I hate to infringe on that friendship, but if the information isn't forthcoming from Captain Saddler, we'll have to go through the back door to get it."

I hated to mention it since Bart hadn't, but had to ask. "What about Roach?"

Bart's lips thinned to a grim line. "I had Interpol wire his dossier to Captain Saddler so they could be on the lookout for him."

Bart pulled into the parking lot at Muir Woods and turned the car facing the single driveway leading in. He rolled down the windows, turned off the engine, and turned to face me.

"And you are going to vanish from the scene, out of reach of Scarlotti, out of my hair while I wrestle with diamond problems and . . ."

He was interrupted by the screaming of police sirens approaching on the road into the park.

Chapter 14

"Bart, that's Sgt. Slade!"

"Slade?"

"The policeman who investigated the murder at the statue and drove Reynard du Pre and me back to the hotel. Wouldn't this be a little out of his jurisdiction?"

"Different county? Sure would," Bart said, whipping the car around and following Sgt. Slade to the other end of the parking lot. "Let's see what brings a San Francisco city cop to Marin County with lights and sirens blazing."

As Bart slammed the car into park, I jumped out of the car and waved at the sergeant as he pointed a policeman to intercept us.

"Sgt. Slade!"

"Mrs. Allan." He stopped and waited for us to catch up. "I didn't recognize you at first. What are you doing up here?"

"Sergeant, this is my husband, Bartholomew Allan. He was meeting with Captain Saddler on these murders while you were investigating the body on Francis Scott Key's lap."

Bart thrust his hand forward. "Just Bart. Thanks for taking Allison back to the hotel this morning. Another one, huh?"

"How'd Captain Saddler get you out here so fast?"

Bart avoided the question. "Who found this one?"

"A couple of hikers cooling off in the creek."

"Same M.O.?"

"Sounds like it."

The park ranger interrupted at that moment to lead the police into the redwoods. Sgt. Slade directed his cohort to keep everyone out of the park and headed into the cool, green shade under the towering giants with us close behind.

"What will Captain Saddler say when he finds out we've horned in on his investigation?" I whispered.

"We'll cross that bridge when we come to it," Bart said quietly.

The woods were hushed and still. Even the scolding of jays and raucous cawing of ravens faded the farther in we hiked. Warblers' cheery songs dwindled as though their merry music was taboo in this place of tragedy.

We crossed the first bridge to the south side of Redwood Creek. The ranger explained it was a shorter, straighter route. This part of the trail on the north side of the creek bowed and wandered.

Redwood sorrel carpeted the forest floor, and sword fern, ladyfern, and bracken fern peeked through rust-colored pine needles. I longed to stop and savor the tranquility, the peace of this quiet enchanted place, to relish the reverence inspired by the majestic trees.

Sgt. Slade and the ranger strode purposely past the Bohemian Grove, past shaded bay trees twisting upward toward the sunlight sifting through towering redwood branches.

We crossed the second bridge spanning the gurgling creek, splashing over moss, lichen-covered rocks and fallen trees, to the shorter trail on the north side of the creek.

Bridge Three was a thirty-minute hike from the ranger station. Today it had taken twenty minutes. The park ranger who'd been standing guard over the body hurried to meet us, apparently relieved to have company.

"Aaron Henscheid," he said, extending a nervous hand to the policeman.

"Sgt. Slade, SFPD."

"Bart Allan, and my wife, Allison."

Aaron's hand was warm and moist with perspiration. He took off his cavalry-style ranger hat and wiped his forehead on his sleeve, revealing thick hair the shade of the redwoods and a sprinkling of freckles the same hue.

"It's over here, wedged under the bridge." Aaron motioned to the boulder next to the wooden bridge.

Bart and Sgt. Slade leaned over the water.

"Looks like someone wanted to make sure it was found right away," Sgt. Slade said. "It isn't hidden. They didn't want it washing down the creek. See how they anchored it between the rock and the bridge?"

"Does this one look like the others?" Bart asked.

"Same type victim, same M.O.—wire around the neck, diamond in the forehead."

"We closed the trail as soon as the hikers ran in with the news. I came immediately and sent everyone already on the trail back out. I've been here alone ever since," Aaron said.

"Good," Slade said. "The less traffic, the better. Forensics doesn't like it when people mess up their crime scene."

"You were right on about Muir Woods, Princess," Bart said.

"That doesn't help this poor guy—or the next victims. We've got to stop them before it happens again, not just count bodies and cart them away after the fact."

"I know." Bart's voice was grim and frustration clouded his blue eyes.

As the medical examiner and the forensics crime crew hustled up the trail behind us, we moved aside to watch them in action. They photographed the scene and combed the area for clues. But this was a heavily hiked trail with hundreds of people tramping through every day.

"How can they tell what's a clue the killers left and what's litter from careless hikers?" I asked.

"They have their ways," Bart said.

I watched, not wanting to but unable to avert my eyes, as they pulled the dripping body from the creek, performed a cursory examination, then zipped it into a body bag. It was something they'd probably done hundreds of times. That didn't lessen the feeling of helplessness that swept over me, or the pity I felt for the poor victim—for all of the victims.

"Bart, I almost feel responsible. Seven bodies in seven days. Where will tomorrow's be found? And what's being done to prevent any more?"

"Word's on the street to the homeless. They're trying to move them to centers in the city, those that will go," Sgt. Slade said, sounding as frustrated as Bart and as sorry as I felt. "We've beefed up patrols, borrowed some help from Oakland and called everyone in from leave. We're doing all we can. All we humanly can."

"They've got people staking out Chinatown, the Presidio, Haas-Lilienthal House, the brownstone on Nob Hill, and both the courthouse and U.N. building," Bart said.

"You mean Captain Saddler believed me?" I gasped.

"Let's just say he's covering all eventualities," Bart grinned, winking at me.

Aaron, listening to our conversation, asked, "Are you one of those psychics that helps the police solve problem cases?"

"Heavens, no!"

"How'd you know about the murders?" he persisted.

"An educated guess, nothing more. I'm sorry I was right."

"Guess we're through here for now," Sgt. Slade said. "Are you two coming back with me?"

I looked at Bart. "If you don't have a pressing need to get back, could we stay a bit?"

Bart turned to Aaron. "Would it be okay?"

"Sure. I've got a few things to do at the station. You won't be more than an hour, will you?"

"No, I promise." I smiled into the young park ranger's sincere brown eyes. "We'll only be a few minutes behind you."

Sgt. Slade and the two rangers followed the forensics crew down the sun-dappled trail, leaving us in a melancholy silence. I took Bart's hand and led him to a bench in the Cathedral Grove. A peaceful air of reverence permeated the pines, much like a chapel. I leaned into the crook of his arm and laid my head back on it.

"Those men must all have families somewhere who worry about them and wonder where they are. A mother, father, sister, brother, wife, or child must be missing them right now. Will they ever know what happened or will they spend the rest of their lives not knowing?"

"Some of the bodies were identified with fingerprints, dental work, ID they found. Those whose families they could locate have been notified. Some will probably never know what happened."

"That's awful. To have someone you love disappear and never know . . ."

"Do you see why I'm so anxious to be baptized—for you to be baptized—so we can be sealed in the temple? If anything happened in this short span of life on earth and we were separated, we'd still have each other after death—for eternity."

"That's a different belief from most churches, isn't it?"

"Yes. But that's only one thing that makes it different. It's not a breakaway from the Catholic Church like most Protestant churches. It's the original church of Jesus Christ, restored to the earth in the latter days. Hence, the Church of Jesus Christ of Latter-day Saints. It was restored with the authority and power to act in God's name. That's what the priesthood is—God's power, delegated to man to do His work here."

"Restored? How?"

"Would you believe by angels?"

I turned and looked up at Bart, expecting to see his eyes twinkling and his face crinkled in a teasing smile. There was no smile. He was serious. I swiveled on the bench to face him.

"Angels? You've got to be kidding?"

"No. I've never been more serious. First Angel Moroni appeared to a fourteen-year-old boy, Joseph Smith, and told him God had chosen him for a special work. The angel kept returning to teach Joseph and when the boy was ready, God sent John the Baptist, then Peter, James, and John to restore the priesthood authority they took with them when they died."

"You really believe that?" I poked him. "This is Bart, the strong, sensible, silent type who takes nothing at face value and believes only what he can see, touch, smell and feel."

"One and the same."

"And you believe angels came . . ."

"I do. And you can, too. All you have to do is ask if it's true, have faith to believe the Lord will answer, and He'll tell you."

I stood up and looked at Bart. I walked away, turned and looked at him again. "We are talking about the same religion that got you through prison in Tibet? The same one Michael and his family belong to in Hawaii?"

"The same."

I was disturbed—more than a little. My mind reeled, my thoughts were a jumble of what I remembered from Bible class and what Bart had told me.

"How far did you get in the Book of Mormon?" Bart asked.

"Only the first couple of chapters. Why?"

"It's a unique and sacred book. Joseph translated it from gold plates written in reformed Egyptian. . . ."

"Gold plates?" I shook my head. "Captain Saddler thought I was inhaling fumes that addled my brain. What were you inhaling? Incense? The fumes of the poppy?"

"I know it sounds farfetched. . . ."

"Try unbelievable."

"Try reading the book. Then ask if it's true. You'll know as sure as I do it is. In fact, you don't have to read the whole thing. Just read Moroni 10:3-5, then ask. The promise is there. It works."

What had I gotten myself involved with? A husband who believed in angels? And gold plates? A husband who was ready to lock me away in "protective custody"? What next?

"Want me to tell you what you're thinking?" Bart asked. "I can even tell you what you're feeling right now."

"Now you're a psychic? Or are angels whispering to you?"

"No, Princess. I've experienced what you're going through. The disbelief, the incredulity of the whole thing. The confusion, the world tipped on its end from what you've always believed. Things are not right—not cut and dried as they were. Then wonder—could it be true? Could it really have happened? And the hope—that it is true. That God really does speak to us today, that the heavens are not closed, that miracles do happen. Am I right?"

I stared at Bart. "You just read me like an open book."

"I told you. I went through the whole thing with Emile in Tibet. For six months I argued and he taught. But you've seen enough miracles in the past two weeks in Greece, the Azores and Hawaii to know more than most people at this point. I wish we'd had time to sit down and discuss this so I could tell you in a logical way. We haven't had an uninterrupted hour since I found you again."

I wasn't sure what to say—so I said nothing. I held out my hand to Bart. He got up and we silently walked out of the Cathedral Grove and down the trail.

"I know it's overpowering. Just take it as slow as you like.

There's no hurry," he stopped and smiled, "as long as we can be sealed in the temple this time next year."

Was Bart crazy to believe these ludicrous things? Was I—even to think about believing him?

A chipmunk scampered for cover as we wandered slowly through the redwoods. Thrushes darted in and out of the trees, warbling their flute song as they played hide and seek in the ferns that grew under the towering trees.

The happy gurgle of Redwood Creek dispelled the disquiet I felt. A peaceful feeling settled over my heart and mind. There would be time to learn what Bart said I could know.

After we'd dealt with the deaths and the diamonds. After we'd dealt with Roach. And Scarlotti.

Chapter

15

The Convention Center filled rapidly as Bart and I claimed two seats near a rear exit. I'd have taken a front-row seat had there been one available, but Bart wanted to be where he could watch the crowd and, I suspected, near a quick exit if he needed one. Were back-row seats to be my lot in life now that I was married to an agent who stayed poised to jump and run at any moment?

"Bart, look at that man's cane. It's just like the one the old man in the museum had the other day. It's so unusual, I can't believe there could be two exactly alike."

"Are you sure it's not the same man?" Bart asked, turning his attention to the well-dressed, gray-haired man who walked with exaggerated decorum down the aisle.

"The one in the museum looked like he was crippled with arthritis or something—he was all bent over—and his clothes were straight out of the rag pile. I was so captivated by the intricate carvings on the cane, I didn't really look at his face, but this man . . ." I turned to Bart. "You don't think it could be the same man, do you?"

"Sorry. I didn't see him. Picture this guy all bent over in different clothes."

"I can't see him. There are too many people between us."

"Follow him down the aisle," Bart said, "and see if you can get a better look. You've got me curious now."

I made my way through the crowd of noisy, animated people all vying for seats close to the podium, trying to keep my eye on the gray head moving in front of me. Being height-impaired didn't help.

I stood on tiptoe when my way was blocked, hoping to keep my quarry in view.

"Excuse me, may I get through?" I murmured, trying to squeeze through a human barricade.

As the tall man blocking my way turned to let me pass, I looked straight up into the sullen dark eyes of the ponytailed fellow in the museum. I quickly dropped my gaze, mumbled thank you, and pressed on down the aisle, hoping he hadn't recognized me, but even more than that, hoping my recognition of him hadn't shown in my face.

A sudden thought struck me—why should it matter if he recognizes you? You were both simply patrons of the museum, weren't you?

Finally catching up with my quarry, I went beyond him so I could come back up the aisle facing him for a better look. This man was clean-shaven where the other man had several days' gray stubble. This man's hair was neatly trimmed; the other's had been shaggier, tousled-looking, but both were only cosmetic differences.

Moving slowly back toward Bart, I passed the man now taking a seat on the aisle. It was the same cane. I was sure of it. The crowd pressed toward the front of the auditorium, and I felt like a fish swimming upstream as I fought my way to my seat.

I was almost there when my path was suddenly blocked by a short, stout body that moved to the right when I did, then to the left as I tried to dodge him. I laughed and was going to say, "Shall we dance?" when I recognized the smiling, pale eyes of the other man in the museum.

"Excuse me. I seem to be going the wrong way," I laughed lamely, and slipped around the man who appeared to be purposely standing in my way.

"You're not going to believe this!" I whispered breathlessly when I'd finally found my way back to my seat. "Not only could that man be the same one in the museum, but I just ran into two other men who'd caught my attention—and I think they recognized me."

"Where are they?"

"Headed down front. I can't see them from here."

"The gang's all here, Princess. Look who just came in."

I turned to see Elekta sashay down the aisle in an elegant eggplant pantsuit. I'd never have imagined anyone with cinnamon-colored hair looking so great in purple—but as usual, she was a knockout. As she scanned the crowd, she spotted us and stopped.

"How are the honeymooners tonight?"

Bart stood and took her extended hand. "Great, and you?"

I immediately stood, which placed me between them. Just where I wanted to be.

"Intensely interested in tonight's lecture. It's rumored they're announcing a new find. By the way, Allison," she said as she finally let go of Bart's hand and turned her attention to me, "thank you for introducing me to Reynard. He's exceptionally talented. I'm going to use some of the pictures he took of my gallery for publicity. He has a natural eye for beauty and design."

"I'm glad you could use him."

"Ladies and gentlemen, if you could please take your seats, we'll get started with tonight's lecture."

Elekta looked quickly around, then turned back to us.

"Is that seat taken? I don't see the party I was supposed to meet."

"Please join us," Bart said amiably, moving into the aisle so she could get in. That put me between them again. Perfect. I glanced at Bart as I settled down and caught a wink and a knowing grin. I squeezed his hand. He was no dummy.

Lights dimmed. A portly, balding gentleman introduced the guest speaker with glowing adjectives—distinguished, renowned, learned, and acclaimed. When Professor Bainston stepped to the podium, Bart's arm slipped around my shoulder and pulled me close to him.

"Just to remind you, you're mine, in case you get carried away with his silvery oratory," he whispered.

Then I got lost in the fascinating world of diamonds. Arthur Bainston was an articulate and knowledgeable speaker filled with enchanting stories and facts about the most beloved of all gemstones.

He began with the story of Jean Baptiste Tavernier, a plump little Parisian of great courage and curiosity, who one day in 1631 began what became a forty-year career as a gem connoisseur and merchant. He was the first European to see the Indian mines of

Coulour, near Golconda, and watch sixty-thousand laborers scrabbling after diamonds under the scorching sun. He crossed deserts and mountains, braved robbers waiting to waylay travelers on his way to Turkey, to the exotic world of the Orient in his passionate search for the most precious stone.

Though I was totally engrossed in Professor Bainston's eloquent speech, Bart was not. His attention focused on a man to my left, down a couple of rows, videotaping the speech. I watched for a minute, but when Professor Bainston mentioned the Koh-i-noor Diamond, I left him to Bart and concentrated on the fascinating history of the fabled stone, anxious to see if he had anything to add to today's research.

"After broad-scale bribery by the little Frenchman, India's Mogul of Moguls, Aurangzeb, opened his treasury to the fascinated Tavernier, the first European to view it. Tavernier was shown the fabulous Peacock Throne studded with 26,733 gems, including an enormous diamond, 108 rubies, the least of which weighed one-hundred carats, and 116 huge emeralds. Today the famed throne, stored in the Central Bank of Iran, is used as the basis for the national currency, since the Ayatollah has no use for ceremonial jewels."

With a tiny key-chain camera, Bart began snapping pictures of the man and his camcorder. At my raised eyebrow, he whispered in my ear, "I know him from somewhere."

Professor Bainston continued his description of the tour of the treasury. "As the grand climax, a great diamond weighing an astonishing 280 carats was placed in his hands. But Tavernier was not enthusiastic over the Great Mogul, as it was known, even though it was probably the largest diamond in the world. It had no history. And as any diamontaire worth his salt knows, the more tempestuous the history, the more exciting the diamond."

Elekta finally moved, stretching her long legs in the small space in front of her, arching and rubbing her neck and shoulders. There was a general shifting in the audience as Professor Bainston paused for a drink of water.

Bart's attention now centered on a man leaning casually against the wall near the exit. Tall, slender, Armani-dressed, probably of Arab descent, extremely good-looking.

"I'll keep my eye him," I whispered. "You can keep tabs on the one with the camera."

"The professor's your man. I'll handle these, thank you," Bart countered.

The incredibly handsome Arab turned to scan the crowd, saw Elekta, and got no further. He watched her stretch, appreciation of her graceful beauty written all over his face.

"And now, the story you are all waiting for, I presume—the affair of the Queen's Necklace. This was probably the most beautiful, valuable collection of matched diamonds of the first water ever assembled into one piece of jewelry. It's ironic that this set of gems, named for the notorious Marie Antoinette, never actually belonged to her nor was ever worn by her."

As soon as Professor Bainston resumed his lecture, he became once again the focus of everyone's attention, even the tall, handsome Arab.

"During the reign of France's King Louis XV, the crown jewelers decided to assemble a diamond necklace for the king's extravagant mistress, Madame du Barry. It took several years and depleted their resources. Then just before the magnificent necklace of 647 meticulously matched diamonds was completed, the king died."

Tall, Dark, and Handsome no longer leaned casually against the wall, but stood ramrod straight, attention focused on the professor. The man with the camcorder continued taping.

"The jewelers approached young Louis XVI, hoping he'd buy it for his queen who'd just given birth. What could be more perfect for one whose extravagance was already legendary? But in a gesture entirely out of character, Marie Antoinette turned down the necklace. Our jewelers were frantic, and on one occasion, Boehmer fell to his knees before the queen. 'I am ruined, bankrupt, dishonored. Unless you buy the necklace, I shall go direct and throw myself into the river.' Boehmer backed away from his threat when the queen seemed to approve the idea."

Titters rippled through the audience. Movement at my side diverted my attention to Elekta leaning forward in her seat, gaze transfixed on the speaker at the podium.

"In 1875, the jewelers received a welcome letter from Jeanne de Saint-Remy de Valois de La Motte, a rumored confidante of the queen, informing them a *grand seigneur* of the realm was interested in the necklace. Prince Louis Rene Edouard de Rohan, a cardinal of the church, had fallen out of favor with Marie Antoinette and was anxious to be reinstated. Jeanne convinced the cardinal she could accomplish his great desire. She hired a prostitute who resembled the queen, dressed her grandly, veiled her face, and arranged a secret tryst under cover of darkness."

Though Bart may not have been entranced by the speaker and his subject, the three he'd been watching were mesmerized. Their total attention was riveted on the professor.

"The bogus queen handed Rohan a rose, saying, 'You know what that means,' then fled into the night as he flung himself at her feet. When Madame de La Motte asked him to act as the queen's negotiator in the purchase of the fabled necklace, the grateful Rohan agreed. He shrewdly negotiated a price of 1,600,000 francs and arranged for delivery of the necklace six months before the first installment was due. The cardinal presented the necklace to the cunning Jeanne to give to his beloved Marie Antoinette, or so he assumed. But the crafty Jeanne and her husband immediately dismantled the necklace, divided the jewels, and the husband departed for London.

"The reckless Madame de La Motte lived lavishly for six months in France. When payment came due, Boehmer went to the queen for payment and the elaborate hoax was exposed.

"The king was furious that his queen's name had been used and her reputation tarnished in this way. Instead of settling the affair quietly behind closed doors, he had a public trial for the cardinal and the lady. A dreadful mistake, leading to additional scandal for a queen already known as the Harlot of Versailles.

"The affair of the Queen's Necklace has been called the prelude to the revolution. Of course, the barricades would have, nevertheless, been erected and revolution eventually ensued. However, had the magnificent necklace hung around the queen's neck for a time as its creators had hoped, her head might have remained attached a few more years."

Professor Bainston paused dramatically, looked over his audience for a long moment, then asked, "And what became of the 647 matched diamonds that made up the Queen's Necklace?"

The audience collectively drew a deep, anticipatory breath. There was total silence. I glanced at Bart, probably the only other one in the building whose complete attention wasn't focused on the professor. He intently studied the faces of those around us.

"What became of the diamonds from the necklace?" Bainston repeated. "With the possible exception of twenty-two stones that later were incorporated into a necklace owned by the Duke of Sutherland, the diamonds so painstakingly assembled by the French jewelers seemed irretrievably scattered. Could they be traced? Could the infamous necklace ever be reassembled?"

The tension, the anticipation, was palpable. The professor certainly knew how to hold an audience. Then he dropped the bombshell.

"Ladies and gentlemen, it is my pleasure to inform you that all of the 647 perfectly matched diamonds have been found. The Queen's Necklace has been meticulously reassembled according to the sketches left by it originators, Charles-Auguste Boehmer and Paul Bassenge, and will be the centerpiece of this extraordinary exhibit of extraordinary diamonds. But there's more. Please return for our concluding lecture tomorrow night and another stunning revelation from the exotic world of diamonds."

The audience rose to its feet with an explosion of applause and exclamations.

Elekta made a beeline for the exit without a word. Tall, Dark, and Handsome held the door open, then followed her out. Camcorder Man shouldered the camera and was close on their tail. Bart grabbed my arm and propelled me through the crowd. We followed them into the night.

Chapter 16

"Wait!" I protested. "I wanted to tell Professor Bainston how much I enjoyed his lecture. Where are we going?"

"To see what's happening. Can you see Elekta or the man standing by the door? Or the one with the camera? Or any of your friends from the museum?"

I scanned the faces swirling around us. "No."

The trio who'd just exited were quickly lost in the crowd pouring from the warm auditorium into the cool night air.

"Now what, Kemo Sabe?"

"Want to fight your way back in to talk to the professor?"

One look at the crowd dissuaded me. "Maybe tomorrow night at the last lecture."

"Then let's find your photographer friend, Reynard, and see if he'd like to do a little night work."

"Develop your pictures?"

"I've run into the man with the camera before, and I think I've seen the Arab. Just can't place them right now."

"If I'd seen Tall, Dark, and Handsome before, I'd certainly have remembered where," I teased.

"I can't believe my bride is ogling other men on our honeymoon!"

"Hold that thought! There may be hope for us yet if you remember we're supposed to be honeymooning." We crossed the street and headed back to the hotel. "Which diamond did they seem most interested in?"

Bart looked at me queerly. "What do you have in mind?"

"Suppose—for argument's sake—any or all of them were interested in lifting one of the diamonds. Which one that he talked about tonight got the most attention?"

"Are you changing your theory about the Jihad wanting the whole shebang?" Bart asked.

"Just exploring all the options. Remember what Dad said before we left, about this event drawing all sorts of low life? What if there's more than one group with designs on the exhibit? Maybe somebody else wants just one diamond for some reason."

"Princess, your imagination never ceases to amaze me. When you figure it out, let me in on it. In the meantime, I'll concentrate on the security at the museum and the activity in town, and you work out this newest wrinkle."

"Did I detect a patronizing tone in your voice?" I demanded, stopping in the middle of the sidewalk.

"Not on your life. Did I detect a bit of paranoia in yours?" he countered.

I laughed, looping my arm through his as we continued our walk. "Just possibly. Captain Saddler has me on the defensive these days."

"Speaking of the defensive!" Bart exclaimed. Something zinged past my head, next to Bart's shoulder. He shoved me into the noisy, dirty bar we were passing.

"Was that what I think it was?" I asked as we darted through the smoke-filled room toward the open back door.

"'Fraid so," Bart said, holding my hand tight with one hand, his gun in his other. The tough-looking crowd parted for the gun and we raced through the alley, zigzagging our way through the remaining couple of blocks to McAllister Street and our hotel.

"Next time, remind me to wear running shoes," I panted, pulling my high heels off as we arrived at the Abigail.

We met Reynard just returning from a photo foray of the city. He seemed more shy and nervous than ever when I introduced him to Bart, but he willingly developed Bart's film in a makeshift lab in his bathroom while we waited in the darkened bedroom. I didn't mind the extra snuggle time it afforded.

Back in our room, Bart produced a compact laptop computer containing his rogues' gallery from a hidden compartment in the bottom of his suitcase and was elated to find a match on both the camera man and the good-looking Arab.

"Nothing on Elekta?" I asked, looking over his shoulder.

"Should there be?"

"I assumed you'd run a check on her, too, if our handsome friend was interested."

"I don't know a male in the world who wouldn't be interested in Elekta. Do you blame them?"

"Just as long as you're not, every other man in the world can do whatever he wants. Did you check her out?" I persisted.

"Yes, I checked her out. She's not in our files. Did you want her to be?"

"There's just something about her. . . ."

"While you're deciding what it is, I need to make a phone call."

I plopped on the bed with a map of San Francisco to plot a course for exploration, just in case we ever did get around to doing the honeymoon thing.

Bart didn't even say hello when his party answered.

"The rats are in the soufflé again," Bart said.

I sat upright on the bed and stared in disbelief.

"Lends credence to our theory," he continued, ignoring me. "I'll meet you as planned. The custodial staff will have cleared out by then and there'll just be us and security." He hung up.

"Rats in the soufflé?" I held up my hand. "Don't tell me. It's another 'specialist in Athens' business, isn't it? Let me guess."

"I can think of something better than guessing games." Bart signaled silence with a finger to his lips. He retrieved the bug catcher from the false bottom of his shaving cream canister and swept the room while we carried on a perfectly inane conversation.

"All clean?" I asked when he didn't find anything.

"Apparently."

"Safe to talk?"

"Depends on what you're going to talk about."

"Rats?"

"How about something more pleasant? Like our honeymoon. Want me to show you what I heard honeymoons are all about?" He rolled across the bed and pulled me on top of him.

"Mmm. Why do I get the feeling you're trying to change the subject?"

"All work and no play makes Jack a dull boy. We've done more work than play since we've been here. . . ."

"So now that you have a couple of hours free, you'll squeeze in a little play to placate me."

"Princess, would I do that?" he protested in mock anguish.

"Of course you'd do that." I rolled over and smacked him in the face with a pillow. "You've done it ever since we got to San Francisco."

He grabbed the pillow from my hands and I lobbed him with another one.

"I suspect you'll do that the rest of our lives," I pouted, snuggling into the crook of his arm, "but it's okay. I knew what I was getting into when I married an In—"

Bart kissed the words right out of my mouth.

"I though you said there weren't any bugs," I whispered breathlessly when he finally let me up for air.

"Who said anything about bugs? Your lips are irresistible when they get that pouty look."

"And you're King Tut! But I get the message. I'll watch what I say. By the way, if I remember correctly, you said, 'I'll' meet you, not 'we'll' meet you." I kissed the hollow of his neck, running my hands over his shoulders and down his arms. "Was that a slip of the tongue, or did you plan to ditch me while you rendezvous with person or persons unknown?"

"Ditch you? Princess, your choice of terms . . ."

"Sorry, Charlie." I rolled on top of him and kissed his wrinkled forehead. "Forget it. I'm going with you."

Bart drew his fingers softly across my lips. "You've pretty well cinched going wherever I go for the time being, at least until I can find a safe place for you." He pulled my head down and softly kissed one eyelid, then the other. "I wouldn't dare leave you alone."

Alone. The thought gave me chills. I didn't want to be alone in this room for any reason. Someone came and went through that locked door all too easily for me to ever be alone here again. Bart must have read my mind.

"By the way, we're checking out when we leave so have your bag packed. It may not be much in terms of a honeymoon, but we do have the whole top floor of the building across the street from the museum and I'll feel a lot better having you where I can keep an eye on you. This is like staying in a major thoroughfare, people coming and going any time they please."

He avoided saying Scarlotti, just as I had done, but we both knew what he meant. That made me feel a little more secure, though I wasn't sure how I'd like sharing the honeymoon suite with Oz doing surveillance.

Thoughts of Scarlotti launched a shudder through my body. Bart responded immediately. His arms tightened around me and, holding me firmly against him, he rotated, covering my body with his, as if shielding me from the world. He buried his face in my hair, kissed my ear, my neck, sending waves of electric current tingling through me.

"You certainly know how to take a girl's mind off unpleasant matters," I whispered breathlessly, sliding my arms around his neck.

"I promised to show you what I thought honeymoons were all about," he said, kissing my nose, my chin, then nibbling at the hollow of my neck.

"I didn't think you knew. Be my guest," I invited.

His lips found mine and kissed all thoughts of Scarlotti right out of existence.

At the appointed hour, we checked out of the Abigail wearing jeans and sweat shirts. I wasn't sad to leave.

"When do I get to know about the rats in the soufflé?" I asked as we approached the Museum of Modern Art to check the security system that should insure the safety of the diamonds.

"The 'soufflé' is whatever current project or case we're working on. Rats are previously known perps."

"Perps?"

"Perpetrators. Someone who's committed a crime. Since Anastasia's area of expertise is terrorists, it's usually someone with a terrorist affiliation. These two haven't been linked directly to a known organization, but have showed up often enough to be suspect."

"You think they're working with the Jihad?"

"Guilt by association."

"Speaking of Anastasia, when are you going to replace the agents you lost in Greece? You can't function very long with just three of you, especially with Mom down and Dad consumed with her recovery."

"Jack was working on that. He'd asked for a couple of explosives specialists from another division of Interpol. Yo, Oz. I'd like you to meet my beautiful wife, Allison, who's in protective custody at the moment. Alli, Oswald Barlow, Agent Extraordinaire. Everything ready?"

Oswald Barlow emerged from the shadows, his deep-set gray eyes fairly sparkling with mischief. He was small, wiry, probably didn't weigh a hundred and fifty pounds after Thanksgiving dinner. Sandy hair fell in disarray across his forehead. I suspected no amount of brushing would keep it in place.

"Ah, the volcano lady!" He shook my hand. "You don't look any worse for the wear. Who are you protecting her from, Bart, the male population in general?"

I looked at Bart in dismay. "Does everyone know?"

"Your reputation precedes you, Mrs. Allan. Besides, in this business, we have no secrets. Everybody knows about everybody else's skeletons."

"That's unfortunate," I said. "Now, how do I get to help tonight?"

"Probably by staying out of the way."

"Bart!"

"I told you why you're here. I can't leave you alone with Scarlotti on the loose. I'd ship you back to New York in a heartbeat, but I'm afraid he'd follow you there, too."

"Give him time to get used to having you around," Oz whispered in mock confidentiality. "Being a new husband, he doesn't know what to do with you yet. When you prove indispensable, he'll be glad he couldn't send you away. If he does, I'll hire you to work for me. I like the way you think."

"It's 1 a.m. Time the guard let us in," Bart said, ignoring Oz.

As if on cue, the security guard opened the door and led us to an office with large maps spread across three desks. Bart introduced me to the security chief, Matt McMillan, and two guards, Sam and Ed. Matt was a big man in every way, taller even than Bart's six foot four inches, solid-looking and broad-chested. Bart took charge immediately, directing the operation like a general making battle plans.

I peeked through the circle of hunched shoulders, looking for an opening as they examined the floor plans of the museum—where live guards would be posted, and where special alarm systems had been installed. I felt like a water boy outside a football huddle.

Bart pointed out soft spots he'd found, Oz added his observations and Sam had one suggestion, but Matt watched without comment, his big velvety brown eyes missing nothing. As the group stepped back, Matt finally broke his thoughtful silence.

"Let's walk through and ah'll show ya' what we've got. Ya'll can test each area and see if we've planned for ev'rathang or not."

His words were slow and deliberate, spoken with a soft Texas twang that evoked images of lean cowboys and dusty cattle drives. And barbed wire fences.

They filed out behind Matt, leaving me standing alone in the office. Bart had forgotten me again. But Matt didn't, bless his big Texas heart.

"Mrs. Allan, could Ah impose on ya'll to help us here?" He stopped the procession, waiting for me to catch up. "We'll need someone to be in contact with the police durin' this test and tell them what we're doin' as we set off these alarms. Least, Ah think we're gonna set 'em off." With a smile warm as a Texas summer day, the big man handed me the cordless phone.

His soft brown eyes reminded me of my grandparent's Great Pyrenees. They'd named the huge dog Argus, Greek for vigilant one, guardian. I suspected this giant of a man had a lot of Argus's special qualities: a gentleness that belied powerful strength and an alertness to things and people around him. Interesting that he was guarding these treasures. I'd have to be careful not to call him Argus.

Matt began with the ground floor where we explored every possible entry and the security measures taken. First floor secured.

"How long will it take the police to get here if the alarms go off?" I asked as we climbed the stairs to the second floor.

"Good question, Mrs. Allan," Matt drawled. "Police headquarters is only seven blocks from here. Timed response was three to five minutes depending on traffic in the area, available units, and other variables."

"Plenty of time for a well-executed escape," Bart said with a frown.

"We'll have three guards on each floor twenty-four hours a day

during the exhibit. That should be a powerful deterrent in itself."
That was the first time Ed had spoken.

I hated to ask the next question.

"You've probably covered this, but what if they gassed the guards—put everybody to sleep with something through the air-conditioning system?"

"You're thinkin' like a criminal now, Mrs. Allan." Matt smiled. "We've got one portable alarm rigged so when the pressure's released, the alarm goes off."

"You mean someone has to have their finger on the alarm twenty-four hours a day?"

"It's a heat-sensitive alarm mounted on the guard's belt. He just has to rest his hand over it to keep it from activatin'. If he were unconscious, his hand'd fall away, the sensor'd cool immediately and the alarm would activate."

"What if he forgot and moved his hand?"

"They've thought about all those 'what ifs' and worked them out, Princess," Bart said quietly as we reached the second floor.

Was I making a pest of myself?

"Ah admire a thinkin' woman," Matt interrupted. "She might come up with somethin' we haven't."

"You've probably thought of every contingency. I just have a curious nature. . . ."

Bart laughed aloud. "That's an understatement. Her first words were 'why' and 'what if' and they're still her favorites. But the questions are always good ones." He put his arm around my shoulder and gave me an affectionate squeeze. "It's just that they're never ending," he said with a sigh.

"What else could ya'll devise to steal the diamonds?" Matt's brown eyes narrowed with intense interest.

"Has the sensor alarm been publicized? Who knows about it? I can think of half a dozen ways to thwart it already."

"Why don't ya'll do your thang here while Ah parry with Mrs. Allan for a few minutes?" He waved the four men away and leaned on the balcony. "All the guards were cautioned not to talk about it. It's new, but not unknown in security circles, been used in other special exhibits. How would ya'll foil it?"

"What if—," I laughed. "Sorry. Ingrained, I guess. Suppose the thief knew about it, clamped his hand over the guard's hand while he disabled him, taped the hand in place, then the rest of the gang knocked the remainder of the guards out with gas? The thieves would have on gas masks, of course."

"The sensor isn't on the same guard all the time. It rotates, guard to guard, floor to floor at random."

"What if one of the guards was in on the heist, waited for his turn with the sensor alarm on the chosen night, and let his accomplices into the museum?"

"Our security guards are screened and bonded. . . ."

"But you've hired a lot of extra help, haven't you?"

As he opened his mouth to answer, an alarm sounded somewhere in the building. Matt grabbed my arm and ran.

Chapter 17

"What's happenin'?" Matt called to the four who were nowhere in sight.

Punching a preset number on the phone with one hand, he barked to the police dispatcher, "Standby. Could be a test, but Ah'm not sure. Ah'll keep the line open and let ya'll know."

With his other hand, he'd grabbed his walkie-talkie. "Heads up, everybody. Report *now* what's goin' on."

There wasn't a sound on the second floor except the crackle of Matt's radio.

"Sam, report," Matt commanded.

No reply.

"Ed, where are you?"

Silence.

I held my breath. Where was Bart? Why didn't he answer the call? Where was Oz? What happened to everyone?

The alarm still rang on a floor somewhere above us, a remote annoyance I wished would cease. At least the diamonds weren't on display yet. Just today the cases had been installed; the diamonds would be arranged tomorrow, and the exhibit open the following day. Maybe. No security, no exhibit.

"Come on, Mrs. Allan. We're goin' up." Phone in one hand and radio in the other, Matt gave me a gentle shove toward the stairs, which we took two at a time to the third floor while he reported on the open phone line to the police station.

"Get 'em ready to roll, Carl. Nobody's tellin' me anything yet. Ya'll know as soon as Ah do who or what set the bleepin' thing off."

Switching hands, he yelled into the radio, "Sam. Ed. Report now."

"Sorry, boss. Thought we'd cornered a live one and didn't want to scare him off before we had him. But there's nobody here," Sam reported.

"Where are you?"

"I'm still on two."

"I'm on three," Ed broke in. "What I can see looks clean. Still looking."

"Oz here on four. Haven't even turned up a mouse so far, but I've got a few more corners to check."

"I'm on five and I don't see or hear anything except the alarm, but I'm still checking," Bart said.

"What set it off?" Matt barked into his radio.

"Can't tell yet," Bart answered.

"Carl, send the cars. Have 'em check out the first floor and the grounds while we cover the rest of the place. We'll call ya'll back soon as we find somethin'." Matt turned off the phone and thrust it into my hands. "Hang onto this and stay close." He wheeled to the stairs and took them three at a time with me at his heels. He moved amazingly fast for a man of his size.

"How in blazes did ya'll get scattered so fast?" Matt asked into the radio. My question exactly. Our conversation had barely begun when the alarm sounded and they hadn't been gone long enough to disburse so quickly.

"We were back near the elevators when the alarm rang. Everybody grabbed a car to a different floor thinking we'd spread out . . . ."

"Found the trouble," Bart interrupted on the radio. "The double doors are ajar."

"We're on our way," Matt responded, breathless from the race up the stairs. "Everybody stay on your floor and be alert."

We rattled across the catwalk on the fifth floor, dodging empty display cases.

Bart stuck his head around the corner. "Can't see anything out here. They'd have to have wings to leave by this door. Did you have the video cameras on tonight?"

"Ah think so. Ah think we decided on a test run of the whole system. Let's see."

We boarded the elevator and while we made the quick descent to the first floor, Matt checked in with Ed, Sam, and Oz. Each reported they'd found nothing on their floor and joined us at the monitors in the security room.

"Back the tapes up thirty minutes, then view on fast forward until you see somethin' move," Matt instructed as each man took a monitor.

I peered over Sam's shoulder as he viewed the second floor and watched us appear as we climbed the stairs. Ed's third-floor cameras scanned a quiet floor, with Ed being the only moving thing recorded.

Oz slid to one side to allow me to see his fourth-floor screen.

"Did something move there?" I asked. "Can you back it up?"

Everyone paused their recorders and crowded around the fourth-floor monitor.

"It was about the time the camera scanned the stairs, I think, and I'm not sure exactly what was there, but I had the impression of movement. There!" I pointed at what appeared to be a shadow flitting across the screen.

"Run it back and slow it down," Matt commanded.

The only sound in the room was the quiet hum of the VCR while Oz played and replayed the short sequence.

"It's like a ghost. Ah'm not sure Ah'm really seein' anything. How'd ya'll ever spot that, Mrs. Allan?" Matt asked, rubbing his chin thoughtfully.

I shuddered at the thought of my own personal ghost and ignored his question. "Could it be the shadow of someone on the catwalk above?"

"I think you've got it! Play it again," Bart said, squeezing my shoulder and kissing my cheek. "Good work, Princess."

"Now that we know what, can you tell who?" Sam asked, peering over my shoulder.

"I'll get back to the fifth-floor picture and see if I can pick up anything there," Bart said, moving away. I went with him, needing his nearness. The brief shadow on the screen reminded me too much of Scarlotti, slipping silently in and out of rooms, in and out of my life.

Matt moved to the fifth-floor screen with us. Bart played the tape on slightly faster than normal speed but not full fast forward. "See anything?" he asked.

"Not yet," I said quietly. We were supposed to be finding jewel thieves, not ghosts. Why did everything remind me of Scarlotti? Why couldn't he just die and stay dead like most dead people? Maybe because he wasn't like most people.

"There! Back it up!" Matt stabbed his finger at the screen. The crew crowded around our monitor in time to glimpse a fleeing figure. It remained on camera only a fraction of a second before disappearing.

"Again," Matt demanded.

Again, and again, and again Bart ran the flash of black. It was so fleeting there was time only to gain an impression of what was on screen. Holding on the image didn't help identify the tall, slender figure dressed in black. Could have been either man or woman. The hooded sweat shirt hid the head and hair and came below the hips. The blip was so brief that male or female characteristics or movement didn't come into play.

"Sam, go see what the cops have found. Ed, you stay and see what else ya'll can find on these tapes. Mrs. Allan, would ya help him? Ya'll seem to have a keen eye for that." Matt beamed his warm, Texas smile on me, then turned briskly to the door. "Bart and Oz, come with me. Let's see where our visitor went when he left the fifth floor."

"Ed, do you mind if I study the fourth- and fifth-floor tapes and leave two and three to you?"

"No, go right ahead, Mrs. Allan. I think I'll start at the beginning of two, then do the same with three and see if we can determine how and when the intruder came in. I'm curious to see if he shows up anywhere else and if we missed him when the museum closed or if he got in after."

I rewound the tape of the fourth floor to a couple of hours before closing time, watching the people in the museum and security watching them.

Individually, the interesting trio appeared. First the tall, bearded man with hostile dark eyes and dun-colored ponytail, better dressed this time and alone.

The cane was the only giveaway to the old man. Today he was neither bent with age and in rags, nor tall, dignified and fashionably dressed. He looked like anyone's grandfather, open-collared plaid shirt, polyester pants and wire-rimmed granny glasses perched on his nose. His hair was slicked back close to his head, shiny with whatever old men put on their hair to keep it looking like they'd just watered and combed it.

The short, stout blond with pale eyes wandered alone, still devouring the art, but also noting security and camera placement.

I rewound the tape to Hostile Dark Eyes and studied his movements. Sure enough. He surreptitiously made notes on a tiny pad he palmed when not in use, and I was sure the notes were not of art objects. The Old Man and The Cane was doing the same thing, but his use of the cane intrigued me. I rewound the tape, examining his movements. He was taking pictures with it!

"Ed, let me show you this in case I don't get a chance to show Matt." I told him as we watched how I'd observed them before in the museum, and of their interest in the diamond lecture the night before.

"I think they're casing the joint, as they say in the movies. See if they're on your tapes."

Ed noted the meter reading so he could rewind the tape to show Matt, then went back to his monitor. I continued through the fourth-floor tape, finding nothing of interest until Elekta appeared, resplendent in an apple-green sheath with cream-colored scarf draped from one short hem to the other. Her portfolio was open and she took copious notes, as usual. *I'd like to see if those notes are really just placement, arrangement, and lighting.*

My thoughts surprised me. Why did I clump Elekta with the three men I suspected of casing the joint? Because when I saw one, the others seemed to be in the area? Because they appeared to spend an inordinate amount of time at the museum? Because they were extremely interested in the diamond lecture? Big deal. So were several hundred other people, including myself.

My eyelids felt like sandpaper on my eyes. A cramp spread across my shoulders and up my neck. I tried first one position, then another as I watched people come and go on the monitor.

Suddenly all pain and discomfort vanished as Captain Jim Saddler appeared on the screen. He wandered through the gallery in civilian clothes, checking out the position of the cameras, the guards, and trying very much to look like an ordinary Joe.

As a police captain, it was his job to make the city safe, safeguard the exhibits, protect the integrity of the museum. Why would he be out of uniform?

I rubbed my aching neck. Ed looked up from his monitor.

"Long day, huh? Let's find out what happened to everyone. They should have been back an hour ago."

He picked up his radio. "Matt, where is everybody? Do you need some help?"

"No. Stay put," Matt drawled over the radio. "We're just finishin' up. We'll be right down."

Switching off my monitor, I stretched, yawned, and sank wearily into the big padded chair behind the security chief's desk. Maps were still spread all over its surface.

"Where would someone hide so they wouldn't be seen at closing time?" I asked Ed.

"Any number of places, but the guards on duty should have checked them," Ed said.

"They couldn't have known that we'd be here tonight. If they were making a dry run for the jewels, you'd think they'd wait to see how the fifth floor was set up when the diamonds were there."

It had to be connected to the diamonds. Scarlotti wouldn't come here looking for me. He'd have no reason.

His presence was oppressive. It was bad enough when I thought he was dead. Now he seemed everywhere, in every shadow.

Chapter 18

Bart gently shook me.

"Let's go put you to bed, Princess. You look like you've had a very long day."

"What did you find out?" I asked, glancing at my watch. Four o'clock in the morning. I must have fallen asleep.

"Whoever was here apparently hid somewhere in the museum before it closed."

"Bet they were surprised to find us here. Did anyone venture a guess as to who our shadowy guest might have been?"

We bid tired good-byes to Sam, who let us out the front door of the museum and locked it behind us.

"No," Bart said. "Everyone agrees it had to be someone checking out the showcase arrangements."

"Does that change any of your plans?" I asked as we stopped by the car to grab our bags before crossing the street to the building kitty-corner from the museum.

"We'll increase security, be more on our toes. In a way, it's better, actually knowing someone's going for the diamonds."

"You don't think the fact that you know about them will change anything? They'll call it off?"

"Not if it's Jihad. That would probably just increase the challenge and excitement for them, to take the diamonds right out of our hands."

"Can you really stop them?"

"That's definitely the plan."

The short walk in the crisp, cool, early-morning air roused me from the sleepy state the warm coziness of Matt's office had induced.

It also reminded me how vulnerable we were in the empty street under the lights. Perfect targets for Scarlotti or Roach, or whoever had been in the museum.

Gleaming glass and brass in the newly remodeled entry rather suited the ornate old building which was our new lodging. A security guard behind a green marble reception desk in the lobby looked up expectantly from the book he was reading.

"Good morning," Bart said.

"Good morning." It was more of a question than a greeting.

Bart flashed his ID. "Bartholomew Allan. We have the top floor."

"Oh, yes, Mr. Allan. They said you'd be coming in early. Let's see . . ." He looked at the note on the register. "I'm supposed to give you another set of keys to your floor."

"Who else has keys?"

"We have a set in the safe here. Yours, Mr. Barlow's, and these. There are only four sets."

"Who has access to the safe?"

"Any of the security guards."

"How many shifts do you have? How many security guards?"

"Three, sir. We each have an eight-hour shift. Oh, and the three who cover Saturday and Sunday."

"What else is kept in the safe? How often is it opened?"

"We keep keys to all the office doors on all the floors, then whatever else the tenants in the building deem valuable enough to need secured. We're usually in it a couple of times a day. Rarely at night."

"I have a proposition for you . . . ," Bart read his name tag, ". . . Hank. For the next few days while we're here and have the top floor, I want all the keys."

"But, sir, that's . . ."

"I'll tell you why. I'm charged with protecting the Princess. It's hard enough with the paparazzi stalking her wanting pictures, but now some kook has threatened her life. I don't need him sticking up the place to get the keys or bribing his way to the keys and breaking in on her. So I'd like to take charge of them, and know that between the three of us we have all four sets of keys secured."

"But, sir . . ."

"Would you give me the name and number of your supervisor?

It's been a long day, and the Princess doesn't need to wait while we argue about this."

"Uhhh . . . right, sir. I'll tell you what. I'll give you the keys, then after I've talked to the manager, if he doesn't agree with the arrangement, you'll give them back?"

"Sure. Thanks, Hank."

Hank opened the door behind him and walked into the large closet that contained the safe.

"Princess?" I asked quietly.

"It was the first thing that popped into my mind. I guess Rick's mistaking you for royalty started it. And I didn't tell a single untruth. You are my princess," he whispered, taking my hand and kissing first the back of it, then turning it over and kissing my palm, sending delightful shivers through me.

Hank returned with the keys. "The silver one's for the elevator, the gold one's for your floor. The elevator door won't open until you key it."

"Gotcha. Thanks, Hank. I appreciate your cooperation, and your vigilance in helping me protect the Princess."

"No problem. That's what I'm here for, Mr. Allan. We've never had royalty in the building before, so it's a privilege to help. Good night, Your Highness."

"It's probably good morning, Hank," I laughed. "Thank you."

We crossed the polished green and black marble floor to the elevator. "I didn't think royalty had to carry their own baggage," I said in an undertone, adjusting the shoulder strap on my heavy bag.

"You're incognita." Bart keyed the elevator and the doors opened immediately.

"Why not just a push button like normal elevators?"

"These are private office suites. When a visitor arrives, they wait in the lobby for someone to escort them up to the office. It's one of the most secure buildings in the area, which is one reason we chose it. The second, of course, is that is overlooks the museum. Couldn't have been more convenient."

The ornate old elevator hadn't been remodeled but it was still decades updated from "Elliot," the English lift at the Abigail.

When we reached the top floor, the elevator stopped and Bart used the gold key to activate the door. It opened into a dark void.

Bart stepped into the darkness and reached for the light switch.

"Wait," I said. "Not yet. The Venetian blinds are still open."

"Good idea." He understood immediately.

Since Scarlotti seemed to know my every move, I was sure he knew we'd checked out of the Abigail and knew where we were now. I didn't need him spying on me from some building across the block.

Guided by the glow of the city lights outside, I closed the shades on the windows of the two outer walls of the huge room.

"Let there be light so I can see what my new home looks like."

"Hope you like it," Bart said, flipping the switch. "I've done my best to make you comfy because, as of now, you are hereby confined to this floor, in this building, in this city, until further notice."

I whirled on him. There was no smile in Bart's blue eyes or on his face.

"You're serious. You're not teasing me."

"No, Princess, I'm not teasing. Since I don't know where your folks are, I can't send you to them for protection. I can't send you back to New York. Scarlotti would figure out a way to be on the same airplane. I can't have you at the museum while I'm dealing with jewel thieves. And I certainly can't have you running loose in the city with Roach around. So I'm afraid this is it."

"Bart!"

"Sorry, Princess. That's the way it's got to be."

"Some honeymoon." I stared at the austere furnishings in the large room. "First Scarlotti imprisons me on an island against my will, now you're trying to confine me almost the same way. Whatever happened to free agency? I'm not a child anymore, Bart. I'm an adult who's used to taking care of myself. I survived just fine all those years you were away." I tried to sound rational and reasonable, but could feel my voice rising angrily with each word.

"That was before Scarlotti," Bart said quietly. "That was before I endangered your life by bringing people like Antonio Scaddano and Roach into your world." The misery in his eyes was evident even from across the room. "If I could change it, I would. I'm sorry."

"You had nothing to do with bringing Antonio Scaddono into my life. That chain of events started before we were born. That's not your fault. But you didn't give me any choice here. You didn't ask me. You told me. You may be used to giving orders, but I'm not used to taking them. I don't like the way it feels. If this is what marriage is like . . ."

As soon as the words were out of my mouth, I was sorry I'd said them. Bart looked as if I'd sliced him with a rusty razor blade. Emotions played across his face like a slide show—surprise at the attack, pain from the source of the attack. His jaw tightened. I could almost hear his teeth clamp shut. He took a deep breath.

"There are some compensations." Bart held out his hand to me. I didn't move.

He motioned for me to follow him to a door at the far end of the room, then paused with his hand on the knob. "I'm not an unjust jailor."

"Is that where the stocks are, or just handcuffs and chains?" I couldn't keep the sarcasm from my voice. I didn't want to hurt him. But I hated what was happening. I felt frustrated, helpless to control my biting tongue.

My husband stood, hand outstretched, waiting for me to respond. I shrugged my shoulders and went to him. As if I had a whole lot of choice anymore.

Bart took my hand and kissed it, his eyes imploring me to understand. Pulling me close, he silently traced the outline of my face, studying my expression.

"Do you have any idea how very much I love you?"

I met his gaze unblinking. "I thought I did."

"Do you trust me? Do you think I'd ever do anything that wasn't in your very best interest?"

A zillion smart answers zinged through my head, but this wasn't the time to be flippant.

"Yes," I sighed. "I do trust you. And, no, I don't think you'd do anything that wasn't in my best interest, but your idea and my idea of what that best interest may be are two different things."

"Oh, Alli. I had no idea when I married you that protecting you was going to be a full-time job. I mean, it was one thing when we were kids trying to keep you out of trouble, but I never imagined you could get into so many . . ."

I slipped my arms around his neck and shushed him with a quick kiss. "Thanks, Lancelot. I really do appreciate the effort. Sorry to be such a nuisance."

Bart's arms circled tightly around me, pressing his lean, hard body against mine, forcing the breath from me. He kissed my neck, my cheek, my mouth. The passion, the urgency of his kiss surprised me, snatching my anger from me as he'd snatched my breath, leaving me limp, powerless to protest further.

Bart swept me off my feet into his arms. I kissed him. How I loved this perceptive, patient, protective, passionate man I'd married.

Bart interrupted my kiss. "If my fuzzy calculations are correct," he kissed me, "we've been married two weeks today," another kiss, "and I haven't carried you across the threshold yet." He kissed me again. "Since this will be your home while we're in San Francisco," another kiss, "it seems appropriate."

I felt him reach for the doorknob, turn it, push the door open, and heard the light switch flick on as he kissed me again.

"Shall I put the shackles on you now, or would you like to explore your prison first, Mrs. Allan?" he asked, setting me on my feet and turning me to face the room.

Chapter 19

I gasped in astonishment.

The room was spacious and elegant. Monet prints adorned three walls and his lush green and rose tones, the deep blues and purples were echoed in the furnishings. Tall green plants surrounded a sofa and love seat in one corner, creating the illusion of an atrium.

The bedroom portion was separated from the sitting room by enough greenery to put a rain forest to shame. A fully equipped entertainment center blocked the view of the bathroom. Accessible to both areas were books, all the latest titles, a stack of CDs for the stereo, and a huge TV set that could be hidden behind handsomely carved wooden doors.

"Voilà. A prison fit for a princess."

"Bart, how did you do it?"

"I called a friend I studied architecture with and he put in an emergency call to his favorite decorator. She dropped everything and got her entire staff over here today. I figured if you had to stay put, it ought to be in beautiful surroundings and complete comfort."

"Gold fixtures in the bathroom?" I asked in disbelief as we toured my new accommodations.

"Well, this floor was the executive suite, the most expensive suite in the building. You know the old joke—if you had keys to the executive restroom, you knew you'd arrived. Well, Princess. You've arrived. All they had to do in here was hang the towels."

"And fresh flowers, too?" I stopped and turned to Bart. "This must have cost a small fortune."

"Only the best for my beautiful princess."

"Does Anastasia give you this kind of expense account?"

"Not exactly. My expense account and my salary together probably wouldn't cover the water bills for all these plants for a month. Your dad told me he wanted me to keep you happy and gave me access to your millions to do it with. I figured this fell into that category and he'd approve. Do you?"

"How do you do it? Spirit me away from my fiancé; convince me to marry you when I don't know if the wedding's an elaborate hoax or for real; spend my money right and left; keep me prisoner to boot—and make me glad it's happening. I must be crazy. Or . . ."

"Or what?" he asked, not sure just yet whether I was teasing or serious.

"Or crazy in love," I said, throwing my arms around his neck.

"I'll accept that diagnosis, as well as the responsibilities and benefits that go along with it. And now, what's behind the final door?" Bart said with a bow and a flourish, mocking the TV announcer.

"I couldn't even guess. What is behind the final door?"

"A completely stocked gourmet kitchen. Well, kitchenette."

"Oh, great. Gourmet TV dinners. Does that mean no more eating out?"

"For the next few days, that's exactly what it does mean. You, m'lady, are off the streets until further notice. But you won't be alone. There'll always be someone on surveillance in the other room. Oz is bringing in a couple more FBI, so if I'm not here, one of them will be."

I wrinkled my nose at him.

"They don't get to use your gold bathroom. They have their own. Plain chrome fixtures. You won't have to heat up TV dinners for them, either. They'll do their own thing and they won't bother you."

"Thanks. Is that all the help you have? Three men?"

"The museum security staff has blossomed to twenty for the exhibit. The generous Captain Saddler parted with five of his men to be on call for the duration of the show. There's Oz and his two, and me. Twenty-seven."

"Twenty-eight."

"Twenty-eight? I only count twenty-seven," Bart said, puzzled.

"Me."

"Whoa!"

"No, don't say anything you'll have to take back later. What say we try out that cushy looking bed over in the corner? It's calling out to my tired body."

"That's not the only thing calling out for your body," Bart laughed lecherously. "I want it, too."

"Bet I can beat you to bed. Will you hang my bag in the closet for me while I explore the gold bathroom?"

At the sound of jingling keys, I peeked around the corner of the entertainment divider, toothbrush poised, to see Bart drop the other set of keys in a potted plant in the far corner of the room.

Thank you, dear husband, I thought to myself smugly. *That may save me from having to pick your pocket in case I become claustrophobic in my poshly padded prison.*

Bart beat me to bed. Finishing my nightly routine, I snuggled into his outstretched arms.

"See?" he said. "This isn't going to be so bad, and part of the time I'll be right in the next room."

"And if you're not, Oz will be."

"Right. Not every girl gets to spend her honeymoon with both Interpol and the FBI."

"Oh, lucky me."

* * * * * *

When I woke at nine o'clock, it was to find the bed empty beside me. I stretched and listened for sounds of Bart in the bathroom. I couldn't believe he could slip out without me hearing him. Guess I'd been more tired than I thought.

Okay. What to do today. Besides breakfast. The thought of breakfast brought back the haunting eyes of the Cat Woman outside the Abigail. I wondered where she was. One of today's to-do's would be to call Rick and find out if she'd appeared for breakfast and if they'd fed her and her cats.

Next. I looked around the room. The Book of Mormon sat upright on the dresser with a note leaning against it.

"When the talk shows get too disgusting, try a dose of this for an uplifting antidote. I'm at the museum. Don't leave this floor." And a happy face! Hah!

I peeked into the outer office to see if Oz was on duty or if one of his FBI counterparts was keeping watch. A stranger with binoculars was at the window watching the museum through the Venetian blind slats. I quietly closed the door, leaving him to do his thing while I did mine.

After a long, leisurely shower and a banana for breakfast—nothing else looked appetizing—I unpacked our clothes and got settled in. Then I flipped on the TV. Nothing even remotely interesting. I started a book I'd been wanting to read, but couldn't get into it. None of the magazines on the coffee table engaged my attention either.

I picked up the Book of Mormon and read with fascination about the Liahona, and Nephi building a ship and bringing his family to the Americas, but when Nephi started quoting Isaiah, I quickly lost interest. Even in Bible class, Isaiah had been hard to understand. Today it was impossible to concentrate.

I found the phone Bart had slipped under the bed. Did he just tuck it out of the way, or was I not supposed to make calls? He hadn't said not to. I called Rick at the Abigail.

"Princess Alexandra! I'm so glad you called. The Cat Woman collapsed on the sidewalk last night. She's in the hospital."

"What happened?"

"I'm not sure. The night clerk told me about it when I came on duty this morning."

"Who's taking care of her cats?"

"He said they scattered when the ambulance came. Only one hung around and it cried all night. There's half a dozen at the back door right now."

"Feed them and put it on my bill."

"Princess Alex—"

"Rick, please. Call the hospital. See if you can talk to the doctor and find out her condition. Tell them you're her nephew and ask if there's a key in her purse so that you can get into her apartment and feed her cats."

"Her apartment?"

"Just a hunch. I'll call you back in thirty minutes to see what you found out."

I found myself pacing the floor and turned on the TV again to occupy my mind with something—anything—besides the frustration at being penned up here. The Discovery Channel had a program on cats. Big cats. Beautiful, sleek, wild cats. A snow leopard prowled her cage, back and forth, the same steps over and over relentlessly. I knew exactly how she felt.

When I thought I'd given Rick enough time to discover the information I needed, I picked up the phone to call the Abigail, then slammed it down again. Bart had mentioned secure phone lines. Should I not have made that call? What if Scarlotti was tapped into the Abigail's line, waiting to see if I'd call to pinpoint my location? No. I was sure he already knew it.

Rick's voice sounded strange when I identified myself.

"Rick, what's the matter?"

"Umm, are you in a safe place, Princess?"

"Yes, why?"

"Ummm . . ."

"Rick! Tell me what's the matter?"

"Uh, is your husband with you?"

"Rick! What's going on? Tell me right now!" I demanded in my most regal tone.

"Yes, Your Highness. When the chambermaid went up to do your room this morning, ummm, the bed was slashed. The pillows were slashed and there was blood all over the bathroom."

"Blood? Whose blood? Was there a body? Do you know who did it?" I sat down on the bed, stunned and shivering.

"No, Princess. I wondered if you might know."

I did. But I wasn't telling Rick. It had to be Scarlotti's reaction to our move. Now he didn't have such free access to me. Then my blood went cold. Roach!

"Rick, is Reynard okay? Have you seen him this morning?"

"He's at breakfast now. Do you want to talk to him?"

"No. Right now I need to know what you found out about the Cat Woman."

"She's in San Francisco General. They let me talk to the doctor because she's so agitated they can't control her."

"What happened?"

"She's diabetic and apparently her diet isn't what it should be. Her blood sugar count was out of sight. They rehydrated her all night and have her back on track now. If they had somebody to stay with her, they'd release her just to calm her down. She kept pulling her IV out and screaming she couldn't stay there. Her babies would die without her."

"Was there a key and an address?"

"How did you know about her place?"

"Just a wild guess."

"It's not in a very good part of town so it can't be wonderful. But she'll have to stay in the hospital because there's no one to go home with her."

"I'll go to the hospital and take her home. Did you get the cats rounded up?"

"We enticed them into a big box and I think we've probably got most of them."

"Good work, Rick. Keep them together. Call the hospital and tell them her niece is coming to take her home. By the way, what's her name?"

"Doris Gray."

"I'll pick her up at the hospital, then we'll come by and get the cats."

"Princess . . ."

"Thank you very much, Rick. I really appreciate your help."

I hung up. What had I done? Bart said . . . Bart expected . . . but that was before someone needed help. I couldn't just stay caged up—no matter how beautiful the cage. Especially if I could be helping someone. And it was broad daylight.

I would just be careful. Very careful.

Chapter 20

I scribbled a quick note for Bart, telling him I was taking Doris Gray home from the hospital and left her address. I told him I'd stay long enough to feed the cats and make sure she was comfortable, then promised I'd return immediately to our honeymoon hideaway, as Bart called it, a term more palatable than prison.

Next, how to skip? I checked the windows for a fire escape so I wouldn't have to bluff my way past the FBI and the security guard downstairs. I was sure Bart had left instructions to stop me if I tried to leave.

I was in luck. There was a fire escape. You just had to be as agile as a monkey to reach it from the window. I called a cab and retrieved the keys Bart conveniently stashed in the potted palm in case the fire escape proved too difficult to return by. Managing the acrobatic maneuver to the fire escape, I climbed down to my waiting taxi.

The old woman's dark eyes lit up when I walked into her hospital room.

"Oh, my dear. Thank you so much for saving me from these savages with their probing needles and tubes. Where are my babies?"

"Rick Reinalles at the Abigail has gathered up most of them, fed them, and they're waiting to be picked up and taken home."

"Home?" Those deep-set dark eyes turned to pools of wariness.

Turning my back on the nurse, I put my finger to my lips.

"Yes, *Aunt* Doris. I'm going to take you home and take care of you and your babies until you're feeling better."

Her eyebrows shot up. Her mouth formed a silent "Oh" of surprise, but she held her tongue. I helped her into her navy sweater, wrapped the faded red shawl around her shoulders, and assisted her to the wheelchair.

Encountering no snags or red tape, I checked her out of the hospital with amazing ease. I wheeled her to the waiting taxi and we went directly to the Abigail. The driver was not happy about loading a boxful of squirming, noisy cats into his cab, but when I opened my purse and flashed his favorite color of green, he relented and put the box into the back seat next to Doris.

I tried to press some money into Rick's hand for feeding the cats.

"No, Your Highness, it's on the house."

"Rick!"

"Oh, sorry, Princess," he whispered. "I just keep forgetting."

The taxi driver slowed, craning his neck looking for the address that hospital personnel found in Doris' wallet.

"You sure there's such a place?"

The Cat Woman opened her eyes and looked around to see where we were.

"Turn left into that alley just ahead."

We were in an older part of town where most of the homes had been torn down years ago to make room for business. The alley was narrow and dark, shaded from sunlight by tall buildings all around. The taxi stopped beside a tiny, run-down cracker box of a house that had no yard left to speak of and one huge solitary tree spreading over the little square roof like an umbrella.

"If you'll please get the box," I asked the driver, "I'll help Doris."

The old woman leaned heavily on my arm.

"My legs just aren't what they used to be," she apologized.

The man brought the box of squirming, yowling cats into the house, put it in the middle of the floor, and eyed the place with a wrinkled nose. The smell of litter boxes was overpowering. I threw open the two little windows, and front and back doors.

As he looked around shaking his head, I had visions of the taxi driver calling the Humane Society or the health department—or worse. Digging into my purse again, I produced another bill, and walked the man to the door.

So Doris couldn't hear, I said in a low voice, "This is to not say anything to anybody, no matter who asks. I'll take care of the cats and get the place cleaned up so the health department won't have to be involved. Or anybody else. Can this be our secret?"

His greedy eyes eyed my purse. I produced another bill.

"Got it, lady. It's our secret. My lips are sealed."

"Thank you." *You leech,* I added under my breath.

Doris wouldn't lie down until she'd supervised the feeding of her precious cats and the emptying of their litter boxes. Only when they were happy and daintily washing their furry faces would she consent to being settled into her bed.

"Why didn't you go to the doctor when you got sick?" I asked as I bathed her face, smoothing her wiry gray hair away from her face onto the frayed, faded pink satin pillow.

"I didn't have anyone to care for my babies," she fretted, stroking the fur of a tabby that curled contentedly against her. I stepped over and around a dozen cats on my way to the kitchen sink on the other side of the tiny, one-room house.

"But if you're too sick to care for them, or the doctor keeps you in the hospital, you're no good to your babies," I argued over my shoulder, rinsing in hot water the piece of towel I used as a washcloth, and dropping a black and white kitten to the floor.

"Do you feed your cats on the cabinet?" I asked, clearing two more that leaped gracefully from cracked gray linoleum to chipped gray tile.

"If that's where they want to eat," she answered weakly. "Who are you?"

"Allison Allan." I picked up the old woman's brush from the littered little table at the side of her bed and worked gently on removing several days' snarls from her coarse gray hair.

"You're not from here. You're staying at the Abigail . . . ," her voice trailed off and her eyes closed.

"I was. We moved. We're on our honeymoon, sort of."

Those deep, dark eyes flew open. "Sort of?"

Before I knew what I was doing, I'd poured out the whole story of our strange wedding, our stranger honeymoon in Hawaii, and our purpose for coming to San Francisco.

The cats had settled comfortably on the end of Doris's bed, and the only sounds in the secluded little house were intermittent purring and my own voice.

Through the open window I heard a car door slam shut somewhere down the alley. The old woman lifted her head off the pillow and grabbed my arm. "What was that?"

A tingling sensation spread up the back of my neck and down my arms.

"Nobody uses this alley except people who are lost or up to no good," Doris said, fear filling her dark eyes. "They'll take my babies away."

I peered through the dirty window in time to see a taxi back out of the alley and a tall, slender silhouette slip through the shadows toward the house.

Panicking, I looked around for someplace to hide.

"Who is it?"

"Someone who mustn't find me," I answered, trying not to alarm Doris by showing my terror.

"Can you climb a tree?" she whispered.

"Yes."

"Get out the back door and hide in the tree. I'll cover for you."

"But he might. . ."

"Hurry up. Get!"

I flew out the back door, picking my way through trash that littered the yard. The tree grew so close to the house that at first glance it didn't seem possible to climb the tree. Then I discovered weathered wood strips that had been nailed there as steps and a knotted rope. Squeezing into the narrow space between tree trunk and house, I climbed the first two steps, then used the rope dangling from an overhead branch to help me up the rest of the way.

Just in time. From the open window I heard Doris ask, "May I help you, young man?"

I held my breath.

The dulcet tones I dreaded came honey-soft. "I'm looking for my wife, Allison. She told me to meet her, said she was bringing you home from the hospital. How are you feeling?"

With his mesmerizing voice, his suave manner, and perjurious tongue, he could convince Doris he really was my husband instead of someone plotting to take my life.

I'd thought I was safe from him in the daylight. Apparently nothing and nowhere was safe from this living, breathing phantom, this nemesis who shadowed my every step.

"Fine, now that I'm home. Thank you for asking. I'm sorry, you just missed Allison by a minute or two. She went to the store for me, to get food for my babies. I sent her by the shortcut. If you go out the back door and through the service entrance of the building right behind me, you come out on the street. There's a little market down the block. If you'd like to wait, she should be back in about fifteen minutes."

No! Don't ask him to wait. He might.

"Thank you anyway. I'll see if I can catch her."

He walked through the open back door, stepping through the garbage with more grace than I could believe, and disappeared into the building directly behind the little house.

As soon as the door shut, Doris called, "Come quick!" I hated giving up the safety of my hiding place, but I certainly didn't want to be caught there if he returned.

"He's not your husband, is he?" she said when I entered the room.

"No. In fact, he's planning to kill me and my husband. How did you know?"

"He has evil eyes. Anyone with a heart as good as yours couldn't be married to someone with evil eyes."

"Thank you, Doris. I'd intended to get you settled, then stay with you for a few hours."

"You need to get on your way to your husband, Missy. Where is he?"

"At the Museum of Modern Art, worrying about the diamonds that go on exhibition tomorrow."

"If you ever need another hiding place, I can tell you a good one."

"I'm all ears."

"Yerba Buena Park, across from the museum, behind the Martin Luther King waterfall. There's a panel that opens up. Only a couple of the maintenance people know about it. My son helped build that. Told me how smart the architect was, putting all the normal maintenance out for easy access, but the difficult stuff only experts should tamper with, he hid behind a panel. If you're ever in trouble, it's the panel on the far left. There's a red outline around a white box about six feet up—twist it. He says somebody's been down there lately working on the passageway to the museum."

She stopped and closed her eyes for a minute. She really was very weak. Maybe I should have left her in the hospital. No, she'd rest better here with her babies.

"At the end of the alley there's a bus that'll take you to the museum. You get there and stay with your husband. And thanks for your help. My babies and me'll say a prayer for you."

"Thank you, Doris. I came to help you, but you've helped me more." I gently stroked her veined hand.

"Always works that way, honey. Always works that way. Just the way the good Lord intended it." Her eyes closed. "My babies and me'll be just fine now that I'm home."

Leaving the windows open for much-needed ventilation, I closed both doors, and quickly slipped out of the dark alley into the warm San Francisco sun. I had to run to catch the bus. It wasn't the right bus, but at least I was away from the area and Scarlotti.

Transferring buses, I got off a block from the museum. When it looked like no one was watching me, I hurried into the alley and up the fire escape only to find the window had locked when I shut it. I couldn't get back in. I should have checked that out before I left. The only good thing to come of it was the knowledge that Scarlotti couldn't get in through the window, either.

Scrambling down the fire escape, I made a quick decision not to go to the museum, but straight back up to our rooms. To my surprise and delight, there was a lobby full of people.

Thinking I was going to be so smart and slip in unnoticed by the guard surrounded by people registering at the desk, I was not only surprised, but agitated when someone called my name.

"Mrs. Allan. Ah've been waiting for ya."

I whirled around and gazed straight into the friendly Argus brown eyes of Matt McMillan.

"Matt. What are you doing here?"

"Your husband sent me to fetch ya. He didn't want ya'll on the streets by yourself, so Ah told him Ah'd pick ya up on my way back from an errand Ah had to run. He's meetin' with Captain Saddler."

"Where are they?"

"Captain Saddler's office. The captain sent a car for us. Ah've got it waitin' round the corner."

He spoke into his radio. "Hey, Jake, ya awake? Mrs. Allan's ready now. Meet ya'll out front."

"If I'm going to meet with Captain Saddler, I really need to change clothes and freshen up," I protested. Anything besides these grungy jeans and sweat shirt that still smelled faintly of Doris' babies.

"Ah don't think ya need to, Mrs. Allan. Ya'll look just fine the way ya are."

In a maneuver that was both gentle and decidedly firm, and that physically overrode my objections, Matt guided me out the door. A long, black sedan with darkly tinted windows met us at the curb.

Matt opened the door and motioned me to get into the back seat. I was half into the dark interior when I saw someone else already there.

"Come on in, Mrs. Allan," a voice spoke from the shadows.

Matt gave me a little shove from behind. A hand reached out and grabbed my arm, pulling me into the seat beside him. A wicked-smelling cloth covered my face.

My last conscious awareness was a curse from Matt as his bulky body fell solidly across my lap.

Chapter 21

I woke with a pounding headache and a mouth full of cotton. My stomach didn't feel too good either. For the second time today I remembered how much I hated the smell of hospitals. I thought chloroforming, or whatever it was, went out with black and white movies.

Oh. I didn't want to think. It hurt my head. I tried to slip back into the gray oblivion from which I was emerging, but couldn't. Thoughts of Bart forced me wide awake. He'd be worried, actually frantic.

I was in a decidedly uncomfortable position on a dusty floor, hands and feet taped. Light peeking under a slit in the door faintly illuminated a mop bucket and broom.

Lying very still for a few minutes, I waited for my headache to subside and my thought processes to clear. For the time being, the pain each movement produced wasn't worth the effort expended.

Through the fog, I remembered Matt. Where was he? I scooted around on the dusty floor to see if anyone else was in the closet but only succeeded in kicking the mop bucket and making a great deal of noise that hurt my head even more.

Who was behind this? Scarlotti?

On my first encounter with Scarlotti, I'd been manhandled by a couple of thugs who grabbed me, drugged me, and tied me up. Was this the same scenario? For some reason, this time I'd felt Scarlotti was working alone.

At first, I'd been too groggy for fear to reach me. Now, as my head cleared, cold, hard reality gripped me. Cold, hard terror. I was right back in Scarlotti's malevolent hands.

Footsteps approached the door, heavy shuffling footsteps. Were they dragging Matt to join me? What would Scarlotti want with Matt?

I shut my eyes and lay still.

The door opened. Someone prodded me with a hard-soled shoe.

"Naw, she's still out cold."

"I told ya to be careful, Floyd. Ya don't give little women as much as you do big men. It'll take her forever to wake up."

"How'd she figure it out, Cal? I thought the boss was a genius to come up with a plan like this. I didn't think anybody else'd ever figure it out, even after we done it. How'd she find out?"

"Who knows? Speaking of the boss, have you ever seen him without his mask on?" Cal asked.

"No. Have you?"

"No. Don't you think that's kind of funny? Always has mask and gloves on and talks to us through that voice changer."

"Not funny, Cal. Smart. If we get picked up, we can't point any fingers. We couldn't identify him if our lives depended on it. That's why we only know the part of the plan we're involved with."

I was prodded again by the shoe.

"How long's it going to take her to wake up?"

"I don't know, Cal. Guess there's no hurry. They don't want her gummin' things up 'cause the deal's going down tomorrow night. We just have to keep her out of the way till then."

"Then they're going to let her go?"

"Ha!" Floyd snorted. "What do you think? They're not telling us everything so we can't blow the whistle if we get caught. Why would they let her go when she knows the whole plan? She might even know the boss. Maybe she's seen his face."

"Maybe that's how she knows the plan—she was cozying up to the boss and he spilled the beans."

"Come on, Cal. Does he seem like that type to you?"

"No. Guess you're right. What do you want to do with her?"

"Just leave her there. She's not going anywhere until she wakes up and when she does, we'll be right here."

They shut the door, leaving me in the dark.

What did I know? Certainly not what Scarlotti was planning. Just that it would be something macabre. Something dreadful. And deadly.

Or were they talking about the diamonds? Had I guessed the terrorist plan? Who knew what I thought their plan was? The answer to that question had me scrambling to get loose.

Captain Saddler knew what I thought of the terrorists' plan. Matt McMillan knew how I thought the diamond thieves could thwart the security system. Were they working together?

It was easy to believe of Captain Saddler after reading of his expensive divorce and court battles. It was not so easy to believe of Matt with those gentle brown Argus eyes. Texans were the good guys with the big white hats, weren't they?

My head was still so muddled I couldn't think straight. So I didn't try. I just concentrated on getting loose from the tape that wrapped my wrists and ankles.

The mop bucket I'd tangled with earlier was the heavy-duty kind with mop wringer attached. It had enough of an edge on one side that I could, by positioning my hands just right, wear through the surgical tape around my wrists. I was just ready to start on my feet when my captors returned.

I laid the tape across my wrists and curled up in my former position just as the door opened. The foot nudged me again, then a finger probed my throat, pressing against my pulse. I had to force myself to lie still and not react to his touch.

"Thought you'd killed her, but her heart's still beating. She's sure taking a long time coming around."

"Then let's go get some coffee."

"Floyd, we're supposed to be guarding her. You go bring some back. I'll stay here."

"Come on, Cal. She's out cold. She's not going anywhere."

"Nah, I'll stay and watch her. If there was a lock on the door, I would, but there's not."

"Then just take the doorknob off. If she comes to and tries to get out, there'll be no handle to turn. She'll be locked in."

"Good thinking, Floyd."

In less than a minute the doorknob was dismantled and I was locked in the knobless closet. While my captors took a coffee break, I took the opportunity to strip the tape from my ankles and find the light switch.

Just what I needed. A small tool box with a large screwdriver. Inserting the screwdriver into the square hole left by the missing doorknob, it was an easy matter to open the door. But I couldn't believe where I found myself on exiting the closet.

Elekta's art gallery with its huge pillars, terrazzo-tiled floors, and wonderfully carved wood. So! She was involved in hi-jinks! Just how, I'd have to find out later. Right now, I was out of here. I thought.

The back door was padlocked. I ran the length of the back room and down the three tiled steps to the showroom, but halfway to the front door a taxi pulled up to the front of the building. I recognized the tall, dark, handsome Arab who'd been with Elekta and immediately reversed direction.

Ducking between the elaborately carved bannisters, I raced up the blue and white tiled steps to the second floor, hoping he hadn't seen me through the glass in the front doors.

But the second floor provided no hiding place. Elekta had prepared this floor for a gallery showing and the balcony overlooked the showroom below.

Removing my shoes, I crept up the stairs to the third floor as quickly and quietly as I could. No need to alert Tall, Dark, and Handsome to my presence in the building until the alarm went out when my captors found the closet empty.

Judging from the boxes and crates, the third-floor offices had been turned into storerooms. But these half-glassed doors were locked. I hurried down the hall, testing, trying doorknobs as I went, hoping to find one unlocked, hoping to find someplace to hide.

His footsteps echoed through the nearly empty showroom. Still no open doors. Then I heard him on the stairs. He was coming upstairs!

I listened, hardly daring to breathe as he stopped briefly on the second floor, then started up the stairs to the third floor. To one of these rooms? Or was he coming after me?

It was impossible to hurry and be quiet, too. My heart pounded wildly in my chest, echoing in my ears. I tried several more doors. Just before he rounded the top of the stairs and entered the long hall, the last door gave way. I almost fell into the room.

I dropped a shoe on the soft cream-colored carpet, grabbed it, and closed the door, searching frantically for a place to hide. The overstuffed furniture in the classy office was centered in the room—away from the wall. No closets, no cubby holes. Tall, Dark, and Handsome advanced down the hall. His footsteps echoed loud and clear, stopping at none of the locked doors. He must be coming straight to this room.

In the split second I had to hide, I flung myself under the massive walnut desk that faced the door and curled up in as small a ball as I could. And held my breath.

The door opened. A switch clicked and light flooded the room. The Arab entered, his footsteps absorbed in the padded carpet. Blinds rippled and rattled as he pulled them up.

He walked to the front of the desk. Italian wing tip shoes peeked under the front panel, inches from where I sat scrunched in an uncomfortable ball.

The shuffling of papers was barely discernible over the wild pounding of my heart. Italian wing tips moved away. I heard the clink of glass and ice cubes, the gurgle of liquid being poured. The Italian leather shoes appeared at the back of the desk.

Tall, Dark, and Handsome sat down in the cream-colored leather desk chair, sipped his drink, and rocked back and forth as he slit open envelopes and shuffled through papers.

If he pulled the chair up to the desk and put his legs underneath, I was a goner. We couldn't possibly coexist in that small space without him discovering me.

The phone rang. He scooted the leather chair closer to the desk and reached to answer it, one leg under the desk, the other stretched out to the side.

"Hello, exalted cousin." He spoke in Arabic with a pleasant, cultured voice. "No, I'm alone. There's no one else in the building." A pause.

"Are you sure that was a wise decision? Kidnapping in this country is a federal offense. It could bring down the FBI on us." Another pause.

"Did you check to make sure your facts were correct before you took this dramatic step?"

It was a very patronizing tone. Was he talking to a woman? Elekta? Probably. And were they discussing me? Probably.

"I'm opposed to killing her. Instead, call her husband and tell him you have her. If he wants to see her alive again, he'll leave San Francisco immediately, calling off whatever force he has at the museum. That will leave the way clear for us to get the diamond. He can retrieve his bride and resume his honeymoon. Everyone will be happy. Except, of course, the British monarchy and Lloyds of London."

A long pause.

"My dear cousin, I don't care how close she guessed. It was just that. Only a guess. Let your big American stew and fret. He has no proof, and neither does your blond Adonis."

A short pause.

"Aisha, my apologies. If you do not have designs on him, it would be the first time. Your appetite for virile young men is well established."

Was this not Elekta he was talking to? No matter. Whoever had designs on Bart would do it over my dead body. Oh. That was unfortunate phraseology.

"Cousin! Your tirade is wasted on my lowly ears. Do as you wish. You always do. I can well understand why the diamond passed through the female line of our family, if all your forebears had your temperament. The blood of the Great Khan and Aurangzeb boils hot in your veins. Unfortunate you were not born a man. If our people accepted a woman as their leader, the House of Qujar would have been reestablished long ago."

He sipped his drink as he listened to her reply.

"Yes, Aisha. I understand. Yes. I shall make sure the body is not found."

My body?

"I'm sorry, cousin. Forgive my slip of the tongue. Your new name does not come so easily as the name I have known you by since we were children. I will do as you wish."

He hung up the phone with a sigh and finished his drink.

"It is unfortunate you were not born a man, my cousin," he murmured. "You would have swept through Europe and Asia as did our illustrious ancestors, uniting our people in the greatest empire the world has seen since the Mughal and Safavid Dynasties. Alas, if only I had your temperament, or you had my body . . ."

He let the sentence hang, pulled the chair close to the desk, thrusting his feet inches from my legs, and settled down with the paper work.

Chapter

22

At first his legs were straight, planted firmly on the floor and still. The longer he sat there, the more restless he became. He crossed one leg, barely missing my knee. Then he uncrossed them, and crossed the other, narrowly missing my elbow.

I couldn't get into a tighter ball. I couldn't make myself smaller. I couldn't move. I could only hope and pray he never connected as he crossed and uncrossed his legs and jerked and jiggled his feet.

A shout from downstairs shattered the quiet of the building. My captors had discovered the empty closet. Tall, Dark, and Handsome pushed the chair from the desk and hurried across the room as the two men clambered noisily up the stairs looking for me.

They clattered down the hall, rattling all the doorknobs until they came to the office. His footsteps merged with theirs in the hall.

Falling over each other's words, they explained what had happened.

"The door was locked when I came," the Arab said. "I locked it behind me. Was it still locked when you returned?"

"Yes, Ahmad," they answered simultaneously.

"Then it's a simple matter of finding her in the building. She's somewhere on one of the eight floors. When you find her, dispose of her. Make sure the body is not found. The more police they have looking for her, the less there will be to guard the diamond."

My captors' footsteps faded up the stairs to the fourth floor. Ahmad returned, shut the door with a sigh, and sat down at the desk again.

I'd readjusted my position while he was in the hall, letting the blood flow back into my tightly scrunched limbs, and put my shoes back on. How long would I have to stay here? Actually, the real question was how long could I remain undetected?

I definitely didn't like the way he spoke of my demise and disposal. So casual. So nonchalant. An ordinary, everyday occurrence. *And don't forget to take out the garbage.*

I tried to concentrate on the conversation I'd just heard to get my mind off his extremely unpleasant declaration.

Everyone knew who Ghengis Khan was, of course. And Professor Bainston had talked about Aurangzeb, Mughol emperor of India who owned the Great Mogul diamond from which the Koh-i-noor was probably cut.

That's what they were after. The Koh-i-noor. It belonged to Aurangzeb's descendants until 1813 when Ranjit Singh, the Lion of Punjab, declared war to obtain it. In 1849 when the British annexed the Punjab region of India, it was in the city treasury of Lahore. The Koh-i-noor diamond was sent to Queen Victoria.

Pieces of the puzzle slowly shifted into place.

The Arab was shifting, too. He leaned back in his chair and yawned, stretching, extending his long legs under the desk. He missed my nose by a fraction of an inch.

Please go somewhere else.

I needed access to that telephone—needed to call Bart, to tell him what they were after and when. And that I needed help, pronto. I'd inadvertently stumbled in their path, blocking the retrieval of the diamond these people felt belonged to them.

Not a good place to be. Fatal, in fact. Way to go, Allison.

Had I been so wrong about the terrorists and the bodies, each one with its diamond stud? Or was there truly more than one plot to get into the museum? I hadn't connected Elekta to the terrorists even though I felt she was up to something besides setting up an art gallery.

How about the three men? Her accomplices? They didn't seem sophisticated enough to belong to the terrorists, but then, what did I know of terrorists? What did I know about anything except translating languages? I was a far cry from that now.

My body was going to revolt any minute. Self-discipline ebbed like an outgoing tide and claustrophobia surged in to replace it.

You can sit still. Think positive. You can do this.

I was saved by the clamorous appearance of my unsuccessful captors, reporting that I was nowhere to be found. Ahmad gave them a scathing denunciation in Arabic. I'm not sure they understood the language, but there was no mistaking the message.

The Arab announced that they would be successful or forfeit their heads. "After all, she's only a woman, and an unsophisticated American woman at that. How difficult could it be to find someone of that mentality?"

I hoped I lived to make him eat those chauvinist words!

As soon as their footsteps headed down the hall, and I was sure all three had gone, my kinked, cramped body unfolded. I grabbed the phone and pulled it under the desk.

I really am a nice person, I thought as I called the operator and asked her to dial the Museum of Modern Art. *Why is everyone so determined to get rid of me? First Scarlotti, and now Elekta and her handsome cousin.*

"Museum of Modern Art. Will you hold, please?" The receptionist didn't wait for an answer. Just put me on hold before I could take a breath.

No! Not now!

I hung up and dialed the operator again, asking for an emergency breakthrough on the line.

"I must talk to Bartholomew Allen or Oswald Barlow immediately concerning the diamond theft," I blurted before the receptionist could cut me off again.

She reported they were somewhere in the museum.

"Send someone to find them right now, and you stay on the line to take down a message in case I'm interrupted. It's literally a matter of life or death."

My life.

Finally comprehending the importance of the call, the receptionist dispatched someone to find Bart or Oz.

"Write this down. Elekta and the Arab are going for the Koh-i-noor tomorrow night. I'm at Elekta's art gallery with three men bent on killing me. Get someone here. . . ."

That was as much as I got out before I heard footsteps returning down the hall. I shoved the phone back on the desk and had barely time to curl into my former torturous position before the door opened.

Ahmad slammed the door behind him, muttering curses on ineptitude and incompetency. He walked behind the desk to the cream-colored leather chair and stopped. Both hands fell to his sides. I could see his carefully groomed fingertips as he clenched and unclenched his fists.

The Arab raised his hands to the desk, tapping his fingers. He moved the phone. *I hadn't put it back exactly where I got it. He knew I was here!*

Ahmad walked slowly, silently, around the room as if searching for a place someone could hide. It was only a matter of time before he arrived at the same conclusion I had. The only place in the room to hide was under the desk.

What to do? Roll out and try to knock him down, hoping the element of surprise would allow me to get away? But to where? I certainly didn't want to jump out a third-story window and I hadn't had time to see if there was a fire escape handy.

Ahmad opened the door. I could almost picture the good-looking Arab looking up and down the hall. Doorknobs jiggled on nearby doors. His footsteps paused in the hall.

Was it be possible he wouldn't think to look under the desk? Could I really be so lucky?

He hadn't moved, hadn't made any noise. I wasn't sure just where he was, or what he was doing. I was only sure of one thing. I wouldn't move a muscle until it was absolutely necessary. As it was, I hardly dared breathe.

The Arab came back into the office without closing the door. He walked to the window, stopped, then crossed the room. A drawer slid open. Papers rustled. The drawer slid closed.

He came back to the desk and sat down in the leather chair. For several minutes, he didn't move. When he leaned to retrieve the brief-case from beside the desk, I thought he'd see me. He opened the black leather case on his lap and placed the papers in it.

Opening the center desk drawer, he rifled through papers, adding the contents to the briefcase.

As Floyd and Cal approached the door, Ahmad set the briefcase on the floor, still open, and went to the door to talk to them. This time he wasn't yelling. This time he spoke so softly I couldn't hear what he was saying.

Their footsteps moved slowly down the hall. My attention was riveted on the papers in the briefcase. The top sheet appeared to be a list of names. Curiosity won over caution and I leaned closer to see what it was.

An unusual genealogy chart. The female line was highlighted—the male names subordinate. I didn't recognize the names at the top, but Alexander the Great appeared, and after him many illustrious names: Babar, first of the Mughal emperors, descended from Ghengis Khan on his mother's side and Tamarlane on his father's.

Babar's son, Humayam, second emperor, and his son, Akbar, the third emperor who raised the Indian Empire to its greatest splendor. Jahangir, fourth Mughal emperor, and his son, Sha Jahan, who built the Taj Mahal and the Pearl Mosque at Agra.

The notorious Aurangzeb, last of the Mughal emperors; Muhammad Shah, great-grandson of Aurangzeb who lost the Koh-i-noor diamond and the Peacock throne to Nadir Shah and Persia.

The list went on through the Qujar dynasty from 1794 to 1925: from Agha Muhammad Khan to Ahmad Shah.

Then the Pahlavi dynasty from 1925 to 1979: Riza Shah Pahlovi, his son, Shah Muhammad Riza Pahlovi who was deposed by Khomeini in 1979. And finally his son, Prince Riza Pahlavi.

The women's names were unfamiliar, but one name appeared frequently—Aisha. In at least every other generation, an Aisha had married an emperor or shah. This was the royal matriarchal line since before Alexander the Great.

Before I had time to turn the page and see where it went from there, footsteps approached the room, then stopped. The three men had returned. They entered the room without a word.

The men spread out, walking around the office as if searching. I froze. They approached the desk, surrounding it. The briefcase was moved. A face peered under the desk.

"Well, I'll be!" one of my captors exclaimed.

"Hi. Are you Cal or Floyd?" I asked, hoping a little humor might lighten the situation.

"Get her out of there!" Ahmad was not amused.

"I'll come. No need to manhandle me." I crawled, very undignified, from under the desk, almost, but not quite glad to be able to finally stand up.

"Who did you call?" the Arab demanded.

Was I better off telling them Bart should be on his way to save me, or make them think they were still safely anonymous?

"The Museum of Modern Art to tell my husband where I am."

"You did not speak with your husband?"

"The receptionist put me on hold and I never got to talk to him." That was the truth.

"Get her out of here," Ahmad commanded, a scowl marring his handsome face. "When you've disposed of her, don't come back. If I need to contact you before tomorrow night, I'll leave a message. Otherwise, we'll proceed as planned."

"Shouldn't we wait till dark to take her out?"

"No. Pull the car up in back. If she lied, the police could be on their way at this moment."

All the while he was giving orders, Ahmad had been sorting documents and filling the briefcase. He clicked it shut. "Now!"

The finality in his tone propelled my captors to action. They each grabbed an arm, literally carrying me to the door and down the hall. Ahmad was close on our heels.

I kept listening for sirens. There weren't any. Had the police quietly gotten into place, and were they waiting for us to come out so they could take my captors by surprise?

At the showroom floor, Ahmad hurried out the front door, and after carefully locking it, hailed a passing cab. I didn't see anyone following the taxi as it pulled from the curb. Where were the police?

Cal and Floyd hurried me through the showroom to the back of the building. I searched the streets through the big windows, looking for Bart, for the police. If they were there, they were well hidden. What if they weren't there? What if no one had come?

I was on a one-way trip out of town.

I stood meekly while Cal keyed the padlock on the back door and opened it. Floyd's huge, strong hand clasped my wrist like vise grips while we waited just inside the door for Cal to bring the car up to the steps.

If the police were waiting for a signal to make their move, I'd certainly give it to them. I whirled and kicked Floyd with all my might where it hurt him most. Doubling over in pain, he let go. I flew down the stairs and headed for the alley, not reckoning on Cal's speedy reaction.

He shoved the car in reverse, whipped it into the street and roared after me, blocking the alley in which I'd intended to escape. I darted for the street, but Cal was out of the car before I reached it. He pounced on me, right there in broad daylight, in the middle of San Francisco, with not a soul around to see.

Where were the police? Where was Bart?

Chapter 23

Cal shoved me roughly into the car, jamming my face down on the front seat.

"Don't even wiggle until Floyd gets here," he growled.

Cal and Floyd were not happy with me. First, I'd brought the wrath of Ahmad down on them by escaping and hiding. Now Floyd hurt so bad he couldn't move.

Cal maneuvered the car to the steps where Floyd waited and reached over the seat to open the back door for him.

"You stay put while I lock the building," Cal ordered.

Right.

As soon as he slid from behind the wheel, I raised up and reached for the door handle on the passenger side. I wasn't about to pass up what might well be my last chance to escape.

I saw the movement out of the corner of my eye, but not soon enough to dodge the fist that plowed into my jaw.

* * * * *

Frequently losing consciousness was unhealthy and dangerous. According to my captors, that would not be an important factor to my health and well-being much longer.

Those were my first lucid thoughts as I lay in the dark, carbon-monoxide-filled trunk en route to who-knows-where. My next thoughts were equally ridiculous—and valid.

Was my marriage and Bart worth all this? My world had been turned totally upside down since Bart reappeared in it. I had been stalked, shot at, kidnapped who knows how many times, locked up against my will, my body battered and bruised. Now I probably had a broken jaw and my death sentence had been pronounced. Twice.

This certainly wasn't what I'd bargained for when I said, "I do." If I got out of this alive . . . No. *When* I got out of this alive, I'd have to do some serious thinking about my life and its future. I wasn't sure if I stayed with Bart I'd have a future.

That was tomorrow. Now, I'd better figure out where we were so I'd know how to get back. If I could. I fought back the overwhelming claustrophobia that choked me and concentrated.

Traffic was heavy. Cal braked a lot. We must be on a bridge. The tires blipped constantly, as they do when crossing the sections in the spans. But which bridge? Oakland Bay? Golden Gate? If I'd been out long enough, we could be north on the Richmond Bridge or south on the San Mateo Bridge.

Why hadn't Bart come? And the police? What if the receptionist thought I was just a kook and didn't relay the message? What if Bart really had been meeting with Captain Saddler? If he was in on the diamond heist, Captain Saddler could have squashed the call, not passed it through to Bart.

What if Bart had no idea what was happening? What if! What if! What if I'd stayed in our room and hadn't taken Doris home from the hospital? Then I wouldn't be in this predicament. My do-gooding certainly didn't do me any good.

I concentrated on freeing my hands, needing to take the tape off, then rewrap it so I could get out of it quickly, if I had a chance.

What if I didn't have a chance? What if they simply took me to a deserted spot and shot me?

I shuddered, fighting the impulse to kick, scream, holler, and pound on the trunk. I rolled into a tight ball and rocked back and forth, willing away the claustrophobia, swallowing hard to keep the contents of my stomach down.

Running my tongue over the tape till I found the end, I pried it loose with my teeth and started unwinding it, trying to keep it from getting raveled and stuck together.

Mustn't dwell on the macabre. Must do everything in my power, then pray. God had delivered me from some tight spots before. I had no reason to believe He wouldn't do the same for me again.

Or would He? I was dragging my feet in discovering the truth about the church Bart said was the true church of Jesus Christ. Would He take that into account when I asked for deliverance?

Miracles hinged on faith. I had faith He would hear and answer my petition. But was I showing faith if I wasn't actively investigating Bart's claim? If, by lack of enthusiasm, I displayed lack of faith, would that be a consideration when I asked for still another miracle of deliverance?

Bart said we were put here on earth to be tried and tested. Well, I was certainly being tried—my patience, my ability to think and act. Even my love for Bart and my commitment to our marriage.

That hit me like a runaway eighteen-wheeler. What had I just been thinking, minutes ago, about whether or not it was all worth it? With that attitude, I'd fail the test for sure.

With a firm commitment to be more zealous in my search for truth and a fervent prayer for divine intervention, I finished freeing my wrists as the car slowed and pulled off the pavement onto a bumpy gravel road. Loosely rewrapping the tape around my wrists, I tucked the slack under so it appeared I was still tightly bound.

Just in time. The road was so rough I was tossed and banged around the trunk like a rubber ball until I wedged myself in. Oh, the bruises I'd have tomorrow. *Let's just hope you're around to feel the pain.*

I tried to estimate how long we drove on the road. It seemed an eternity of bone-bruising potholes and teeth-rattling bumps. Then the car slowed and stopped. *No! Not yet! I haven't loosened the tape on my feet!*

Please, Father, be with me now and have a legion of guardian angels standing ready.

Car doors opened. Total silence. What were they doing?

"There! See it blow! That's the place I told you about. It'll be perfect." That was Cal's voice.

Footsteps approached. Keys rattled. As they opened the lid, fresh, pungent sea air swirled through the trunk, borne on a cool evening breeze. I inhaled deeply, elated to breathe something besides carbon monoxide.

"Take your clothes off down to your skivvies," Cal directed Floyd. "Otherwise we'll be soaked to the skin. I don't want to ruin my nice jacket, and I don't want to be wet and itchy with salt water all the way back to town."

I turned my eyes away from the disgusting, naked beer belly when Floyd stripped his shirt off. Cal was smaller and firm-fleshed, but no more attractive.

Floyd grabbed me roughly and sat me up in the trunk, then hefted me over his shoulder like a sailor's duffle bag and followed Cal down the rocky beach.

"It's a good thing for you the boss said we had to make it look like an accident." He swatted me squarely on my fanny which was in a far too convenient place for him to reach.

"If I had my way," *another slap,* "you'd pay," *smack,* "big time," *a harder smack,* "for what you did to me."

Floyd's zeal increased at my expense. "I'd break your fingers," *slap,* "one at a time," *whack,* "then your toes. . . ." He grabbed my foot and tried to twist it. The tape around both ankles prevented him from breaking it immediately. "And then an arm and a leg. I'd even let Cal practice carving with his new knife. Hey, Cal! Wait up! How about if we have a little fun before we dump her in the hole?"

"Like what?" Cal asked.

"Like I break a few of her bones, and you practice whittlin' with that new sticker you got."

I really hated Floyd's enthusiasm. His voice was high with excitement, like a kid planning a fun trip to an amusement park.

"You heard what he said. It has to look like an accident. They don't want a murder charge added to the list if they get caught. She'll be just as dead when the hole gets her."

"What if she swims out?" Floyd asked, reluctant to be deprived of his fun.

"Nobody gets out anymore. The last half dozen who tried it all ended up being caught by the tide and carried on into the cave. They had to send divers rigged with ropes to get the bodies. Even professionals won't go near it anymore. The whole area's off limits to swimmers."

That didn't sound encouraging, whatever they were talking about. Then Floyd dumped me off his shoulder onto the ground.

A long bridge was silhouetted against the fiery setting sun. Sand dunes prevented me from seeing anything of the horizon. There was just water blowing like a geyser from some rocks—a blowhole.

"We timed it perfect," Cal gloated. "The tide's just coming in. Bring her over here and we'll sit her on the edge. After the water blows, it'll suck her back down in the hole. Good-bye, Ms. Meddler."

"How did you get out when you did it?" Floyd asked.

"We'd come about noon when the sun was high. You have to look for the light out of the cave or you get disoriented and swim the wrong way. I almost didn't get out once. That was my last time."

"What if she's a good swimmer?" Floyd argued.

"The current's really strong. It'd take her right out into the bay, which everybody knows is full of sharks. We had an old rowboat waiting to pull us in as soon as we surfaced. She's got nothing. Come on, Floyd. The odds against her getting out are higher than winning the lottery."

"Nothin' says we can't up the odds." Floyd grabbed my tennis shoes, pulled them off, and tossed them into the water.

"Now carve her feet up so if she does swim out, she'll attract the sharks before she can get to shore."

Cal's tone was that of a patient parent to an insistent child.

"Floyd, her hands and feet are taped. She can't swim. It takes a strong swimmer knowing where the entrance to the cave is to get out. The sun's almost set. She can't see the entrance. The tide will carry her to the back of the cave, and they'll never find her body because nothing comes out of there unless you go in and get it. Come on. This is the local lover's lane, and we're likely to have company pretty soon."

Floyd picked me up, almost gleefully, and threw me over his shoulder again. He scrambled behind Cal over the wet rocks to the blowhole, stumbling once and nearly dropping me.

"You're awful quiet. Don't you have nothin' to say?"

"I'm praying," I answered, biting back the barbs I wanted to sting him with.

Better keep quiet and not get another crack on the jaw. You'll need all your wits, sharp and focused, not addled by a blow to the head because of a smart mouth.

We got drenched by a blast from the blowhole. As soon as it subsided, Cal got in position and guided Floyd to "the spot." He plopped me down unnecessarily hard on the wet rock, my feet dangling in the dark hole below.

Please, dear God, let me see that glowing sun and find my way out.

I wasn't worried about the swim. I was a strong swimmer. I'd learned in the ocean on the Santa Barbara coast, spent long summers in the waters of Greece, exploring caves and coral reefs. What did worry me was becoming disoriented and swimming the wrong way. A fatal mistake.

Icy water blasted upward, piercing my jeans like a thousand icicles. It drenched me, left me breathless. I shut my eyes. Inhaling and exhaling deeply, I got one last good breath before hard hands pushed me and the receding water yanked me into its swirling, frigid, inky depths.

Chapter 24

Caught between the force of the tide flowing into the cave and the water rushing back out of the blowhole, I was tumbled about till I didn't know which way was up, much less which way was out.

Tearing frantically at the tape on my wrists until it was off, I fought for control, spinning in a circle, searching for light. I might as well have been swimming in ink. There was no light. Nothing penetrated this cave.

Think. There's got to be a better way. A quicker way. I could only hold my breath for a minute and a half. That was all the time I had.

Against the current! The way out is where the water's coming in. Relaxing, I let the current carry me for an instant, then whipped around and swam into it.

The current was strong, forcing walls of water into the cave. I fought it, slicing it with my hands, swimming like a porpoise with my bound feet. I wasn't going anywhere. Wasn't making any headway. But I'd be driven back into the cave if I relaxed. My eyes burned from the salt water.

Then I saw the red glow like fire on the water. The setting sun. *Thank you, Father.*

I blew air from my bursting lungs and propelled to the opening, using the jagged rocks to work my way through the current and out of the cave.

Air! I need air! I clawed my way toward the surface, frantic to fill my lungs with something besides water. *Hold on. You can do it. Hold. Hold. Don't breathe. There's no air there. Hold.*

I exploded out of the water like a dolphin, just not as high and graceful. Nothing in this world ever felt so good as that fresh air in my lungs. I lay back, floating spread eagle, taking in great gulps of the wonderful, life-giving stuff.

Suddenly the water around me erupted, dancing in little spurts and splashes. Gunshots! I'd forgotten about Cal and Floyd watching for me to surface!

I threw one arm in the air and yelled, then slid beneath the choppy waves, swimming underwater parallel to the shore. I'd probably been easy to see with the sun glimmering on the water. I had to get out of that spot and hope they bought my act. They must think they'd hit me with one of their shots and go away so I could get out of this icy water, pronto.

I rolled onto my back to breathe so I didn't have to stick my whole head out of the water, hoping I was hidden in the rolling waves. My next priority was to get the tape off my feet.

The cold was taking its toll. My muscles were cramping, movement getting slower and slower, and my fingers could hardly work. I struggled with the tape, finally finding the end and peeling it off, then played submarine again.

Something brushed against my leg. Tentacles wrapped around me, pulling me back under the freezing black waters. Kicking and fighting, I pulled one slimy thing from my arm as another wrapped around my leg. I finally got my head above water, drinking in great gasps of air. The thing relaxed its grip on me. I lay back in the water, too tired to swim away.

The sun was gone. Night fell. I was cold, colder than I could ever remember being. And tired. I rolled over and looked for my abductors. They hadn't given up. They'd driven the car close to the rocks and beamed the headlights across the water, searching for me.

The thing reached for me again. I grabbed the tentacle, only to have it come off in my hand. Seaweed. I was in a bed of seaweed. No giant octopus. No man-eating squid. Just seaweed.

Keeping as much on top of the water as possible, I slipped through the watery forest toward the shore some distance from my persistent captors.

My movements were sluggish, my thoughts tumbling over each other like a litter of newborn kittens. Hypothermia must be tightening its icy grip. I had to get out of this frigid water.

Moving lights on the beach caught my eye. It was a minute before it registered in my muddled mind that my captors were leaving. And another long minute before I realized why.

A second car had driven out to the rocky point. Someone to help! If I could reach them, they could get me back to town. Back to Bart. Back to warmth and safety.

I increased my efforts, spurred on by the promise of a hot shower. If only this part of the Pacific was the temperature of the waters around Hawaii. Concentrating on memories of our swim in warm, clean, crystal-clear water, then lying close to Bart on white sand with sun hot on our bodies, I swam doggedly, ploddingly atop the waving, moving seaweed.

I clung to those warm thoughts, feeling my body start to shut down, to slow almost to a stop. My mind kept wandering. I wanted to go to sleep. Simply close my eyes, and go to sleep. I was so tired I didn't care if I ever woke up.

Allison! If you go to sleep, you never will wake up.

I forced myself to move, to shake my arms, to kick my legs. My feet touched bottom, a muddy, squishy bottom, and immediately slimy seaweed entangled my legs.

Frantically, I pushed it away and laid across the surface of the water to stay clear of the threatening tentacles. I could see the beach now. I could make it.

When my hands touched the bottom, I stood and immediately sank to my knees in thick, sticky, gooey, muddy sand. As I pulled one foot out, the other sank deeper in the mire.

I tugged at the seaweed for leverage, but it slipped through my stiff, cold fingers. The harder I fought it, the faster the bog swallowed my legs. Like quicksand.

I yelled for help. Surely the people in the car could hear me. They'd pull me out. But there was no sign of acknowledgment.

Up to my waist now in the gooey muck, I screamed louder, panic-stricken. Why didn't they come? Every minute that passed, I sank deeper. Every movement I made pushed me further into the quagmire instead of freeing me.

"Allison. Stop struggling."

I looked around to see who had spoken to me. No one was

there. I was alone on the beach. I was being swallowed alive in freezing liquid death, but I was definitely alone and hearing things.

Frantically, I fought against the mud which was now up to my arms. The icy water came to my chin.

"Allison. Stop struggling. Relax."

The voice sounded clearly in my ears over the lapping of water on the shore, over the crashing of waves on rocks down the beach. Was I hallucinating? Or had death's angel come for me?

"Allison. Don't move."

"Dad! Where are you? I can't see you? I'm over here."

"Stop moving. You'll stop sinking."

"Help me, Dad. Can you see me? Can you reach me?"

"You'll have to help yourself. There's no one to help you. Relax. When you move, move slowly."

An icy shudder ran through me, colder than the water lapping at my shoulders. Dad wasn't here. But once again he knew, somehow, when my life was in danger and I needed help beyond my own abilities.

I stopped moving, stopped thrashing and flailing wildly, and relaxed. I would die with dignity. That was his final contribution to my life. I could do that for him.

Telepathing my last message, I told Dad that I loved him and Mom. Then I resigned myself to death by hypothermia or drowning, whichever came first, as the quicksand pulled me under the icy black water.

But I didn't sink deeper. The water didn't get any further than my shoulders. Move slowly, he said. Dad wasn't telling me how to die. He was telling me how to live.

Your mind really is muddled, lady! Get out of here before the cold shuts it down permanently. Remember what you know about quicksand.

When water is forced upward through sand, the grains are pushed apart and the sand swells. It loses firmness and can't support weight.

Concentrating on moving one foot just a little bit, slowly, carefully, I moved my leg in a slight circle, loosening the mire's grip, then inched forward, one leg at a time, one foot at a time. Slowly, very slowly, I worked my way up till I was only waist deep, and shivering uncontrollably.

I didn't know which was worse, being in the frigid water, or out of it. At the snail's pace I was moving, I'd surely freeze to death before I escaped. But I was making headway.

The farther out I got, the firmer sand seemed to be on the bottom and the less dense on top, but progress was agonizingly slow.

At last, the bog was only up to my knees. Quivering from head to foot, I slogged through the mucky, smelly mess to firm ground, ready to collapse in an exhausted heap on the beach.

The engine on the car turned over, lights piercing the darkness across the water. They were leaving!

Panic and fear-inspired adrenalin projected me down the beach and across the rocks in the direction of my last hope. If they left me, I wasn't sure I'd survive the bone-chilling, teeth-chattering hypothermia that already had my mind and body numb.

The long, low car backed around a quarter-circle, lights shining away from me.

"Stop! Take me. Stop!" My mouth wouldn't form words properly. My speech was slurred. I stumbled and fell, my feet so cold they wouldn't work right.

Music blared from the open windows, too loud for the occupants to hear my cries.

The car pulled forward slowly away from me, up the gravel road leading to the highway, and with it went warmth and safety.

"Don't go! Help!" I staggered after the car, terrified it would drive away and leave me alone.

Bright red brake lights lit up the night.

"Help!" I wobbled toward them, barefoot on the sharp gravel, falling, crawling to my feet and staggering again toward the car.

The music stopped. Slowly, the car backed toward me. It stopped. A head poked through the open window. I swayed unsteadily forward, stepped on something sharp and fell to my knees.

"Help!"

A girl screamed, drew her head back in the window and the car peeled out, spewing rocks and gravel at me like shrapnel.

They left me.

I crumpled in a heap in the middle of the gravel road and cried, too cold and tired to move. My thoughts were a confused garble that made no sense.

If I hadn't been sitting on sharp rocks that poked unmercifully through my sodden jeans, I might have stayed right there and gone to sleep, never to wake again. Pain finally penetrated my muddled mind, forcing me to move.

Picking my way carefully over the rocks, I reached the side of the road where I only had to contend with sand spurs. I headed toward the highway, trying to think why I needed to get there. I had to do something, but I couldn't remember what.

My teeth chattered so violently I kept biting my tongue. Wet, muddy jeans chafed my legs; my dripping sweat shirt was stiff with cold. All I wanted was a hot shower and a warm bed. I concentrated on that as I stumbled through the sand, stopping to pick needle-pointed sand spurs from my bare feet.

At last I reached the highway. But cars sped by so fast, no one could see me, or if they did, they couldn't have stopped. I just stood there, too numb to think, too numb to move, too tired and cold to pursue my objective, even if I could have remembered what it was. I backed off the pavement into a sign post, and slid to the ground.

Wrapping my arms around my mud-caked knees, I laid my head down and closed my eyes, weary, bone-weary. All the way through.

Suddenly tires screeched in gravel. With great effort, I raised my head. A car pulled off the road and ground to a stop a few feet away, blinding me with its headlights. I wanted to block the light with my hand, but it wouldn't move. I dropped my head again. It was too heavy to hold up.

"Ma'am? Are you okay?"

A hand touched my shoulder.

"Ma'am, are you all right?"

The hand lifted my chin. Another pried open my eyelid.

"What's your name? What're you doing out here?"

I tried to tell him. Something garbled and unintelligible came out instead. He went away and came back in a minute. A blanket covered my shivering shoulders.

"I've radioed for the paramedics. They'll be here in a few minutes. Can you talk? Tell me your name."

Whoever he was, he was concerned about me. He rubbed my hands, trying to get the circulation moving, trying to pull me out of my stupor.

"Miss, talk to me. Tell me who you are. What're you doing here soaking wet?" He pulled me to my feet and, supporting me with his arm around my waist, tried to get me walking, moving, keeping me from slipping into a fatal sleep.

"What's your name?" he insisted. "How did you get here? Why are you wet?"

I rested my heavy head on his shoulder and struggled to focus my tired eyes. The first thing I saw were flashing lights. A policeman! He'd tell Captain Saddler where I was.

Sirens wailed in the distance, coming closer. Coming to take me to Captain Saddler. I couldn't let them take me. Pulling away, I tried to stand by myself, to tell the policeman I was okay, that I didn't need his help. But I did. My quivering legs wouldn't hold me up on my own. How could I get away if I couldn't even walk?

Another car ground to a stop at the edge of the road. A car door slammed.

"Allison! Here you are, my darling! Where have you been? What happened to you? You're dripping wet."

No! No, no, no!

"Where did you find her, Officer? She's been lost for hours and needs her medication immediately."

He pulled me from the side of the policeman and scooped me into his arms.

"I've got to get her to our hotel and administer her injection or she'll go into shock."

"Looks like she's on her way right now," the policeman said. "Paramedics are coming and can . . ." The police radio crackled, broadcasting a description of someone wanted by the police as a witness.

It was me they were talking about! I reached for the officer, trying to push away from the arms that held me tight to get free.

"Can't wait. Might be too late." Scarlotti wheeled and ran with me to the waiting car. And there was nothing I could do.

Chapter 25

Scarlotti dumped me on the front seat, wrapped the blanket around me like a straightjacket, and buckled the seat belt. I couldn't have moved my little finger if I'd had the energy, which I didn't.

He slid into the driver's seat and backed the car away from the police car, then peeled into the traffic just as the policeman made the connection between the broadcast and me. The cop ran out to stop us. Scarlotti hit the gas and the car leaped forward, swerving toward the officer. At the last second, the officer leaped clear.

"Allison, you have more lives than a cat." Scarlotti's mesmerizing, malevolent voice penetrated the gray fog I was slipping into. "First you elude me at the old woman's house, then swim away from the blowhole. You escape the bog that should have swallowed you alive, and survive hypothermia that should have claimed you an hour ago."

His statement shocked me.

I rolled my head toward him, struggling to speak the words my lips were almost too cold to form.

"You saw?"

He brushed the long black hair back and turned his face toward me, dark eyes mocking, his handsome face marred only by the evil I saw there.

"Of course. I got to your building just as you tried to sneak back inside. When they shoved you into the car, I followed you to the building on Van Ness. I didn't want to be deprived of the pleasure of watching you die. When they took you from there, I again followed the car. The blowhole was a rather ingenious idea. Too bad they didn't know what a strong swimmer you are. But even I thought the bog would get you after you'd been in that frigid water for so long."

He'd watched everything, waiting to see me die!

Sirens screamed behind us. The policeman had taken up the chase. I glanced at Scarlotti. A sneer curled his perfectly formed lip. He geared down and slid the car into the other lane, weaving in and out of traffic, inching away from the flashing lights.

"No dimwitted cop can stop me." Scarlotti's laugh sent shivers up my spine. "None of them are smart enough. In a few hours, we'll be back in Hawaii, and no one will ever see you again. I'm glad you survived, Allison. I want you to pay in a very special way for killing my father."

His atrocious arrogance ignited a burning inside that began to warm me all the way through. I tried to wiggle my fingers, getting the blood flowing back into them, making them usable again. Slowly I rubbed my icy feet against the floor mats in small movements, hoping Scarlotti wouldn't notice.

When the opportunity came, I had to be ready to move. My feet needed to be able to run, my hands to free me from the seat belt, from Scarlotti's grasp.

We crossed a bridge. I had no idea which one, unsure even of which way we were going. The policeman hung in there, not closing, but never getting too far behind.

A big truck, an eighteen-wheeler, loomed in the headlights in front of us. Scarlotti whipped around it, cutting too close in front, forcing the driver to veer off the shoulder.

Mistake. Traffic flowing onto the freeway from an on-ramp left Scarlotti nowhere to go and the truck sped up behind us. His lights were blinding. The huge silver grill filled the rear view mirror. I jumped when the air horn nearly blew us off the road.

While Scarlotti was busy looking for a way out of the moving roadblock, I busied myself wriggling my arms up under the blanket. Inhaling deeply, scrunching my empty stomach toward my backbone, I slipped one arm under the seat belt, then inched the edge of the blanket under the belt toward the door, freeing my hand to move when I needed it.

Suddenly the truck bumped the back of the car, then acceler-ated, pushing us down the highway. Scarlotti let out a string of oaths that burned my ears. He struggled to keep the car steady, laying on the horn, trying to move the car in front of us or the one beside us.

It was as if they were all intent on keeping us penned in right where we were. Then I saw the helicopters. A newscopter and a police chopper. These people were listening to their radios as the newscopter broadcast the chase. They *were* trying to box us in.

An exit ramp appeared ahead. Scarlotti spun the wheel as he hit the gas pedal. The car flew off the freeway with the truck still on our bumper. Air brakes screamed and hissed behind us. The truck was stopping. We weren't.

Scarlotti's maniacal laugh died in his throat as we raced around a blind corner straight into a road block. The spotlight from the police chopper illuminated what looked like an escape route.

Scarlotti headed for the handicap slope of the curb and the wide sidewalk behind it. The car careened on two wheels, taking out a stop sign. We hit a grassy slope and topped the little hill as the heli-copter's lights revealed what was on the other side. A lake.

Not again.

"Another time, Allison. There will be another time." And Scarlotti opened his door and leaped out of the car before we cleared the grass.

It was surprising how calm I felt. The car hit the water nose first. It didn't sink immediately, just settled into the water slowly. The whole world moved in slow motion.

I just sat there watching the water rush in Scarlotti's open door, watching the cold water cover the seat, freezing my legs, my knees, my body. Again.

I simply sat there. Numb.

Someone jerked the door open and fumbled for the seat belt.

"Are you okay?"

"No."

"Where do you hurt?"

"Everywhere."

"Did you hit the dash?"

"No."

"Do you have any broken bones?"

"Not yet."

He shined the light in my face.

"Are you okay?"

"No. Wet, cold, miserable."

The policeman picked me up, dripping blanket and all, and waded through waist-deep water toward the grass at the edge of the small man-made lake.

A helicopter hovered over us, whipping the water into little whitecaps, stirring up the wind like frigid arctic air swooping down from Canada. I would never be warm again. Or clean.

Another helicopter swooped low above the grassy hill we'd flown over on the way to the lake. Before it even touched down, a figure leaped from the open door and raced toward us.

"Allison!"

Relief and joy surged through me at the welcome sound of my husband's voice.

Bart grabbed me from the arms of my rescuer and stumbled back onto the grass. He sat down, took the dripping, freezing blanket from my shoulders and someone replaced it with a dry one.

Taking my face in his hands, he looked at me closely in the lights from the choppers and cars.

"Princess, talk to me. Are you okay?"

All I could do was shake my head.

"Did he hurt you?"

I shook my head.

"Are you injured?"

I shook my head.

"Allison, talk to me! Are you all right?"

"Don't like being married. Too hard." My head dropped to his chest. If I hadn't been so cold and miserable, I would have cried, but my tears would probably have frozen on my cheeks.

Bart got to his feet and carried me to the helicopter that had settled onto the grassy hilltop.

"Get my message?" I asked as he put me, shivering, on the seat.

"Which one? That you don't like being married or that tomorrow night is the heist?"

I dropped my head back on the seat, too tired to hold it up.

"Get us to San Francisco General," Bart told the pilot as he climbed across me into the other seat.

I shook my head. "Hot shower, hot soup, and bed."

"I think you need to be looked at."

"No."

"How close can you get us to Yerba Buena Park?" Bart asked the pilot as we lifted above the chaotic scene.

"How close do you want to be?" the police pilot countered.

"We're staying across the street."

"I'll see what I can do."

"Catch Scarlotti?" I asked, knowing full well he'd slipped through their fingers.

"Scarlotti!"

"Scarlotti was driving."

"But I thought . . ."

"Too many mysteries." I was too tired to think about it, much less talk about it. I needed to get out of my freezing, wet, stinking clothes and get warm. I smelled like rotten eggs. Or rotting seaweed. I lay my head against Bart's chest as he held me close and turned off my thoughts to anything other than a hot shower.

Good to his word, the pilot set the helicopter gently in the center of Yerba Buena Park. Bart lifted me out and carried me across the street into the black and green marble foyer. A policeman met us at the door. I didn't even care what he was doing there. Captain Saddler could go hang. Nothing, or no one, would keep me from my hot shower.

Bart set me on my feet long enough to dig the keys from his pocket, handed them to the policeman and picked me up again. A good thing. My rubbery legs wouldn't have held me up for thirty seconds.

The policeman keyed the elevator and got on behind us. No one spoke on the ride to the top floor. Putrid aromas from my bog-covered clothes overpowered the little enclosed elevator. Holding the door to our suite open for us, the officer followed us inside and joined the agent at the window.

"Not coming with us, is he?" I asked as Bart carried me on into the bedroom portion of the suite.

"As soon as you're clean enough to get close to, you get to share bracelets with him." He said it with a straight face but he couldn't hide the facetious tone in his voice, nor the concern in his eyes.

Bart deposited me in the bathtub and stripped off my wet, smelly clothes while the hot water in the shower steamed up the bathroom. Then he peeled off his own clothes, nearly as wet and foul-smelling as my own.

"What are you doing?"

"Can you stand up alone in the shower?"

"No."

"I didn't think so." Bart threw our wet clothes out the door with instructions to dispose of them. He deserted me for a minute while he put soup in the microwave, then helped me out of the tub and into the shower.

Nothing ever felt so wonderful. At least, nothing I could think of at the moment. To be both clean and warm—and safe—was bliss beyond description. I curled up and leaned against him, totally content.

"Oh, no, you don't," Bart said, pulling me to my feet and turning off the water.

"Don't what?" I asked, trying to keep my eyes open.

"Don't go to sleep in the shower. You've got to stay awake long enough to tell me what you found out. Then you can sleep for a week. In fact, I'd be happy to know you were safely in bed and out of harm's way."

I pulled the huge towel around me and sank down on the toilet seat while Bart rubbed my feet and legs dry. He stopped, sat back on his heels and looked up at me.

"Why did you leave here?"

"Doris needed someone to take her home from the hospital."

"I need you . . . alive. Will you try to remember that? Please." The pleading in his voice stabbed me with guilt that I'd put Bart's needs after those of a stranger.

"I'm sorry," I murmured, repentant, remorseful, but struggling to keep my eyes open.

"I love you, Princess." Raw emotion, too close to the surface, stopped him. He touched my cheek, then gently kissed my lips. "I need you," he whispered, the words catching in his throat.

Bart finished towel-drying my hair, then picked me up and carried me to the bedroom. I curled up on the bed with the damp towel wrapped around me, chilled again now that I was out of the hot shower.

"How about getting into bed instead of sleeping on top of it?"

"Mmmm. I'm fine."

Nevertheless, I was vaguely aware that he peeled back the covers, tucked me snugly under the blanket, then sat on the edge of the bed with a cup of soup in hand.

"Stay awake long enough to eat some soup. It'll warm you from the inside and you'll stop shaking."

"Later."

"Allison?"

I opened a tired eye and tried to focus on his face.

"Two things before you fade entirely. Tell me what you found out about Elekta and the Arab. Who's helping them?"

I struggled to stay awake, to remember, to think clearly enough to make sense. He put a spoonful of soup to my lips. It tasted good and warmed me, but I was so sleepy.

"Elekta is Aisha of the House of Qujar. The Koh-i-noor was passed down through the matriarchal line for thousands of years . . ."

Bart shook me. "Princess, have another spoonful. I'm sorry, but I've got to know what you know."

"I'm tired."

"Besides that. Who's working with Elekta?"

"Two men and a masked boss, tomorrow night."

"Do you know when?"

"No."

He let me fall back on the pillow and stood.

"One more thing."

I opened my eyes again, but gave up trying to focus on his handsome face and closed them.

"Do you really not want to be married anymore?"

Fighting to stay awake, I reached for his hand. "Come, hold me," I said.

Bart slipped between the covers and I wrapped my arms around him. He kissed my forehead, my eyelids, my nose, and had just found my mouth when the phone rang. His warmth departed as he left the bed.

I let myself slide into the welcoming black velvet void without even caring who was on the phone.

Chapter 26

Something pestered me awake. I didn't want to be awake. But it needled and wheedled its way into my subconscious, wresting me from that marvelous undemanding nether world that was warm, clean, and safe.

I tried to push it away, tried burrowing under the covers to escape it and the morning sun. Lying very still and willing my body and mind back into black velvet oblivion didn't help. Finally I gave in and let the subliminal do its thing.

The question wormed its way from deep in my subconscious to center stage in my mind. Matt! I sat up in bed, thoroughly awake. What happened to Matt? My last memory as they covered my face with the cloth in the car was his heavy body falling across my knees. What had they done with Matt?

Bart, of course, was gone. Disappointment steam-rolled me back on my pillow. I'd had the romantically mistaken notion that I'd be the first of Bart's concerns when we were married. I should have known better. If my father would put his work before his family, why wouldn't Bart, who'd been trained by him? But then, men saw things differently than women; if they were doing their job well, they were doing what was best for the family.

Why hadn't Bart mentioned Matt last night? Too preoccupied with his errant wife? Probably. I had been thoughtless and selfish where Bart was concerned. He had enough problems on his hands preventing the diamonds from being lifted out from under his nose without me complicating things.

I looked at the clock. Ten o'clock. Newspaper headlines caught

my eye. "Diamond Discovery on Exhibit." Bart had propped the
paper up on the dresser so I'd be sure to see it. Retrieving the newspaper, I sank back into the pillows to read it and the little love note
Bart had scribbled. I felt better knowing he was, at least, thinking of
me as he raced off to save the diamonds or the world or whatever.

While I'd been freezing to death in San Francisco Bay, Professor
Bainston had been giving his final lecture—and announcing the
discovery of the century. A 1,541.9-carat diamond, the largest found
in this century, and in fact the largest diamond found since the fabled
Cullinan, would be exhibited beside two other uncut gems.

The Rangoon, Myanmar museum was loaning the 21,500-
carat ruby discovered in 1996, a flawless beauty measuring four by
seven inches. Its display mates would be a sixty thousand-carat
sapphire, the largest in the world, along with the largest pearl. A
cortege of Myanmar guards would protect the three huge stones for
the exhibit's duration.

Interesting. So besides the Koh-i-noor which we knew Elekta
and company were after, we now had three large uncut stones that
were of immense value. What if . . . ?

I jumped out of bed and pulled slacks and a silk blouse from
the closet. No. On second thought, this trip to San Francisco had
been very hard on my clothes. I tossed them on the bed and grabbed
a pair of jeans and a sweat shirt from my suitcase. I was just tying the
laces on my tennis shoes when someone knocked on the door.

"Who is it?"

"Oz."

"Just a minute." I grabbed my brush and ran it through my
hair on my way to open the door.

"Good morning, Oz. What's up?"

"You are. Bart said you should sleep well past noon and if I
heard you up before then, I should check. Are you okay?"

"Of course. He's such a worry wart."

"He has reason to be, Allison. You're lucky to be alive. I can't
believe you left here yesterday knowing that Scarlotti and Roach were
prowling the city."

"As it turned out, neither of them were the immediate danger."

"Well, it won't happen again. Bart gave me a strict injunction to watch you until he gets back. I'm not to leave your side for a minute, and we're not to leave this floor."

"Oz, I've got to talk to Bart right now."

"Sorry, Allison. He's gone. Said he'd come back here as soon as he got through."

"Can't you call him? Beep him? I need to talk to him right away."

Oz glanced at his watch. "I don't imagine he'll be too much longer—and no, I can't reach him. He didn't say where he was going. Can I help?"

I opened my mouth to tell Oz what had been bouncing around in my mind since I read the newspaper, but shut it instead. Someone on the inside who knew my theory about the diamond theft had told someone on the outside. That's what got me into trouble yesterday. *And leaving when Bart asked you not to.*

"Do you need to be watching something right now?"

"Yeah. You."

"No, I mean, aren't you supposed to be doing surveillance or something? We could talk while you do that. You could keep an eye on both your responsibilities at the same time."

"Kill two birds with one stone," Oz laughed as we moved from the bedroom door to the window in the outer room.

I winced. "I'd rather you didn't put it that way. Too many people seem to have that idea in mind for me already."

"You must know something very important they don't want known." Oz turned and looked me straight in the eye. "Do you?"

"Only what I'd guessed. If my conjecturing was correct, then someone would have reason to silence me. Except, by doing away with me after I'd spouted my theories, it should just validate their accuracy. They'd be better off to ignore me and hope the authorities would, too."

"Unless you reached the right ears with your theories and were convincing enough to make them do something about it. And you were." Oz turned back to the equipment at the window.

"What do you mean?"

"Bart didn't tell you what the phone call was that pulled him away from you last night?"

"Phone call?" Then I remembered Bart's warm body slipping away from mine as I succumbed to blissful sleep.

"I was too tired to ask. What was it?"

"Captain Saddler caught the body dropper. They'd staked out all the places you'd suggested as possibilities, and the Pacific Union Club—the brownstone—was the next drop."

"Who was it?"

"They don't know yet. That's where Bart was all night. He came back to check on you this morning and leave a newspaper, then left again," Oz laughed, "giving me instructions to make sure you stayed here even if I had to handcuff you."

"I promise you won't have to resort to that. What are you watching for?" I looked out the window at the crowds below.

"People. Patterns. Anything out of the ordinary—or even too ordinary."

"Speaking of people," I took a deep breath, hoping I wasn't making a mistake, "has Matt been around?"

Oz looked at me with a strange expression.

"Around?"

"You know, at the museum," I stammered, wishing I hadn't said anything.

"You mean, is he out of the hospital and back at the museum? When they grabbed you, they hit Matt on the head and dumped him in an alley, apparently thinking he was dead. Somebody found him and called 911. He came to in an ambulance on the way to the hospital. The receptionist relayed your message to Bart right after Matt bullied his way out of the hospital and stormed back to the museum. The building was empty when they got there. Those next few hours were some of the worst in Bart's life. He was frantic."

"I wasn't sure he got the message. When the police never came . . ." I let the sentence drop, unfinished, but Oz was quick to snap it up.

"You thought they'd either killed Matt or he was in on it."

"Yes," I admitted, ashamed I'd had doubts about Matt's allegiance.

"Unfortunately, it's sometimes hard to tell the villains from the valiant. I assume, by the way you couched the question, you weren't sure whether you could trust me, either." His gray eyes sparkled and an impish grin spread across his face.

I felt a blush spread across mine. "Guilty as charged," I said, embarrassed that I would suspect Oz.

"Allison, can I be frank?" The smile vanished and the gray eyes darkened.

"Of course."

"Sit down for a minute."

I plopped into the nearest of the occasional chairs scattered about the large room. Oz grabbed a folding chair, placed it backwards and straddled it, folding his arms across the back.

"My first impression of you was a gal who really had it all together. You're sharp; you're gutsy; you grasp things quickly; you're confident in your own abilities; you handle yourself well . . . and in this case, you're way out of your league. These guys play dirty, and they play for keeps. You can't just go bopping around the city alone."

"But . . ."

"No buts. I can think of three very good reasons right up front you can't." He held up three fingers, pointing as he named them.

"One: Scarlotti vowed revenge for what your family did to his. All he needs to reach your parents and your husband is to get his hands on you first. Two: A terrorist group, Jihad, Hamas, or Hezbollah, issued a contract on Anastasia to one of the world's most deadly assassins. There's no reason to believe that you aren't now included in that contract since both your parents and your husband are involved. Three: You opened your pretty mouth and told someone about a plan to steal the diamonds. That someone was in cahoots with the jewel thieves. You stand between them and millions of dollars worth of diamonds. Do you think for one minute your life is worth five cents on the street?"

"But . . ."

Oz held up his hand. "I'm not through. Neither Scarlotti nor Roach would kill you right away. You'd be the bait to get to your parents and your husband, and the cause of their death. Of course, you wouldn't have much time to feel bad because you'd be dead, too. If the Jihad is actually going after the diamonds, you'd tie Bart's hands if you were captured. He'd let them take the jewels in exchange for you, but he'd come out on the short end. All he'd get back would be your dead body and they'd have made off with the diamonds."

Oz was right. I had been impudently thoughtless and brazenly careless. I got up and walked to the window, staring down at lines of people waiting to get into the museum across the street.

"Sorry I was a little hard on you, Allison." Oz put his arm around my shoulder and gave it a squeeze. "Forgive me?"

"There's nothing to forgive. You were right, Oz. Completely. I should have thought things out before I acted. Mom always said I was too impetuous. I just wasn't concerned about my own safety as much as I was about helping Doris. I didn't stop to think about my actions endangering Bart or my parents."

Oz went back to his surveillance, changing the subject as he scanned the scene below through binoculars.

"You certainly have a flare for attracting interesting characters. Doris is the woman with the cats?"

"Yes. She's all alone and had no one to help her."

"What about the Frenchman?"

"He didn't know anyone in this country."

"And the Englishman?

"Professor Bainston? He's just here lecturing on diamonds . . . oh! I see what you mean."

Oz's laughter was contagious.

"You missed one other character," I said, pulling a face. "Captain Jim Saddler. He's on the negative side of the list, though. The other three are positives."

"Positives?" Oz asked.

"Pleasant to be around. Captain Saddler's obvious misogyny makes him a negative with a capital N."

"Real woman hater, huh?"

"Haven't you talked to him? He's so blatant about it, I'm surprised someone hasn't cut out his blasphemous tongue, although I read where several have tried to sue the pants off him. Not very good PR for someone constantly in the public eye."

"He's done a nice about-face regarding one gal I know." Oz turned and smiled. "I think he'll be a little nicer than the last time you saw him. You may even luck out and get an apology."

"I won't hold my breath waiting for that one." I stopped, puzzled by what I saw on the street below. "Aren't all the diamonds already on display? If the exhibit's open, surely everything's in place."

"It is. And it's an incredible array of jewels. Why?"

"Don't you think it's a bit odd for an armored truck to be

picking up something—unless they've taken in so much in admission already this morning. . . ."

Oz grabbed his radio. "Matt! Are you there? What's the armored truck doing at the museum? Come in, Matt."

"Ed here, Oz. Matt's gone. What's up?"

"You've got six armed guards getting out of an armored truck out front. They're heading for the museum empty handed. Is a pickup scheduled?"

"It'll take a minute to check," Ed said.

"Ed, alert the guards to be on their toes. Something's funny. I'll be right there."

Oz grabbed a camera and turned to me. "Allison, I need two things. Your solemn promise you won't leave this room for any reason, and your help filming everything that's going on down there. The video camera's set—I've turned it on. Use this camera and take pictures of everything you see. It has an action-sequence feature. Just keep pressing your finger on this button and it'll keep taking pictures. Promise?"

"I promise. Get out of here."

Oz, gun already in hand, threw one more instruction over his shoulder as he keyed the elevator.

"Grab that set of headphones on the desk, put them on, and keep me informed about what's going on out front. You'll have to be our eyes from up here."

I adjusted the headphones and attached mike and turned to the window as the elevator doors shut. The telescopic lens on the camera gave me a clear close-up of the scene below. The guards looked authentic enough, and were certainly well armed. But I'd never seen so many with one truck before. Usually only a driver and a delivery person, and possibly one in the back guarding whatever their payload happened to be.

"Oz, can you hear me?"

"Loud and clear, Allison."

"The guards have Uzis. Is that normal?"

"Not to my knowledge. Thanks. What else can you see?"

"A garbage truck just pulled into the alley beside the museum and drove behind it. Must be a heavy garbage day. There were four men hanging off the corners besides the two in the cab."

"Whoa, boy. Ed! Sound the alarm! Get the cops here on the double. I think we got big trouble!"

Chapter 27

What if I've just sounded a false alarm and the guards and garbage men are real? I didn't have time for self-recrimination before several well-dressed men stepped out of line, pushing their way through the crowd that had parted for the armored guards.

Oz was running across the street, dodging traffic at the intersection.

"Oz, do you have plainclothes men in line?"

"Don't think so."

"Six men in sport coats, turtlenecks, and slacks will reach the front door about the same time you do. Be careful. They may or may not be trouble." I clicked a picture just in case.

"Good work. Ed, did you hear that? Possible six more behind the guards. Is everyone in place? Where in blazes is Matt?"

Instead of a confrontation at the front door with the six men, Oz slipped through the gift shop. If it wasn't thronged with people, he'd make the lobby at the same time the six did, right behind the guards.

"What else is moving, Allison?"

I scanned the scene below. A colorful line of people, two and three deep, snaked down the street toward the corner of Howard and Third. Suddenly the end of the line erupted. People scattered in every direction.

A semi-truck screeched into the intersection, jackknifed, and overturned, sliding with a metallic crash into the curb. The street light toppled to the pavement. Screams of people near enough to be hit by flying glass joined the sirens in a cacophony of clamor and confusion.

"Oz! A semi just overturned at Third and Howard!"

"Is the intersection blocked?"

"Yes."

Oz swore. The direct route from the police station was blocked. More gunshots from the museum. Then the irritating, unmistakable buzz of helicopters caught my attention. I scanned the skyline. Above a tall building southeast of the museum, three sleek helicopters hovered like mosquitos looking for a place to land.

Not waiting for the chatter on the earphones to clear, I broke in over the top of Sam yelling directions.

"Oz! Three small, unmarked choppers in a holding pattern not far from the museum. Getaway vehicles?"

"Good work, Princess." Bart's most welcome voice filled my headphones.

"Bart! Where are you?"

"Leaving Captain Saddler's office. We were on our way, but your last message changes things. We've just radioed for a police chopper. Looks like we've got our hands full this morning. Keep up the commentary. I hear you loud and clear."

"You'll need more than one helicopter. There are three waiting in the wings. But Bart, I'm only assuming they have anything to do with the robbery. And there are lots of people down on the street who could be hurt. How do we get them out of the way?"

"The first squad car should be there any minute. They'll handle it. I see our choppers coming."

Gunfire and shouts filled the earphones. People fled, screaming, from the museum through every exit. The museum had been packed with people. That would only hinder Oz and his men. And provide hostages for the gunmen. I felt powerless in my ivory tower with only a camera in my hands.

Suddenly three men appeared on the museum's fourth-floor balcony, each clutching a hostage. Immediately the helicopters flitted forward, nose down, tail up.

"Bart! Men outside on the balcony with hostages. The helicopters are moving in."

"Gotcha! Our buggies just arrived. Getting airborne now."

Police cars screeched into the street below. Uniformed officers swarmed through the intersection, shepherding the throngs of people out of the area.

Right behind them, a SWAT team arrived. Armed, black-clad men poured out of the van.

The first two small, sleek helicopters swooped low over the museum, ladders trailing like trolling lines. Two jutting wings of the museum complicated the pilot's attempt to hit the "sweet spot" with his ladder.

When the chopper's dangling ladder finally came within reach of the gunman, the struggling hostage prevented him from grabbing hold. The gunman flung the hostage against the wall, shot him, then leaped to the ledge of the balcony to catch the ladder.

The third helicopter hung back. Suddenly, a police chopper swooped over the hesitating helicopter, a hawk stalking a blackbird. Number three darted away. Not far or fast enough. It exploded in a ball of fire and fell out of the sky in flaming pieces, shot down resisting the police.

Helicopter number two dipped, wheeled, and headed toward the Bay Bridge with a police chopper right on its tail.

As chopper number one peeled away from the museum, the gunman on the ledge lunged for the ladder, connected, and clung, swinging in a wide arc under the chopper. A police helicopter twice its size hovered above it, forcing it down in Yerba Buena Park across the street from the museum where it was quickly surrounded by police.

The man dangling on the ladder bailed out into the fountain instead of smashing into the Center for Performing Arts. He was dragged out, dripping, and cuffed by grinning cops.

Remembering the camera in my hand, I snapped a few delayed pictures. I'd missed the action shots Oz told me to take. Hopefully most of it was on the video camera.

"Did anyone check out the men in the garbage truck in the alley?" I asked.

Bart answered. "The SWAT team got them and the cherry picker. You missed that, Princess, but that was about the only thing you missed. The police, instead of the gunmen, went in through those fifth-floor double doors."

The noise and confusion in the headphones from the museum was overwhelming.

Oz yelled he'd been hit. Ed was down and not moving.

Sam was pinned down by the two gunmen who'd lost their helicopter escape and gone back in to fight it out, keeping their hostages in tow.

"Princess, keep your eyes open," Bart commanded through the earphones. "From your vantage point, you can spot things men on the ground can't see. I'm going into the museum now, but I'll still be able to hear you."

"Please be careful. And Bart . . ."

"Yes?"

"I really do like being married."

"Gotcha."

I could almost hear his grin over the headphones.

The big police helicopter dropped down over Yerba Buena Park. Bart and two uniformed officers jumped to the grass and raced toward the museum, joined by the two cops who'd dragged the gunman from the fountain.

Tires squealed around the corner directly below and a car screeched to a halt. The door flew open before the car stopped moving. Matt McMillan's big frame unfolded with incredible grace and speed. He caught Bart at the museum's entrance.

Matt and one officer took the doors on the left. Bart and his man took the doors on the right. The two cops went through the revolving door in the middle.

Sirens again rent the air. Two ambulances peeled into the parking lot next to the museum. EMTs unloaded a gurney and raced toward the entrance.

"Medics are here, Bart," I reported. "How's Oz?"

"Bleeding, but breathing. Ed's dead. They got five of the gunmen. The rest are holed up on the fourth floor. The SWAT team's got them pinned down. We're going up."

I watched as Oz was wheeled out to the ambulance and hustled on board.

"Hang in there, Oz," I said, not realizing I'd spoken out loud.

"I'll be right back, Allison, as soon as they pump some of that life-giving red stuff back into me. In the meantime, keep me posted. I don't want to miss a thing."

"Oz! I thought you were out of this."

"Not on your life. They promised they wouldn't take my radio away if I'd be a good boy and not get excited. I want a blow by blow from your front-row balcony seat. And a recap of what I missed. Okay?"

I described the scene below as the ambulance pulled away, and gave a quick recap of the gunman's daring attempt to get away by leaping to the ladder only to end up in the fountain.

The action was taking place in the museum now and I was missing it all. Even the radio was fairly quiet with only intermittent comments.

I picked up the field glasses to scan the street ten stories below and see what other little dramas might be taking place. My first surprise was the old man with the cane, and not far from him were the two men who were always in the museum—the tall, dark, pony-tailed one and the shorter, fat man with the light-colored eyes.

A cab pulled into the intersection. Before the police could wave it on, the passenger door opened and long legs appeared in a dramatic pose. Just long enough to get the cops' full and undivided attention. Then Elekta bounded out, notebook in hand. What I wouldn't have given for a parabolic mike at that moment. I'd loved to have heard the story she was laying on the police. Whatever it was, she'd been convincing enough to be allowed to stay near one of the police cars. Probably told them she was a reporter. I could tell them a whole lot more. And would.

I scanned what faces I could see, hoping Reynard had heard of the robbery attempt and had come with his camera. He wouldn't beat the media this time, but he might get some pictures that would be profitable for him. Too bad he couldn't have caught that great shot from the helicopter ladder to the fountain.

I thought about calling the Abigail Hotel and having Rick send Reynard over, but I didn't dare leave the window. Bart was depending on me to be his eyes from up here. Or was he just making sure I was out of his hair and out of harm's way while he was tied up with the robbery?

I continued scanning the sidewalk, watching the crowd press against the line the police had thrown up to hold them safely back. Some had fled from the museum; some had been waiting in line to see the exhibit; some were just onlookers drawn by the excitement.

There was no excitement now except inside the museum, and I wasn't privy to that.

Then I felt prickles up the back of my neck and the uneasy feeling someone was watching *me.*

Certainly no one on the ground. I was on the tenth floor. They couldn't see me from down there. With the binoculars, I checked out the windows of buildings that faced this one. There weren't many. With the Center for the Arts and Moscone Convention Center facing us . . .

Without turning around, without hearing a sound, I somehow knew *he* was here in this very room with me.

"Bart," I said quietly, hoping the quiver in my voice didn't transfer over the radio. "Can you hear me?"

"Yeah. What's happening, Princess?"

I hesitated to interrupt what he was doing. I certainly didn't want him worrying about me and getting shot when he needed to be alert to what was going on around him. But I needed him a lot more right now than either the diamonds or the police did.

"Have you got them yet?"

"Still working on it."

"Can they manage without you?"

"What's the matter?" Bart demanded.

"Scarlotti—," was all I got out before the headphones were ripped from my head.

I whirled to face my personal phantom.

Long, silky, black hair fell across one side of his face. Graceful, slender fingers brushed it aside, revealing a perfectly-formed, handsome oval face.

"How did you get in here?" I demanded, staring in disbelief at this specter who seemingly could not be kept out by walls, guards or locked doors.

"I told you there'd be another time, Allison." Scarlotti's seductive voice sent chills of terror down my spine.

"But how?" I persisted, backing slowly toward the window.

"The same way you got out yesterday—the fire escape."

"The windows were locked."

Scarlotti dangled a small device in front of me as he narrowed the distance I'd just put between us.

"Glass cutters. Come with me, Allison, before your husband misses your inane chatter and comes to find you."

"I don't think so, Scarlotti. Bart's gone to a lot of trouble, not to mention expense, furnishing this wonderful little honeymoon hideaway. I think I'll just stay here and enjoy it."

"I wasn't giving you a choice." Scarlotti grabbed for me, the pleasant expression on his handsome face contorting into an ugly mask of malevolence.

Seizing the folding chair Oz had been sitting on, I threw it at him.

"Stop it!" I screamed. "Just stop it! I'm sick to death of being threatened and drugged and kidnapped and people trying to kill me. Go away and leave me alone!"

Scarlotti stopped, as surprised by my outburst as I was.

"My dear Allison, I can deliver you from all of that. In fact, that's why I'm here. To end your miserable life." Each step he advanced toward me, I matched retreating.

Hurry up, Bart. I can't play cat and mouse with this monster for long.

"My plan was to take you back to Hawaii, lure your family there, and let you watch each other die a little at a time with my marvelous drugs. However, I've changed my mind."

"What diabolical scheme have you devised this time?" I asked, trying to keep Scarlotti talking as long as possible while I felt my way backwards around the room.

"I've decided to use your impulsive, heedless nature against you. You broke the window to get out again, but this time your agility was impaired by your trauma of yesterday and you fell into the alley below to your death."

"Why would I have to break the window? It opens easily from inside."

"You're a smart girl. You figure it out."

"Because you cut a portion of the window to get in. It will seem I was so frantic to be free I broke the window. My death must appear as an unfortunate accident so my husband will blame himself for locking me in and not come after you with a blood lust."

"He'd never catch me."

"Because you're far more clever than he is," I said sarcastically.

"Allison, I do regret that I must kill you. You're the only woman

I've ever met with enough wit to offer me any challenge and enough sensitivity to understand me. But I could never forgive you for killing my father."

"Actually, it was the FBI, but I'll admit the two by four to the head probably didn't do him any good."

Scarlotti lunged for me. I tried to sidestep his grasp and fell over a box I hadn't seen between the chair and the window. I went down hard.

Scarlotti pulled me to my feet, twisting my arm behind my back.

"It's time to be rid of you." Scarlotti pushed me toward the bedroom door.

Bart should have been here by now. Hadn't he been able to get away? Hadn't he understood my plea for help? Or worse, had he been shot trying to leave the museum to help me?

"I'd like to be rid of you, too, Scarlotti. Why don't you just crawl back into whatever hole your father dragged you out of to watch him kill my mother, and leave me alone."

"You're an unfinished item. I hate loose, dangling threads."

"And what about my family?" We were at the bedroom door. *Stall, Allison. Don't go in there. If Bart's not coming, you've got to do this on your own.*

I grabbed the door frame with my free hand as we went through and used it as leverage to throw all my weight back against Scarlotti. He staggered back a step and recovered.

"Sorry. You've already used that trick." Scarlotti twisted my left arm till I cried out, pushing me into the bedroom. "The fall will be exhilarating, and the stop at the bottom will be so quick, you won't feel a thing."

"If it's so much fun, you go first," I said, looking for a weapon, anything I could find to stop him.

Grabbing a wooden statue from the bookshelf as he propelled me past it, Scarlotti smashed the window, sending glass flying everywhere.

"Now climb on that chair and get on the fire escape."

"Not on your life, Buster."

Trying to jerk free from his grasp, I elbowed him viciously in the stomach. Scarlotti held on tight, wrenching my arm higher. Gasping for breath, he shoved me toward the overstuffed chair and lifted me on it, forcing me onto the windowsill.

"It's time I was free of you."

Chapter
28

"She is a lot of trouble, isn't she?" Bart said as he stepped through the bedroom door. "But I'm getting used to having her around—and the excitement she generates—so I'd like to keep her just like she is." He pointed his gun at Scarlotti and all levity vanished.

"Let her go and step away," Bart demanded.

"As usual, your timing is off," Scarlotti sneered. "One little shove and she's gone forever. Put down your gun and lock yourself in the bathroom, or out she goes."

"Not on your life, Scarlotti. If I put the gun down, you'll push her anyway. Release my wife and move away. Now!"

"Do I understand this correctly? You're making demands of me while I hold your wife's life literally balanced in my hand?" Scarlotti's evil laugh sent chills through me. He was like a cornered wild animal, unpredictable and dangerous. One tiny shove and I'd be history, a splotch on the sidewalk one hundred feet straight down.

"How high is your trust level today, Princess?" Bart asked in voice that was strangely calm and quiet considering my current circumstances.

"Depends," I said over my shoulder. "What did you have in mind?"

"In one minute, I'm going to put a bullet into Scarlotti's chest where most people have a heart. He may push you through the window. If I tell you that you'll be all right, will you trust me?"

"Was that kind of trust implied in our marriage vows? I don't remember Bishop O'Hare saying anything about that." *Whatever he was trying to tell me, I wasn't catching.*

"It was. And I distinctly remember you said you'd trust me with your life."

"I did say that, didn't I?" I took a deep breath and said a quick prayer. "Okay. Fire when ready."

I searched the sky for a helicopter, the ground for a net to catch me when I fell. Neither were in evidence. I couldn't turn to look up. Maybe someone had suspended a rope for me.

But Scarlotti tightened his hold around my waist and pushed me off the ledge so he could perch on the windowsill where I'd been. I dangled precariously in space, totally dependent on Scarlotti's arm, and subject to his whim.

"You're a fool to think you can scare me with your threats, as if it mattered whether I lived or not. You killed the only beings who cared about me—my father, then my beloved lion, Kat. Now it's payback time."

Without warning Scarlotti let go of my waist and flung himself backward out of the tenth-floor window, laughing insanely as he fell. The look of evil delight changed to surprise as a hand grasped my wrist and Scarlotti fell alone. I looked up into Matt McMillan's big, brown eyes.

"Gotcha!" Matt was lying on the fire escape, leaning far over the edge, feet hooked in the wrought iron bars to hold him—and me—as I hung by one arm.

Bart grabbed me through the window and pulled me inside. He didn't say a word. Nor did I. We just held each other tight until I stopped trembling. His arms around me had never felt so good.

"Are you okay, Princess?" Bart whispered finally as he stroked my hair.

"Other than being scared sick, I'm fine, thank you. Excuse me, please."

I ran to the bathroom and threw up.

Bart graciously left me alone. The only thing worse than being sick was having someone watch you be sick. As I came out, Bart finished talking on the radio to Matt in the street below.

"It's finally over, Princess. We have a body to bury this time." Bart held open his arms and I quickly filled them.

"Are you sure he's dead?" I asked, not daring to believe I was actually free at last from this nightmare.

"As dead as they get. Even Scarlotti couldn't survive that fall. Matt verified it."

My knees buckled as a rush of relief hit me. I could hardly imagine life without constant fear, without searching shadows for the dreaded silhouette, without the terror that sensuous voice incited.

"Are you up to a little more excitement?" Bart asked, holding me at arms' length so he could look at me. "I'd like to leave you here, but frankly, I don't trust you. If there's trouble within a ten-mile radius, it'll find you."

Before I could answer, Captain Saddler's voice came on the radio. "Been listening in, Allan, and I'm sending your wife a present. She's on her way over so let her come up."

At that minute, the guard at the desk downstairs called on the phone to report we had a policewoman waiting in the lobby.

"Wonder what that's all about," Bart muttered. "Let's go get her."

"I'll be fine," I told Bart as we got on the elevator. "You need to get back to the museum. Go ahead. I promise I'll stay right here and save my nervous breakdown until your diamonds are safe. If Captain Saddler's sent me a jailor, you won't have to worry about me at all."

"Not on your life. I don't want you out of my sight." Bart held my face in his hands. "You'll go with me. Just promise you'll stick to me like my shadow."

"But stay out of your way while I'm doing it," I laughed as the elevator doors opened and a petite uniformed policewoman with gray-streaked hair stepped in and extended her hand.

"I'm Liz Bizby," she said, a slight Hispanic accent in her husky voice. "Captain Saddler sent me to keep an eye on Mrs. Allan."

"We're just on our way back to the museum," Bart said.

"I think Captain Saddler meant for me to remain here with Mrs. Allan," the policewoman stated in a tone clearly implying she was used to being obeyed.

"Captain Saddler may have that in mind, but I don't. From now on, Allison goes where I go and you can come along if you like."

They squared off and faced each other, determined to do it their own way.

"Bart! I just remembered! Elekta is out there. If she discovers I'm still alive, they could abort their plan and we'd never catch them.

Unless you want to arrest her now on attempted murder and take a chance on letting the others get away."

The radio crackled with voices from the museum. I could tell both Bart and Liz needed and wanted to be there, not here.

Liz reached for the elevator buttons. "You're on the tenth floor?"

I nodded. She pushed the button and spoke into her radio.

"Captain Saddler, Liz here. Permission requested to do something unorthodox."

"More Liz-biz?" came the reply.

"Yes, sir," Liz answered with a slight smile, her dark eyes sparkling mischievously.

"Granted. Just stay within the realms of reality this time."

Bart keyed the elevator doors open and Liz surveyed the penthouse suite at a glance, then turned to me.

"We're pretty close to the same size, Mrs. Allan. If you've got something I can wear, you could put on my uniform. We might get away with the deception."

We headed for our private portion of the suite while Bart went to the window to watch what was going on below and keep abreast of the confrontation at the museum.

Liz stopped abruptly as we stepped into the bedroom.

"Ay Caramba! What a place!"

"It was supposed to double as a honeymoon hideaway and prison for me, but it turned out not to be as secure as Bart hoped." I pointed to the glassless window and explained briefly as I opened the closet and gave Liz her choice of what was hanging there. She was already out of her uniform. I stared in surprise at her very brief and very sexy leopard-print panties and bra.

Liz laughed at my expression. "They remind me that I may be playing a man's rough game, but I am all woman and whenever possible, I play it the woman's way. That's what Captain Saddler meant by Liz-biz. I always try to find an alternative. My little Spanish grandmother taught me that."

Liz was bustier than I, but my black sweats were adequate for her, and her uniform, though loose, transformed me.

"Where's your makeup?" Liz asked.

"Here in the bathroom, what there is of it. I only do eyes and lips."

"That'll do. I just need some eye liner. We're going to age you a little." I sat on the toilet seat while Liz sketched a few age lines lightly around my eyes and mouth and along my forehead.

"Has that woman ever seen you with your hair any other way than this?"

"No. I usually wear it this way."

"Good. Put it up on your head. Do you have some talc?" Liz rummaged through my toiletries, while I ponytailed my hair.

"Sorry, I don't."

"What does Bart have?" Liz dumped out Bart's shaving kit. "Ahh. This will do nicely." She pulled out some foot powder and threw a towel around my shoulder.

"Tip your head way over. We're going to lighten everything that sticks out from under the hat. Unless she gets up close, that woman shouldn't recognize you. All she'll see is the uniform."

Liz placed the cap on my head. I stood up and looked in the mirror. It was amazing. At a glance, I wouldn't have recognized myself. The uniform, made for a more voluptuous figure, hung loose, giving me a rather dowdy appearance instead of the sharp figure Liz cut in it.

Liz grabbed the towels off the racks and folded them into a neat stack.

"What's that for?" I asked.

"When was the last time you looked at a Hispanic chamber-maid in a hotel and paid any attention to her? They all look just alike. It will appear that you came across the street to retrieve a cham-bermaid and some towels. There is a lot of blood there. Let's do it," Liz ordered.

Bart turned as we entered the outer room and gave a long, low whistle. "Wow. Talk about a transformation!"

As we headed for the elevator, I grabbed the headphones Scarlotti had ripped from my head a short time ago and shuddered. He was a sick, evil man, but even so, I felt sorry for him. No one should die like that. *But he chose to,* I reminded myself. At least Bart hadn't had to shoot him.

"What's going on?" Oz complained into the headphones. "You aren't keeping me up-to-date."

"Haven't they sedated you yet?" Bart asked over the radio. "You think all we've got to do is keep you up to speed?"

"I was talking to your beautiful wife, Allan, not you. Allison, your commentary quit. What happened?"

"Scarlotti decided to come calling in the middle of the action at the museum. We had to take a few minutes to deal with him." I paused, a shiver running through me as I remembered his face when he fell. "He won't be a problem anymore."

"We're on our way back to the museum," Bart added. "Allison can bring you up-to-date later."

"Got the message," Oz answered. "I'll stay out of your hair as long as I get the full report when you're done."

As we whipped through the lobby, Bart tossed the guard a key and directed him to have someone repair the broken window in our bedroom.

"Can you bring me up-to-date?" I asked as we headed across the street to the museum, keeping close to Bart. Before he could answer, Elekta darted from behind a police car and headed straight for us.

Liz eased herself into position between Bart and Elekta with me on the far side. I turned my head the other way.

Bart waved the nearest cop over without breaking stride. "Keep everyone back, please." He motioned to a disappointed Elekta, looking absolutely ravishing in a key lime shorts suit. It wasn't fair that someone so beautiful should be so evil. This woman had ordered my death without any apparent remorse.

"Catch you later," I said under my breath as we hurried into the museum. "We'd better catch her later, and put her elegantly clad body in prison clothes!" I muttered as much to myself as to Bart.

"Thou shalt not covet," Bart laughed as he pushed me through the revolving door, "even thy neighbor's long legs."

"I wish the Golden Rule said 'Do unto others as they have done unto you.' The suffering that woman caused me . . ."

The levity ended abruptly. Fatal fingers of crimson flowed from bodies littering the black and white marble floor. Ed's was one of them. A museum guard, two men wearing sport coats, and three of the armed guards completed the body count. The first floor had the deadly atmosphere of a morgue.

"I forget you're not as used to this as I am. Can you handle this, Princess?" Bart said as I gasped at the horrible scene. "It's pretty gruesome."

I swallowed hard and took a deep breath.

"Yes."

He took a long look to be sure I really could before he turned on his radio and spoke into it.

"Matt, where are you?"

"Fourth floor. SWAT team just got everything under control. Come on up."

We took the steps two at a time with Liz right on my heels, stepping over a body on the second-floor landing and passing two more on the third floor. I wondered how long before the museum could reopen. And whether or not Elekta would still try for the Koh-i-noor.

Matt met us at the top of the stairs and stared in momentary confusion from Liz to me before he spoke. "Ya'll probably don't want to bring Allison up here. It's not a pretty sight."

"It can't be much worse than what I've already seen. By the way," I said, extending my hand to Matt in gratitude, "thanks for grabbing me. You can hold my hand any time you want."

"Mah pleasure, pretty lady. Was shure glad to see you get back okay." He put his hand to his bandaged head. "I wasn't sure but when I got this we'd lost ya for good."

"Guess it's a good thing we're both survivors."

"Or just bad pennies," Matt drawled with a laugh. "We just keep turnin' up, no matter what. The experience did appear to age you a tad though," he laughed. "What's with the get-up?"

"We want Elekta and everyone involved in yesterday's attempt on my life to think it was successful. They're after the Koh-i-noor and we want to catch the whole kit and caboodle red-handed."

Matt coughed. "'Scuse me. Ah'm so dry Ah could spit cotton." He wheeled his big frame around and headed for the water fountain.

Bart had gone to talk to Sam and I quickly followed. This time I was going to be where Bart needed me to be.

Suddenly something wet dripped on my arm from above. Blood. I looked up to see a body draped across the catwalk above me.

It was one thing to find dead bodies all over the place, quite another to have them drip on me. Liz offered me a towel.

The mop-up took the rest of the day. Forensics people from the crime lab spent hours photographing and scouring what seemed to be every inch of the museum. Detectives relentlessly questioned all involved. Liz finally stopped dogging my every footstep and went back to her own duties.

Ed and the museum guard were the only two fatalities on our side. One of the diamond thieves survived. He'd tried to turn his own gun on himself at the end, rather than be captured, but Sam shot it out of his hand.

He was identified as a member of a new fanatical militant branch of Jihad. They'd launched their holy war against the infidels and capitalism. To finance that war, they were going to use rich capitalists' own wealth to destroy them. The huge new diamond would have been the start of a nice nest egg.

As soon as the police were through, Helen Hunicutt, the museum's curator, danced anxiously through the museum, checking for damage to her precious charges. Her long, slender fingers clasped and unclasped as she cornered Bart.

"When can we open again?"

"I imagine as soon as you can get things cleaned up," Bart said, "but you'll have to ask Captain Saddler how much longer they need."

She flew off to find the captain. If it had been me, I'd have sent Matt or some man to ask. They'd be much more likely to get permission than she would. He could purposely delay the opening for days just because a woman was dependent upon his authorization. I wondered how Liz had managed so easily with her request.

I wasn't looking forward to my first confrontation with Captain Saddler, though I knew it couldn't be put off forever. Fortunately, he and Bart had been busy in different areas of the museum and we hadn't had to meet yet.

Imagine my surprise when Ms. Hunicutt fluttered past us toward her office, a worried smile on her face.

"What did he say?" I asked, surprised at any semblance of a smile.

"Tomorrow morning if we can get it all cleaned up! I'll have to call in special crews, but we'll do it. Now I have to call the newspaper."

"Just step outside and make your announcement. Every reporter in town must be there." *And some who aren't, but are pretending to be,* I thought.

"Great idea. Thank you, Mrs. Allan." She darted to the elevators, pushed all three buttons, and straightened her skirt and hair nervously as she waited for one to open.

Bart turned from his last conference with Matt. "I'm starved. How about you?"

"Thought you'd never ask. What do you have in mind?"

"Something hearty in a quiet place where we can talk without interruption of any kind."

"Do you like Indian?" I asked. "I don't know about hearty, but I do know a place that's about as quiet and secluded as you could want."

"Lead on, McDuff."

"Going somewhere, kids?" Liz appeared at my elbow.

"To eat. Want to come along?" I asked, hoping she'd say no.

"I think Bart can handle any trouble you could conjure up tonight. I'll give you a rest, but I'll be back tomorrow to meddle in your lives." She smiled and waved us off.

Bart grabbed a couple of policemen to run interference through the herd of reporters shouting questions and thrusting mikes in our faces, and we made our escape to the car.

It wasn't quite the escape we'd envisioned. Two cars pulled out of the parking lot right behind us.

Chapter

29

As the light changed, Bart squealed out of the parking lot and whipped into traffic. The two cars were trapped at the light. A wave of relief hit me. I didn't want to contend with press, bad guys or anybody.

"Whither to, m'lady?"

"The Maharini is on Post Street between Van Ness and Polk— just a couple of blocks from the infamous art gallery. Speaking of the art gallery, what are your plans for Elekta, Ahmad, Cal and Floyd?"

"Cal and Floyd?"

"Elekta's strong-arms who dumped me in the blowhole to drown."

"You have a lot to tell me," Bart said, pulling my fingers to his lips, "and I want to hear every word. As for Elekta, we've got a tail on her. She can't sneeze without half a dozen detectives saying *'Gesundheit'*. She'll lead us to Ahmad and your kidnappers sooner or later. Unless they scrap their plans because of today."

"They won't. Aisha, alias Elekta, wants the Koh-i-noor in the worst way. It's been in her family for hundreds of years. I think she feels it's her legacy. I doubt she'll let anything stand in her way now that it's out of the Tower of London. If she misses this opportunity, I'd bet she'd even try for it there. I think she believes she might be an acceptable leader to her people by bringing the Koh-i-noor home again, even though she's female, and, therefore, inferior."

Bart raised his eyebrows.

"Ahmad's words, not mine."

"Never mind Ahmad. Tell me every step you took from the time I left you yesterday morning until I found you last night, soaking wet, freezing, and half dead—and smelling to high heaven," he added, wrinkling his nose.

I recounted my escapades, telling Bart when I got to the part about Doris that, after dinner, I'd like to stop by and check on her.

My narration reached the blowhole at the same time we arrived at the Maharini. By this time, the slight sprinkling of rain that started as we left the museum had turned to a steady downpour.

"You're sure about this?" Bart asked, looking doubtful at the rather plain exterior of the restaurant.

"Appearances can be deceiving," I said. "Prepare for a real surprise."

I requested the upstairs dining room and laughed at Bart's stunned expression as we entered the opulent fantasy world created on the second floor. Hundreds of yards of mauve fabric lavishly draped the ceiling. Private booths, separated by intricately carved panels, enclosed low tables.

As we reclined on elegant pillows covered with sumptuous fabrics, Bart leaned over and kissed me. "Convenient choice. There are not many restaurants where you can dine while making love."

We were interrupted by the waiter as he arrived to take our order. Bart ordered fish curry. I thought the lamb vindaloo sounded more interesting.

"Now. The rest of the story. Cal and Floyd drove you where to dispose of you?" Bart rolled over on his stomach and propped a tapestry pillow under him so he could stretch out and watch me, complete with police uniform and powdered hair, as I related my ordeal.

Our dinner arrived as I finished my tale. Bart just shook his head.

"I don't know how you manage to have so many people intent on doing away with that beautiful body. You know, if someone wrote that, even as fiction, it would be too far out for any editor to accept."

"I know. That's me. Totally unbelievable," I shrugged, attacking my lamb vindaloo. "Bart!" I said with a mouthful. "We have another problem."

"I'm not sure I want to hear this. Is it going to ruin my dinner?"

"Probably. You remember the old man with the cane and the two other men who were always hanging around the museum?"

Bart nodded, intent on his fish curry.

"I think they're planning their own little larceny."

Bart set his fork down and put his hand on my forehead.

"You don't feel like you have a fever, but you sound delirious. A third attempt at the diamonds?"

"They were all in the street this morning in front of the museum. . . ."

"So was half of San Francisco. Give me more than that. It's not that I don't believe you," he added, "it's just that I have a hard time keeping up with your leaps in logic. There's a good bit of imagination sandwiched between the logical, and I think I must be imagination-impaired. Walk me through it."

I described my thought process—they were always at the museum, had been filmed taking pictures of the security systems, were at the lecture, on the street during the robbery attempt, and . . .

"And you have this feeling," Bart finished with an understanding smile. He leaned over and kissed me. "After your track record last night and today, even Captain Saddler will listen to anything you have to say."

"Last night?"

Bart's smile vanished. "I wondered why you didn't ask. You don't know, do you?"

"Know what?"

Bart stared at his dinner, separating the fish from the curry, then mixing it together again, avoiding my gaze.

I took his fork from his hand. "Tell me."

"They caught the killer at the brownstone last night."

"Oz mentioned that."

I waited for more. Bart was quiet.

"Am I missing something significant here?"

It was apparent he was looking for a way to tell me something unpleasant.

"Okay," I said. "We'll play Twenty Questions. Were the murders connected to the diamonds? The killer *was* one of the terrorists, wasn't he? Was I right about the political statements they were trying to make?"

Bart put his finger gently to my lips.

"Roach *was* the killer."

My mouth dropped open. I leaned back against the cushions. "That's a real surprise, except Roach was tied to the terrorists, you said."

"Roach had a contract to exterminate Anastasia. He only had three of us to go when this all started."

"Then what was he doing in San Francisco? None of you were here."

"I imagine since we were in this part of the world—Santa Barbara isn't that far from San Francisco—they also assigned him the matter of the bodies. That's his *forté*. That *we* came to *him* was either a happy accident, or brilliant strategy on his part. We'll never know."

"Why?"

"He's dead."

"I thought he was in custody." I leaned forward on the table.

"He was."

"Bart! You're driving me crazy! Stop feeding me a sliver at a time."

"Captain Saddler had each place you named staked out. Every man and woman he could get his hands on was on the street. Every target was so saturated that if a body was dropped anywhere near the spot, they'd catch the killer. It worked. They called me immediately."

"The phone call that took your warm body away from mine?"

"I didn't think you even noticed," he said, leaning across the corner of the table to kiss me.

"I noticed. Go on," I urged.

"Captain Saddler hoped I'd recognize the suspect—my 'underworld connections,' he said."

"Did you?" I bit back the acid comment I had on Captain Saddler.

"Not right away. It took a couple of hours for me to figure out he was wearing a disguise. We peeled off the very real looking mustache, eyebrows, and goatee and found a friend of yours."

"Mine?"

"Reynard du Pre."

That was like a slap in the face. I slumped on the cushions, stunned.

"Reynard was the killer? But you just said it was Roach." I was thoroughly confused.

"It was. When the face hair came off, I recognized Reynard from the night he developed the pictures for us. He tried to use that as a lever to spring himself, but by that time, we'd accessed Interpol's fingerprint files and identified him. Then we removed the fake nose and cheek padding and found the real man—the Roach I recognized."

I shook my head in disbelief. "Reynard seemed like such a nice guy. And his story was so convincing. I can't believe it. I'm usually a better judge of character than that."

"When I think of you out there in the fog with him alone . . ." Bart didn't finish. He abandoned his dinner and pulled me down on the cushions in the corner, kissing me with a hunger born of fear—for my safety, for my life, for our lives together.

"Actually, we were only alone a few minutes," I murmured between kisses. "The police got there right away."

Bart looked at me.

"The joggers surprised him, caught him placing the body on the statue. Then you came. He didn't know who you were. If he'd had any idea you were my wife—and Jack and Margaret Alexander's daughter—you'd probably have joined the body on the statue's lap."

I shuddered, grateful to be snuggled in Bart's arms. "But why didn't he try something after I'd introduced you and he'd made the connection?"

"I imagine since he'd been adopted so nicely into your little circle, he figured he'd bide his time and find out where Margaret and Jack were hiding. That would make his job much easier. Then he could fulfill his contract and do away with us all."

"You said he was dead. What happened?" I asked.

"Cyanide capsule. He bit into it as soon as I recognized him as Roach and he figured there was no way out."

"Do you realize it's only been twenty-six days since you came back into my life?" I said. "Eighteen very long days since we were married? And in that short space of time, I've been chased, shot at, nearly drowned in the Mediterranean, had an airplane blown out from under me, fallen into a volcano, survived a hurricane, been kidnapped and drugged at least twice, stalked continually, shoved in a freezing blowhole and left to drown or freeze to death. . . ."

Bart's lips got in the way of my list. His kiss took my breath away and muddled my thinking.

He pulled away slightly, enough to see my face, and ran his finger down my cheek to my chin.

"And your point is?"

"I'm not sure I can survive this marriage until our first anniversary, and I'm not talking about first year. I'm talking about our first month."

Bart was quiet. His finger outlined my bottom lip.

"And?" he breathed the question softly.

Before I could reply, Bart's radio beeped. He ignored it to wait for my answer. The radio was too distracting. I wanted his full and undivided attention when we continued this discussion. I handed him the radio, knowing it would not only end the discussion, but our quiet dinner as well.

Bart listened for a minute. "We're on our way." He dug for his wallet and got to his feet. "Sorry to interrupt your dinner, Princess. Duty calls."

"Not as sorry as I am. I was looking forward to the *gulab jamun*."

"The what?"

"Dessert. Sweet cake dripping with passion-pink pomegranate syrup."

Bart pulled me to my feet and threw some money on the table. "Next time."

As we drove along glistening streets, I adjusted the uniform hat.

"How long do you suppose I'm going to have to be a policewoman?"

"Until Elekta and crew are apprehended."

"I can hardly remember what it was like not to have someone wanting to kill me—not to have to search the shadows as I pass, wondering if Scarlotti's lurking there. And now to have both him and Roach gone—it's almost too good to be true. When I go back to New York . . ."

"When you what?" Bart almost shouted.

"When I go back to work. Saroya said she'd cover for me for a week. I've only got a couple of days left before I have to be back at the U.N."

"I'm getting signals I don't understand and I certainly don't like. First you don't want to be married, which I attributed to your harrowing experiences in San Francisco Bay. Now you're going back to New York. Where did I miss something? Correct me if I'm wrong, but I somehow had the impression that we were happily married."

Bart whipped into the museum parking lot. A yellow-slickered policeman immediately appeared at the window. Bart flashed his ID.

"Captain Saddler and Matt McMillan are waiting for you in the security office," he reported.

"Thanks. We'll go right in."

Bart parked the car, turned off the ignition, then turned to me.

"What's going on, Alli? I have to know before we get out of this car."

Chapter 30

"Bart, we can deal with this later. It's not as important as protecting the diamonds."

My husband stared at me dumfounded.

"Not important? You're talking about leaving me and that's not important?"

Bart's radio interrupted us again. We both ignored it.

"I'm talking about going back to work, not leaving you, and that discussion will keep."

The policeman knocked on the car window.

Bart opened the door but remained in his seat. "*That* will be the first item of discussion. Allison, do you love me?"

"You know I love you. What a question!"

"Are you committed to this marriage?"

"Bart," I exclaimed in amazement and exasperation. "Of course I am. What's going on in that male mind of yours?"

"We have a contract, not a covenant. Contracts are easy to break—especially in view of the rather rocky start we've had. I know you've been through a lot, but it won't be like this forever. If I thought you were even considering leaving me, they could have all the diamonds in the world. They're not as important as you are . . . as we are."

Matt burst around the corner of the museum into the parking lot. "Allan! Get your buns in here. Saddler's going apoplectic."

"Contract's not in danger," I assured Bart as we got out of the car and ran through the rain. "I just hope we're not."

Matt hustled us into his office where an agitated Captain Saddler paced the floor.

"Where in blazes have you been, Allan? I ordered everyone in place before the museum closed at nine o'clock. You're late." Captain Saddler glared at Bart, then yelled at me. "Sergeant, I'm sure you have an assignment. Get to your post."

"She is," Bart said. "She's my back-up."

Captain Saddler opened his mouth to say something and shut it again. Matt took the opportunity to focus the group back on the setup for the night.

"Personally, Ah think we're bein' a little optimistic thinkin' the thieves will try for the diamonds tonight. Ah'd lay off and let things quiet down if it were me."

"That's what they want us to think," Bart said quietly. "We can relax tonight because nobody in his right mind would hit the museum after a try this morning."

"What does your psychic wife think?" Captain Saddler asked sarcastically.

"That they'll try tonight because we won't be expecting them," I said, stepping toward Captain Saddler and looking him straight in the eye.

Saddler peered at my name tag, then looked closely at me. "Bizby?"

He tore the hat off my head. "Mrs. Allan! You're impersonating an officer. I can have you arrested for that."

"You gave permission, Captain Saddler. A little thing called Liz-biz."

He glared at me. I glared right back. Finally he gave up.

"We've already been over the set-up," he said, turning to the group of guards and police watching our confrontation. "Any questions?"

"I feel a little overdressed with a gas mask in a museum," one of the new guards said. "Is it necessary? I haven't carried one of these since the war."

"If you'd been here this morning, you'd have no trouble thinking of the museum as a theater of war instead of a theater of art," Bart said, handing me one of the articles in question. I hung it on my belt like everyone else.

"Listen up," Saddler growled. "In five minutes the guards in the museum start ushering people out. When they're gone, the doors'll be locked, the police in front pull out, and it'll appear everything has quieted down for the night. You have your assigned posts. Get to 'em. If a mouse moves in this place, I want to know about it. Matt, you stay here with me. We'll direct this from the control room."

The security guards and police hustled out of the room. I wasn't sure whether they were anxious to get into position, or simply out of the volatile presence of Captain Saddler.

"Where's our spot?" I asked Bart as we turned to leave.

"Fifth floor."

"I want to be next to the Koh-i-noor."

"I think we can arrange that," Bart said, signaling to Liz Bizby.

"Anything to report?" he asked so only the two of us could hear.

"Jim kept him too busy and never left his side," Liz whispered. "Even went to the john with him. I'm sure he didn't have time for a phone call to anyone."

"Good. Thanks, Liz."

"What was that all about?" I asked as we made our way up the stairs through throngs of patrons leaving the exhibit.

"Tell you later."

Later there wasn't an opportunity. As the last patron left, we made a thorough search of the entire fifth floor to make sure no one had stayed behind. Others did the same below us. Then everyone moved into position.

Five security guards patrolled the fifth floor. The dozen colorful Myanmar guards stood silent sentinel over the newly discovered diamond and its magnificent ruby, sapphire, and pearl display mates, their curved scimitar swords poised to protect the precious uncut gems. Even with lights dimmed, the glitter of diamonds in the room was incredible.

"Can I look?" I asked Bart, who'd taken his position near the catwalk where he had a clear view of all the display cases.

"Go ahead. You can't get into too much trouble with all of us watching," he teased. "Just stay outside the red line on the floor and don't lean over the red ropes or you'll activate the motion sensors."

The diamonds were enclosed in three, four, and five-foot-high glass-domed cases, clustered in groups so patrons could enjoy and examine the jewels from various angles while winding along serpentine lines drawn on the museum floor.

Professor Bainston was right. Though the Koh-i-noor wasn't the most beautiful, it was the most fascinating. It was apparent why Elekta would attempt to regain her legacy even with all the security protecting the historical gem.

Wandering the exhibit, examining the royal treasures of several nations, and the incredible collection from the Smithsonian, I found myself suddenly drowsy and fighting to stay awake. The Myanmar guards were no longer sharply erect, but saggy, drooping. I turned to see Bart slip his gas mask on and motion to me to do the same. He put his finger to his lips and pointed to the guards.

Slipping quietly beside the Hope Diamond, I crept to the nearest of the native guards and grabbed his gas mask, thrusting it into his hands with a signal to be quiet. He moved to the next guard, who went to the neighboring guard until they had silently rotated positions and all had on gas masks. The patrolling guards noted the movement and did the same.

The museum was quiet. Five floors of dead silence. But the atmosphere was alive with an electric air of expectancy. Even the guards stopped patrolling and stood listening, waiting.

A soft sound from the catwalk brought all eyes to Bart. He motioned everyone to the floor. Play dead. Everyone dropped quietly where they were, curled so their gas masks were hidden. Not wanting to be down in the middle of the showroom, I crept to the wall between the Queen's necklace and the exquisite Orlov diamond. The Koh-i-noor was right in front of me. A door creaked. The elevator hummed to life. I tried to peek out from under my hat without moving my head. The gas mask not only prevented me from seeing clearly, it created a case of claustrophobia that would cause big problems if I had to sit here very long.

Sudden movement near the uncut Burmese diamond set my heart pounding. Out of the corner of my eye, I watched a shadowy figure approach. This was the diamond the terrorists came for this morning. Were they going for it again?

The figure paused at the Black Orloff, then continued past the Premier Rose, the Taylor-Burton diamond, and the pair of magnificent pink diamonds, the Sea of Life and Light of the Eye.

Suddenly a second figure appeared silently at the Koh-i-noor and was joined by the first. Both were dressed in black tights and sweat shirts, wearing gas masks and hoods. It took every ounce of self-restraint I could muster to sit still but I couldn't move till Bart did.

How did they plan to take the diamond without setting off the motion or heat sensors? That would sound an alarm at the police station and bring the police running. But they should know that if they'd done their homework.

They checked their watches. One retrieved two items from the other's backpack. They attached them to the goggles on their masks. Night-vision facilitators. Another watch check. Suddenly the lights went out, plunging the place into total darkness.

The quiet of the museum was breached by noise from outside. Tires screeched. Horns honked. People screamed. Glass shattered. Pandemonium broke loose on the streets of San Francisco.

The power was out. That meant no street lights. No traffic lights. And no alarms at the police station. Captain Saddler and Matt wouldn't be able to see anything on the monitors. Video cameras wouldn't film the two in the act.

A power tool buzzed to life in front of me. Bart moved in with a single shout that brought all the guards to their feet. Footsteps pounded up the stairs. Beams of light flashed disco-style with them.

In the dim light, I sensed more than saw one of the thieves drop to the floor and crawl toward me. The figure turned the corner, bumping the brass stand that held the red velvet rope, and headed for the rear of the room.

"Oh, no, you don't!" I jumped the shadow moving quickly away from me just as Bart reached the other one.

Mine wasn't giving up without a fight. Hands ripped the gas mask from my face as we rolled on the floor. I tore at the hooded figure, snatching the mask and night goggles off. With an oath, the thief struck out, connecting hard to my cheekbone. I fell against a display case, giving the fleeing form time to get to its feet. In seconds, I scrambled to mine and gave chase.

Footsteps pounded across the catwalk from one direction as flashlights illuminated the escaping thief going the other. I caught the thief at the open elevator doors and grabbed at the hood dangling down the back. Instead, I got a handful of hair. I yanked with relish.

This was the person who had consigned me to the freezing waters of San Francisco Bay. This was the person who ordered my death. She wouldn't get away.

Elekta, of course, had other ideas. She elbowed me in the stomach, knocking the wind out of me. I had both hands in that shoulder-length cinnamon hair and wasn't about to let go. Elekta couldn't turn to get at me, but she kicked and elbowed viciously, screaming threats in Arabic that made me sorry I could understand the language.

Suddenly I felt lightheaded and dizzy. The gas! Elekta should be affected, too. Her cursing stopped. Her struggle to be rid of me didn't, though it lessened.

In one last burst of desperate energy, Elekta grabbed the open elevator doors and dragged us both through. But it wasn't the floor of the elevator on which we rolled as we fell. It was the roof of the elevator cage.

The hatch was open. Elekta fell across it and tried to scramble down inside. I wouldn't let go of her hair. I knew I was blacking out. I was so drowsy I couldn't keep my eyes open. But I wouldn't let go, even after she managed to wriggle through the hole. I leaned over, pulled waist-deep into the hole by Elekta's weight hanging from my tightly clenched hands.

Suddenly the lights came on. Bart hovered over me, covering my face with the gas mask. He pulled Elekta back up through the hatch.

"You can let go, Princess," he said, voice muffled by his mask. "I've got her. She won't get away."

"I know," I said, still clutching the long silky strands. Too muddled to think straight, I only knew that as long as I kept hold, Elekta would not escape.

Shouts from the first floor echoed up through the museum. Bart stepped through the door to see what the excitement was all about. Elekta lay quietly across my legs, unconscious from the gas. I guessed it wouldn't hurt her or Bart would have brought her a mask, too.

Suddenly the elevator doors closed and the car started slowly up. I looked up. There seemed to be no clearance. When the elevator reached the top, we'd be crushed. Without thinking, I released my grip on Elekta's hair and shoved her headfirst through the open hatch.

There was no time to lower myself feet first. I dove in right behind her. The elevator came to a smooth stop as I landed squarely on Elekta, one arm twisting grotesquely under me as I tried to break my fall.

Chapter 31

The elevator doors slid quietly open and Bart rushed in. I gasped in pain as he raised me from the floor.

"Don't touch my arm." I tore the mask off with my good arm and threw it on the floor. I'd rather be unconscious than have that horrid thing on a minute longer. "What happened? Who started the elevator?" I asked, wondering who else wanted to kill me.

"When the power came back on, it must have automatically activated to finish the cycle to the fifth floor," Bart said, helping me from the elevator. "Apparently one or both of them hid on top of the elevator before the museum was closed."

"Why weren't they crushed?"

Bart leaned me up against the wall and wrapped his handkerchief gently around my bleeding arm.

"Compound fracture," he muttered, shaking his head. He went to find a chair for me. I slid to the floor, too weak-kneed to stand by myself. A breath of fresh air from the open double doors wafted by. The gas was being cleared out. Elekta would wake up.

I dragged myself to the elevator door to make sure she was still out, holding my shoulder to keep my arm from moving. Captain Saddler appeared at that instant. "What do you think you're doing?" he growled.

"Checking on my prisoner," I snapped, in no mood to be bullied.

"Where's your husband?"

"Gone for the Boy Scouts. I'm in need of a good deed."

"There's no need to be sarcastic."

"You're right. Put some cuffs on her so I can stop worrying

she'll get away and I can pass out in peace, will you please?"

"Very funny, Mrs. Allan." But he complied.

Just in time. Elekta was rousing and I was in no condition to tangle with her again. This time she'd try to kill me herself. And probably succeed.

Bart returned with a chair and saw me on the floor.

"Ambulance is on the way, Princess. Hang in there another couple of minutes." He slid to the floor beside me so I could rest my head against his shoulder.

"What was the shouting all about downstairs a minute ago?" Bart asked as Captain Saddler dragged Elekta out of the elevator.

"Sam thought he saw someone using one of the service doors as the lights came on, but there was no one in the hall when he got the door unlocked."

An alarm rang in the back of my mind. I knew something. But what? I struggled to clear my addled mind. Then I remembered.

"Bart! There's a service tunnel connecting the museum with Yerba Buena Park. It comes out at the Martin Luther King waterfall."

Captain Saddler let go of Elekta and grabbed his radio, barking orders to the police out front. In less than a minute his radio crackled with a reply. Three men in city maintenance uniforms emerged from a panel as the cops ran across the street to the waterfall. They detained the men for questioning.

"How in blazes did you know about that tunnel?" Captain Saddler thundered.

"Be nice to me and maybe I'll tell you," I said, no longer intimidated by the blustery captain. My arm hurt so bad nothing else mattered, especially not this raving misogynist.

"Will you tell me?" Bart asked, kissing my cheek gently and holding my good hand.

Sirens wailed through the night. I hoped it was the ambulance. It couldn't get here fast enough as far as I was concerned, as much to treat my arm and stop the pain as to get me away from the unpleasant captain.

"Doris told me about it when Scarlotti followed me to her house, in case I needed a hiding place."

"The Cat Woman?" Bart asked.

"Yes. Her son helped build it."

"The Cat Woman?" Captain Saddler echoed.

"One of Allison's service projects," Bart explained. "My wife is a compassionate soul who can't stand to see someone in need and not do something about it. She escaped from our room to take the woman home from the hospital to be with her cats. That's when Elekta's men grabbed her."

"So if you'd stayed put and minded your own business like you were supposed to —," Captain Saddler started.

"I wouldn't have found out about Elekta and Ahmad's plan for the Koh-i-noor, or the tunnel."

Elekta came to about that time. She sat up and raised her cuffed hands to rub her head. Then she saw me. There was no mistaking me for a policewoman this time. I didn't have the hat on and my hair had tumbled back around my shoulders. And Bart was holding my hand. Her eyes grew round in surprise, then narrowed with hate.

"You little meddler," she snarled.

Elekta lunged for me, but Bart stuck his foot up to fend her off and caught her in the chin just as Captain Saddler grabbed for her and caught her hair.

Elekta screamed in pain. Not from the foot to the chin. She grabbed her head and rolled on the floor.

"I didn't hurt her that much," a surprised Captain Saddler protested.

"I did," I said. "That's how I stopped her when she tried to get away. When she went through the elevator hatch, I still had hold. She couldn't touch the floor. And she may have landed on her head when I pushed her through so we wouldn't be crushed."

Captain Saddler looked rather stupid with his mouth hanging open. Bart finished and clarified my explanation. I hurt too much to say any more. I touched the handkerchief. It was dripping with blood. I shivered, suddenly cold.

The sirens wound down outside and stopped. The elevator hummed beside us. When the doors opened, a gurney burst through followed by two emergency medical technicians. Lifting me carefully to the cart, they covered me with a blanket. Bart held my hand as they wheeled me back into the elevator and punched the ground-floor button.

As the doors closed, Captain Saddler shoved his hand between them, forcing them open.

"Get her the best surgeon you've got and bill me personally," he said quietly to the tall, black EMT nearest the door.

I wasn't supposed to hear that, but I was glad I did. It made the pain in my arm almost worth it. Almost.

As we exited the elevator on the ground floor, three men in maintenance uniforms and handcuffs were just being brought in from Yerba Buena Park across the street.

"Well, guess who?" I said as they wheeled me past the angry trio.

"Your three men," Bart said. "Why am I not surprised? You were right on all three counts. How did you manage that?"

"Pure luck," I said through gritted teeth as they jostled the gurney into the ambulance.

* * * * * * *

The first things I saw when I opened my eyes were two deep blue pools hovering over me. *Déja vù*. I closed my eyes, waited till the room stopped moving and opened them again. Bart was still at my side, his blue eyes filled with worry and concern.

"I thought you were going to sleep your life away, Princess. How do you feel?"

I tried to reach for his hand and my arm wouldn't respond. No wonder. I was in a cast from my shoulder to my fingertips.

"Don't try to move or they'll put you in traction. I promised the doctor you'd be very quiet and wouldn't need it. I figured if you were all strapped in, your claustrophobia would have you climbing the walls as soon as you woke."

"Thanks, Galahad. How long have I been asleep?"

Bart glanced at his watch. "About twelve hours. We got here just after midnight and it's noon. Are you up to visitors?"

"Depends. Who is it?"

Bart opened the door to the room adjoining mine. "She's awake."

There was a rustle of sheets and the squeak of wheels. Dad

pushed Mom into my room in a wheelchair.

"Allison! Are you okay?" Mom asked anxiously.

"Mom! Are you okay?"

"Apparently everyone is okay," Dad laughed.

"How did you know where I was?" As I tried to sit up, Bart quickly pressed me back against my pillows.

"The same way I knew you were freezing to death in San Francisco Bay," Dad said, "after I finally tuned in to you. I was totally focused on Margaret's illness for days. I've never been sure whether our link was a blessing or a curse. When I know you're in trouble and I'm too far away to help, it's a blasted curse." Dad leaned over and kissed my forehead.

"It was a blessing to me once again. Thank you." I squeezed his hand with my good one.

"Mom, I assume from the color in your cheeks and your sparkling eyes they decided what your problem was and cured it."

"Scarlotti had put a rare, slow-acting poison on the arrow he shot me with. If the arrow itself didn't kill me, the poison would. It was something from the Far East. None of the doctors were familiar with it."

"But you're all right now?"

"Still weak, but the Sansonne Clinic released me when I promised to stay in the hospital here for another few days. When I finally received the antidote to the poison and your dad could think of something besides me, he got in touch with Bart and found you were here."

"The Sansonne! You were in Santa Barbara all the time?" I said.

"Is this a private party, or can anybody join?" Oz asked from the door.

"All ambulatory patients cheerfully invited," I laughed.

Oz wheeled his chair into the room with one hand and rolled his IV beside him with the other. Bart introduced him to my parents.

"*The* Jack Alexander?" Oz said extending his hand, surprise written all over his face. "I'm honored, sir. They tucked us into bed at night at the FBI Academy with the adventures of Jack Alexander and Anastasia. This must be his lovely silent partner, Margaret," he added, shaking my mother's hand. "No wonder Allison was light

years ahead of us on this investigation. And speaking of the investigation, who's going to fill me in?"

"Yes. Tie up all the loose ends for those of us who missed out," I said.

"We were lucky this wasn't a seasoned group of terrorists," Bart
said. "They considered all infidels inferior and stupid. They used
Roach to drop the bodies. When Allison stumbled across Roach in
Golden Gate Park and took him in like a stray, he took advantage of
it. Why didn't you tell me about the bed slashing, Princess? I had to
find out from the investigating officer who went to the Abigail to
retrieve Roach's belongings."

"I thought it was Scarlotti and didn't want to worry you," I
said. "Did Roach set the fires, too?"

"The old man and his two accomplices were responsible for the
fires. The ponytailed one, Ned, is his son. Ned's son was involved in
gangs so Ned put his kid's buddies up to arson and gang flare-ups.
Ned took care of the stickups himself."

"What was the purpose?" I asked.

"Diversion, as we thought. The old man was a professional
jewel thief in Europe. He wanted one last heist to retire on. The
blond was Doris' son. He knew about the tunnel—their way in and
out of the museum. They just timed it wrong. The museum was
crawling with cops when they got there. The power was off, and the
place was full of gas. If they'd chosen any other night, they might
have gotten away with it."

"They actually thought they could steal all those famous
diamonds and not get caught?" Mom asked.

"They were only after the Queen's necklace," I said, looking at
Bart. "Right?"

"Right."

"How'd you figure that out?" Oz asked.

"The terrorists wanted the newly discovered uncut Rangoon
Diamond—the least traceable when it was cut, and worth the most
to them on the open market."

Bart nodded. "Word of the discovery leaked out in the diamond
world long before it was announced to the world in general."

"Elekta and Ahmad were after the Koh-i-noor because of its
history for their people and the political power they hoped it could

give them," I continued. "All the rest of the diamonds are too famous and well-documented to be worth anything to anyone except a private collector who could never show them to anyone—or someone who was heartless enough to have them cut. But that would diminish their value. The Queen's necklace was the next obvious target because it was totally unfamiliar to all but the very few who'd been involved in reassembling it."

"Bravo," Dad said. "Good thinking."

"Did they catch Elekta and Ahmad's accomplices?" I asked, delighted and embarrassed at Dad's praise.

"All three of them," Bart said.

"Three? I thought there were only Calvin and Floyd."

"You mean there's something your psychic wife didn't figure out?" a voice growled from the door. I knew the voice. The face was hidden by a huge bouquet of long-stemmed peach roses, my favorite.

"A peace offering," Captain Saddler said as he propped the roses against my cast. "I apologize for all those nasty things I said at lunch and humbly ask your forgiveness." He paused. "And want to know if you'd like to come to work for me."

I stared open-mouthed at the audacity of the man.

"I take it that's a *no*," he said.

"You can bet your badge on it," I said, not really believing he'd actually apologized, much less offered me a job.

Captain Saddler shrugged, a slight smile curving his mouth. He wasn't bad looking when he smiled.

"Well," I laughed, changing the subject quickly, "too bad nobody brought cake and ice cream. We could have a party. The gang's all here except Matt. Why didn't you bring him along?"

"You asked about Elekta's two accomplices," Bart said. "She and Ahmad had three. Floyd, who worked for the power company, to short-circuit the power, and Calvin, a former racer, to drive the getaway car."

"And someone on the inside to help take care of the guards," I guessed, jarred by disappointment in the big Texan. "When I told Matt how I'd circumvent their system, I must have accidentally stumbled on the method they'd devised."

"Too close. Which forced Elekta's hand," Bart added. "She had to get you out of the way before somebody took you seriously and rigged a new security system. They conked Matt on the head to take the heat off him when they kidnapped you."

I shuddered. "Good thing my guardian angels were on duty when he was at the window. He could have let me fall with Scarlotti and finished what Cal and Floyd didn't."

"Probably not," Captain Saddler said. "He knew I was watching from below. It behooved him to save the maiden in distress and make hero points instead of casting any more suspicion on himself."

"Captain Saddler and I put our heads together when we heard Matt's story and found a lot of weak spots," Bart said. "Jim had Liz investigate him. Matt didn't pass muster. That's why Jim never left his side from the time we got you down to the museum till Elekta and Ahmad hit the museum. We didn't want him reporting to Elekta that you were still alive and we knew their plans."

"Then Elekta was the boss Cal and Floyd had never seen and only heard through the voice changer," I said, tidying up one more loose end in my mind. "She thought, being from that very chauvinistic world, that they wouldn't respect a woman boss."

Everyone was quiet for a minute.

"The elevator!" I exclaimed. "If they hid on top of the elevator, why weren't they crushed when it went to the top and opened on the fifth floor? There wasn't enough clearance. . . ."

"Actually, there was," Bart interrupted. "Just barely. You had to lie very flat and be very slender."

"You mean I have this broken arm for nothing? I didn't have to dive through that hole!"

"No," Captain Saddler said emphatically. "And you didn't have to push Elekta through first. I can't believe you'd think of saving the life of the woman who ordered your death before you'd save your own neck."

Mom reached for my hand. "It would never occur to Allison to put herself before someone she perceived to be in trouble."

"Bart, my condolences. You'll never have a minute's peace as long as she's around." Captain Saddler slapped Bart on the back. "But you'll never be bored, either." He actually winked at me as he strode out of the room. "And the offer of that job still stands."

"You've had enough excitement for awhile," Dad said as he kissed my cheek, "and so has your mother. If you two are good, the doctor might let you have dinner together tonight." He wheeled Mom back to her room, ignoring her protests.

"Guess that's my signal to leave you two alone," Oz said, dragging his IV stand toward the door.

"You have a quick grasp of the obvious," Bart said. "You're a good man."

"So are you," I said softly, pulling Bart's head close to mine so I could kiss him.

"Flattery will get you everywhere. But we have some serious talking to do."

"As a matter of fact, we do. Do you really believe the Book of Mormon was brought by an angel?"

"Where did that come from?" Bart asked in surprise.

"I thought of it when I mentioned my guardian angels. Do you actually believe an angel brought the book?"

"Absolutely," Bart said with quiet assurance.

"How can you be so sure?"

Bart paused. "I told you. I did what Moroni instructed. I asked with real intent, believing that God would give me an answer."

"And?"

"And He did. The Spirit bore witness that it was true. Did you finish reading the Book of Mormon?"

"No. I guess I had too many things on my mind. I couldn't get through the Isaiah quotes."

"You and a lot of other people. If that stops you, skip over the Isaiah chapters and finish reading the rest of it. I promise you'll be glad you did."

"But why an angel? Why not a man?" I persisted. "I have no trouble believing in my guardian angels, but I have a hard time believing God would send an angel with a book."

"It's not just any book," Bart said. "The Book of Mormon contains Christ's dealings with the peoples of ancient America. Basically, it's the gospel as it was when Christ was on the earth. When the apostles were martyred, the apostasy occurred and the truth was lost. It had to be restored. God chose to do it through a fourteen-year-old boy. He received the book from the angel who had charge of it when he was on the earth as a man. There's so much to tell you, I don't know where to start."

"I'm a willing listener if you can keep the bad guys at bay long enough to teach me."

"My turn for a question now. What do you mean, you don't want to be married anymore? And you're going back to work?"

"Bart, put the 'Do Not Disturb' sign on the door and shut it. Then lock the door between Mom's room, and come here."

"I recognize that *I have a plan* look. What's on your devious female mind?" he asked as he followed my directions.

"Bring your shrewd male mind over here and see if you can figure it out," I said, holding the covers open invitingly.

"You wouldn't dare."

"I seem to recall a warm body next to mine the other night before the telephone called it away."

"And?"

"And it felt awfully good."

"What if they kick us out of here?"

I smiled my most enigmatic smile.

"We'll reconnoiter another honeymoon locale."

About the Author

Lynn Gardner describes herself as an avid storyteller. In building the plot and characters of her first novel, *Emeralds and Espionage*, she did extensive research on the countries described in the novel, and carefully gathered information on the FBI. She had first-hand knowledge of the military aspect from her career-Air Force husband.

A writer's workshop at BYU-Hawaii provided the opportunity for research on the setting for her second novel, *Pearls and Peril*, and intensive research in San Francisco, one of her favorite cities, furnished her with material for *Diamonds and Danger*.

Lynn and her husband, Glenn, make their home in Quartz Hill, California, where Lynn is director of the stake family history center. They are the parents of four children.

Among her many interests, Lynn lists reading, golf with her husband, traveling, beachcombing, writing, family history, and spoiling her four granddaughters and two grandsons.